D1443274

Compromises

Compromises

Joan Hohl

KENSINGTON BOOKS

KENSINGTON BOOKS are published by

Kensington Publishing Corp.
850 Third Avenue
New York, NY 10022

ISBN 1-57566-076-8

First Zebra Paperback Printing: April, 1995
First Kensington Hardcover Printing: March, 1996

Printed in the United States of America

Chapter One

Oh, hell!

Frisco Styer stared at the telephone receiver clutched in her hand. Heaving a long-suffering sigh, she refrained from flinging it onto the cradle and instead gently settled it into place on the console.

It was mid afternoon, and so far the day hadn't been anything to write home about. To begin, a throbbing sinus headache had awakened her an hour before her usual crawl-out time of six-fifteen.

Frisco was never scintillating in the morning. She wasn't grouchy, just quiet. So, naturally, she had seated herself next to a chatterbox on the bus to the office; she had had little choice, really. It was the last empty seat on the S.E.P.T.A. vehicle. Never had the ride seemed quite so long from her center-city-Philadelphia apartment complex to the stop nearest the accounting firm of Manning and Manning, where she had risen to the position of senior manager in the accounting and auditing department.

Then, having arrived at her office chattered nearly to a state of brain numbness, she had received the information that a client, one of her original, and the largest of her private accounts, had somehow forgotten to include a few vital receipts in the tax package he'd delivered to her last week. Of course, Frisco had worked late last night, completing that client's tax-return forms.

Ah, springtime . . . Wasn't it grand?

The sinus medication, which had just begun to take hold, went into a decline, and so did Frisco—for all of five minutes. But, being a scrupulous as well as an excellent C.P.A., she then proceeded to rework the material.

She finally finished and was having a much-needed coffee break when the phone call came from her father. She knew at once that all was not well; the panic edging Harold Styer's voice was a dead giveaway.

"I need to talk to you, baby."

Frisco was immediately wary; her father only used the childhood endearment when he wanted something—something he knew would upset her.

"What's wrong, Dad?" She had to work to keep the impatience from her tone. And then she felt guilty. But, Lord, her father was a trial at times.

"I'm in trouble."

Alert the media.

The cynical and ungenerous thought made her feel guiltier still, resulting in a softening of her voice, her tone. "What sort of trouble, Dad?"

"Financial, but I can't discuss it over the phone," he answered. "Suppose I meet you after work today, buy you dinner," he suggested, then added as an extra sweetener, "I'll make reservations at Bookbinder's."

Ever since the first time her father had taken her to Bookbinder's when she was four, Frisco had loved the place; she was just a pushover for good clam chowder, even now, twenty-eight years later.

"Okay, Dad," she said, stifling a sigh. "What time?"

"Six, six-thirty?"

"Six will be fine. See you there."

" 'Bye, baby." The relief in his voice was as loud as a shout. "And thanks."

Nuts.

Releasing her visual lock on the innocent phone, Frisco leaned back in her chair and closed her eyes. Her sinuses had gone ballistic. Her cheekbones hurt. Her upper teeth hurt. Pain streaked her temples.

Being an only child had its down side as well as its perks. Being an intelligent go-getter as well as a mature only child had even more down sides.

Frisco was tired, and finding it harder with each passing day to stay vigorously on top of both her professional and private life.

When had her life begun falling apart?

She contemplated the question while sipping the now-tepid coffee. Her life used to be interesting, fun, an invigorating challenge.

No more. Lately, rather than the taste of ambrosia, her life, privately and professionally, had the rank aftertaste of bitter herbs. The invigorating challenge had diminished into a daily grind, with precious little of anything interesting in it, never mind fun.

Who said feminism was liberating, anyway?

With increasing frequency of late, Frisco found herself thinking that she would relish the opportunity to meet the fabled woman or women who had started it all. She had a few well considered, and what she deemed intelligent, questions to put to that early intrepid female—or those females—the first and to her mind foremost being: Were you nuts or what?

The vote, and the concept of equality, were certainly fine ideals . . . but really, the results!

Frisco hadn't always felt quite so militant about the original militants.

On the contrary. She had been gung-ho and go-get-'em all through college. She had rallied, debated, and protested—

done just about everything. It had all been great fun. Invigorating. Inspiring.

After graduation, armed with knowledge and a degree to prove it, and disdaining a cushy job with her family's corporation, Frisco had gleefully set forth to storm the bastions of male-dominated companies.

It had been a brief skirmish; she had acquired the very first position she went after. She and one of her best friends, who had been—and still was—extremely militant, had smugly toasted each other with champagne afterward.

Flushed with victory, Frisco dressed for success, anchored a chip to her shoulder, and strode with arrogant confidence into the corporate world.

Big deal.

That had been over ten years ago.

Ten years can appear to pass in the blink of an eye . . . or the crawl of a worm.

After ten plus years of *making* it, Frisco had long since lost her youthful enthusiasm.

Although the principles were exhilarating, the practicalities proved exhausting.

What had caused the sweet beginning to turn so sour?

And when had this bone-deep, nagging loneliness seeped into her life?

Frisco frowned at her now-cold coffee . . . and the introspective spurs.

As to the first of those spurs, perhaps the realities of living had soured the sweetness.

In a word, she simply was . . . tired.

How in the hell did women with careers, husbands, and kids survive, never mind handle it all? Frisco wondered in stupefied admiration, staring into what had become yucky-looking coffee, as if hoping to find answers there.

She had only herself to consider.

And she was *tired*.

Tired of being it all, doing it all, having it all. *It* wasn't the *all* that expectation had promised. Now she wanted to rest.

She didn't want to bring home the bacon, or fry it up in

the pan. She hated bacon; she wasn't too crazy about cooking either, come to that.

What Frisco did want was to kick back, preferably on a hot beach, with a cold glass sweating in her hand.

Alone.

That last longing thought reminded her of the second of her introspective spurs; why did she suffer these periodic lapses of wrenching loneliness?

Was it because of being mateless, without a significant other, someone with whom to share the day-by-day trials and tribulations?

Baloney.

She made a face, and shifted restlessly in her expensive, butter-soft leather, swivel desk chair.

Who needed a male around, constantly getting under foot, making demands on her time—and person—and cluttering up her world with his opinions, his self-absorption, his dirty socks and underwear?

It wasn't that she didn't like men, unlike a few of her more militant friends, who disdained them, considering males an alien species. There were some males Frisco genuinely liked, even admired, others she did not like, and still others she merely tolerated or ignored altogether.

But there was not one she loved . . . in the romantic sense.

She had tried the significant-other routine; he had believed no legal commitment translated into no reason to practice fidelity. And besides attempting to be a stud to the female population at large, he'd left his dirty socks and underwear about, littering the bedroom floor.

She had sent him packing.

And, notwithstanding his belief that he was a gift from the gods to women, their sex hadn't been anything to shout about. Frisco grimaced. Hell, she hadn't even ever had the satisfaction of a mild orgasm, let alone the earthshaker she had heard and read about.

All things considered, she concluded there was more satisfaction to be derived from an occasional binge on really fine chocolate.

She didn't need a man, she reasoned. She needed a rest. And that was precisely what she was planning on having. All the arrangements were made. She was to fly out of Philadelphia International a week from the coming Sunday.

Frisco sighed and closed her aching eyes. She had been so looking forward to spending two long, glorious weeks in Hawaii, surrendering her body to the sun and her mind to the sweeping strains of Tchaikovsky caressing her ears via the headset of her new Walkman.

The very last thing she wanted or needed was to receive a call, a cry, a whimper for help from her father.

The phone rang.

Frisco jumped, staring at the instrument as if it had somehow monitored her chain of thought.

It rang again.

With a faint self-conscious laugh at her wild imaginings, she set the coffee cup aside, straightened in her chair, picked up the receiver, and answered in a professionally brisk tone of voice.

"Frisco Styer."

Business as usual.

Harold Styer slumped back into the soft leather of his executive desk chair, a heartfelt sigh of relief whooshing through his trembling lips.

If anyone could help him it was Frisco, he assured himself, pulling a fine cotton handkerchief from his pocket to mop his damp brow.

She would find a way; there was no one else he could turn to, no one except . . .

Harold shuddered. The only other person he could think of was his wife, Gertrude, the true love of his life. He couldn't ask her to help him, daren't breathe a word to her about the trouble he had gotten himself into. The truth would surely shatter Gertrude's illusions about him. Before he'd bare his soul to her, hurt her, see the love in her eyes dimmed by disappointment and despair, he'd sell his soul to that corporate devil, Lucas MacCanna.

A deeper shudder made Harold quake. A fresh spurt of perspiration slicked his brow. He stared with sightless, fear-darkened eyes into the blackness of his self-created hell.

Frisco would think of something. Harold had always been secretly in awe of his only child, because of her intelligence, her quick mind, her decisiveness.

Yes, Frisco would figure something out, some way to extricate him from this financial morass.

She has to, he thought with desperate hope. Because if she couldn't . . .

Harold pushed the very idea away, escaping his unsettling thoughts by sitting upright and reaching for the phone.

He had to call Gertrude, tell her he wouldn't be home for dinner this evening.

Chapter Two

Making an early escape from the office, Frisco arrived at the famous restaurant on Walnut Street a little after five forty-five. Fortunately, the table her father had reserved was ready and she was seated at once.

Weaving through the room in the wake of the rather attractive blond maître d' on the way to the table, she was not unaware of the masculine glances, blatant and surreptitious, skimming her body.

Frisco had a good figure. She worked at keeping her tall form slender and well toned. Although she actively detested exercise and dieting, she did both, regularly. There were the odd on-and-off moments when she asked herself why in hell she bothered. She loved food, the good stuff as well as junk. And she loved to eat. She had precious little time to simply kick back. Spending the majority of that free time punishing her body with muscle-crunching workouts, as well as denying herself the foods she loved, was not at the top of her list of fun things to do.

Then again, as she frequently reminded herself, she liked looking as attractive as possible.

Today, she knew she was particularly presentable. She had enhanced her reed-slim form with a severely cut black suit, and had softened the austere effect with a white silk blouse with a cascading jabot of fine lace. In contrast to the somber attire, her bright, gold-flecked green eyes and unruly mass of shoulder-length chestnut hair became a focal point, drawing the eye to her delicately formed, nearly classical features and creamy complexion.

Frisco had long since grown accustomed to slow appraising glances; she looked damn good, and she knew it. It had not always been that way.

From childhood straight through the vulnerable teen years, Frisco had epitomized the ugly duckling. Her older cousin, teasing brat that he'd been, had dubbed her "Sticks." She had hated the nickname, and her cousin.

Growing up and becoming older hadn't improved the relationship—Frisco still didn't like her cousin, though she did do a better job of hiding her feelings.

Gertrude Styer—with the cloudy gaze of mother love, Frisco felt sure—had serenely maintained that, like the ugly duckling, her daughter would reap the benefits of a metamorphosis into a lovely and graceful swan.

Frisco had never believed it. Looking at herself in her bedroom mirror, all she had seen was a gangly girl, taller than her contemporaries, angular and seemingly all bones, awkwardly sticking out at ankles, knees, pelvis, elbows, and shoulders, even on her thin face. To her critical view, her hair, more red than brown, and a riot of long spiral curls, did nothing to improve the overall picture. Then, in addition to everything else, though sparkling white, her teeth were big, and she had an overbite. In her dratted cousin's words, "Frisco has such buck teeth, she can eat an apple through a knothole in a fence."

It was all rather depressing, so Frisco had avoided mirrors whenever possible. She also had avoided her cousin, whose straight teeth she sorely longed to kick out. She still avoided him; he hadn't improved a great deal with age.

Well, honestly, she was later to reflect in sheer amazement, how could a discouraged fifteen-year-old know that within five years her mother's assertion would prove correct? How could she imagine that a few pounds here and there—in all the right places—would soften and smooth the angles into neatly rounded curves, or that the agony of two years with a mouth full of binding metal would give her a smile to rival a TV toothpaste commercial or, for that mater, that long riotous spiral curls would come into vogue?

Yes, since the miraculous transformation, Frisco had grown accustomed to admiring masculine glances. She enjoyed them. But, having a clear and sharp memory, she never took them for granted.

A smiling waiter promptly appeared to inquire if she would like a drink while she waited. Setting the menu aside, she ordered a glass of white zinfandel, then sat back in her chair to unwind a bit . . . before her father put in his appearance and proceeded to crank her up again.

As usual, the restaurant was packed with laughing, conversing patrons. Savoring the delicate taste of the wine, she let her gaze wander around the room, unobtrusively observing her fellow diners.

They were a mixed bag, male and female, young and not so young, all shapes and sizes, their attire ranging from the very casual to business suits and dresses. There were even a few, those at a large round table, decked out in glittering evening clothes. A pretheater group? Frisco wondered idly.

Whatever. She gave a careless mental shrug that didn't quite come off, even in her mind.

Everyone appeared relaxed and up, the evening before them. Everyone, except the diner at her table. She concealed a self-deriding smile behind the glass she raised to her lips, and silently chided herself for her lack of enthusiasm.

It certainly wasn't the fault of these people that she had lately begun feeling inexplicable and confusing stabs of loneliness, or that she had been experiencing a recurring sense of the meaninglessness of her life and lifestyle, or even that she wasn't looking forward to the coming discussion with her father.

Deep in her moody introspection, she didn't notice that gentleman approach the table.

"Am I late, or were you early?"

Think of the devil.

"I was early." Frisco produced a smile for the man seating himself opposite her; it wasn't all that difficult, for trying as he could be at times, she did love her father. "I believe you're right on time." To save me from my own dispirited thoughts, she appended silently, fortifying herself for whatever was to come by gulping down the rest of the wine.

"Another?" As he asked, he raised his hand to signal for the waiter. The man materialized at the table even more promptly than before.

"Sir?"

"Another for my daughter," her father said, not bothering to wait for Frisco's reply. "And I'll have a perfect Manhattan, just so . . ." He went on to explain his preference.

Frisco studied her father during his brief exchange with the waiter, and could not deny a flash of admiration for the urbane picture he presented to the world.

At fifty-nine, Harold Styer was still a very attractive, vital, and virile-looking man, more like a distinguished diplomat than a titan of industry—which of course he really wasn't but pretended to be.

Standing not quite six foot, and with his trim figure enhanced by expertly tailored clothes, his passage invariably caused many male, and even more female, heads to turn as eyes came alight with speculation.

Harold was not unaware of his effect on the opposite sex; in fact, it added a spring to his jaunty step. But his saving grace, as far as Frisco was concerned, was that, although he reveled in the interest evident from the distaff side, he never stepped off the path of fidelity. Had he done so, and had she heard of it, she would have turned on him like an enraged female grizzly, ripping him up one side and down the other.

Frisco adored her mother.

Fortunately for Harold, so did he, and Frisco knew it.

"Have you already decided?" He glanced up from perusing

the menu to frown at hers, which lay folded on the table to one side of her.

"Umm." Frisco nodded. "I don't need it. I know exactly what I want."

"You always have," he murmured, giving a slight shake of his head. "You never cease to amaze me."

Uh-oh, Frisco thought, somehow managing to keep her smile in place. Her father's problem could prove to be worse than she'd hoped. Not only was he being complimentary, he was obviously about to employ delaying tactics, putting the moment of truth off until after they had eaten. Not wishing to ruin her appetite, maybe?

"Why should my knowing what I want amaze you?" she asked, going along with his ploy, but also genuinely curious to hear his answer.

"Let's order first," he said, once again raising his arm to signal to the waiter. "We can talk over dinner."

Their orders were taken, including one for another "just so" Manhattan for him. Frisco declined. Toying with the delicate stem of her still half-full wine glass, she attempted to draw him out—and to the point.

"Rather than me, shouldn't we discuss the problem that precipitated this meeting?"

"In due course," he said evasively, frustrating her effort, and her. "Let's enjoy our meal."

Meaning, of course, that the discussion to follow would not be enjoyable, she mused, unsurprised.

"All right," she agreed, too tired, and unwilling, to fight him and the persistent, if lessened, pain in her head, "Then tell me why I have always amazed you."

"Well, from the time you were still quite small, you have always known exactly what you wanted." His smile was a little crooked, thus engaging. "In addition to that, you have always seemed to know exactly how to go about achieving your goals or acquiring what you want."

"Oh, really, Dad," she scoffed, laughing. "You make me sound like some strange phenomenon or something."

"Not at all," he scoffed back. "You simply have your head

together, have had for a long time." He paused, sitting back to allow the waiter room to serve their soup and his drink. "There's not a thing strange about it."

Frisco inhaled, savoring the aroma of clam chowder riding the steam rising from the soup in the bowl the waiter set before her. She taste-tested a sip of the creamy broth before replying to her father's comment.

"If you say so," she finally murmured, smothering an urge to laugh aloud at his contention. How could he know that she was going through a spell of self-doubt?

He didn't pursue the subject, so she let it drop. The conversation during the meal was sporadic and banal, but Frisco could see the tension building in him. He gulped two more drinks, and when he ordered yet another when the waiter came to clear the table, she called a halt.

"Okay, Dad, you've had enough liquid courage," she said, waving the waiter away. "Suppose you tell me what this is all about."

"Unless something's done, I'm going to lose the business," he blurted out in a hoarse voice rife with nerves. His eyes were stark; his face pale.

"What?" Frisco stared at him in astonishment; he had to be overstating the case. At least, she fervently hoped he was.

The "business," The Cutting Edge Surgical Instrument Company, had been owned and run by her mother's side of the family for over a hundred years. Upon the death of Frisco's grandfather five years ago, her mother had inherited fifty-five percent of the company stock, and a controlling interest in the firm. Unwisely, as had been obvious almost from the beginning, Gertrude had handed over control of the business to her husband. Harold had quickly proved he lacked both technical and managerial skills, as well as a basic concept of fiscal responsibility. Yet, to this day, Gertrude was clueless as to the enormity of her blunder.

She worshiped Harold.

Busy with her own life and career, Frisco rarely set foot in the corporate offices of The Cutting Edge. And so, although she had been fully aware of her father's ineptitude, she had

had no idea that the situation had deteriorated to such an alarming degree.

"I think you'd better explain."

Harold's head snapped up at the sharpness of Frisco's voice, and he rushed into speech.

"I'm in debt, deeply in debt," he said with unusual forthrightness.

"How deep?" Frisco demanded. "And to whom?"

He drew a quick breath. "Several million," he blurted out in a strained voice. "To three casinos in Atlantic City, and two others in Las Vegas."

'Stunned speechless, his daughter could do no more than stare at him in shocked disbelief for long seconds, feeling her stomach churn sickeningly, certain the color was draining from her face. But his bombshell was only the beginning. Before she could find her voice, or the words to say, her father hit her with another salvo.

"I . . . I've borrowed heavily from the company." He swallowed with visible difficulty. "And now the company's floundering. We can't meet our outstanding debts."

Jesus. Frisco feared she was in danger of losing her dinner. While her stomach heaved, her mind refused to function. Swallowing the brackish taste of fear and seafood, she fixed a drilling stare on her father.

"How could you?" she finally managed to ask in a stark whisper. "Does Mother know?"

"No!" Panic flared in his eyes. "And I don't want her to. You must promise me that."

"But—"

"Frisco, please!"

"All right. All right." Her head was now pounding. "But—" she said again, only to be interrupted again.

"That's not all of it, Frisco." He hesitated, swallowed, then confessed. "There's more."

"More?" she repeated dumbly, not at all sure she could absorb any more.

He nodded, and quickly tossing back the remainder of his

drink, motioned to the waiter for another. "I . . . I'm afraid there's going to be an attempt at a takeover of the firm."

"A corporate raider?" Frisco shook her head, as if to clear her thinking process. She had believed the days of the hostile takeover were long gone.

"No, no." Light glistened on the sweat beading Harold's frown. "More like a friendly takeover."

"Friendly!" Frisco exclaimed, her frown mirroring his. "Who? What *friend*? And how?"

"The man who supplies our steel."

"MacCanna?" Although she had never met him, she knew of him, of course. That would have been the case even if he hadn't supplied the steel for the company; his reputation always preceded him.

From all she had read and heard, Lucas MacCanna was one tough cookie. The stories circulating for years about him were almost legendary. He was lionized because he epitomized the fabled American boot-strap success story, and he was said to be a self-admitted chauvinist into the bargain.

Taking a skeptical, cynical view, Frisco wasn't sure she believed any of the hype—with the possible exception of his reputed chauvinism. From her own experiences, as well as in tales related to her, it was quite often the movers and shakers of the world who were the biggest offenders in their relations with women, though they might give lip service to the concept of equality.

Yet, curiously, she couldn't recall hearing as much as a whisper about him in regard to any particular woman. So, doubting the veracity of the legend, she had never voiced an opinion, one way or the other.

It was patently obvious, however, that her father not only believed the stories, but was impressed by them and intimidated by the man.

"Yes, MacCanna." Harold trembled, then went on in a strained whisper, "I have reason to believe he has been buying up company stock. I don't know how much of it he has managed to obtain but . . ."

He didn't finish, but then, he didn't have to; Frisco got the picture. With enough of the stock, some proxy votes, and some board members in his corner, MacCanna could pull something off.

"Help me, baby." Harold's ragged, desperate-sounding plea jerked her to attention.

"How?" For the life of her, Frisco could not imagine what he expected of her.

"Do . . . *something.*"

"What?"

"I don't know." He mopped his brow "But there's got to be an answer."

"Well, if there is, I can't pull it out of a hat." Frisco lifted her shoulders in a manner indicating her feelings of helplessness. "I'm an accountant, Dad, not a magician. I need more information."

Harold glanced around at the tables nearest to them, and it was only then that she became aware of the buzz of conversation and the occasional burst of laughter coming from the diners surrounding their table.

"I can't go into detail here," he said, taking another quick look around him. "Can you come to my office?"

"When?" Frisco smothered a sigh of resignation.

"It will have to be tomorrow." Harold at least had the grace to appear apologetic. "MacCanna made an appointment with me for nine Friday morning."

The day after tomorrow. Why not? That would give her less than one full day to come up with a solution, Frisco thought, not even attempting to smother another sigh.

"Okay, Dad. I'll take my car in to work tomorrow morning, then leave the office at noon and drive out to the plant." From somewhere, she managed a faint smile. "I'll let you buy me lunch in the employee cafeteria."

Chapter Three

"So, how long do you figure you'll be gone?"

"As long as it takes."

Lucas raised his eyes from the briefcase he was shoving papers into, a wry smile curving his thin lips at the sound of a long-suffering sigh from his brother.

Michael MacCanna didn't return the smile, he sighed again. "Do you think you could be just a bit more precise? I mean," he went on, his disgruntlement evident in his tone and his impatient expression, "couldn't you give me an estimate?"

"Why?" Lucas went back to shoving papers into the case. "You can hold the fort for a while, can't you?" The paper he held crackled as he flicked his hand, indicating not only the average-size, rather austere office but the entire complex and adjacent steel mill as well.

"Well, sure, but—"

"What?" Lucas snapped shut the case, then straightened to frown at the younger man. "We went over everything yesterday, Mike. You're up to speed on all the current contract deadlines, as well as pending deals. What's the problem?"

"Oh, I don't know." Mike shrugged. "I guess it's just that you've never done anything like this before."

"Like what?"

"Like taking off without leaving a schedule of where you'll be, what you'll be doing, and when you'll be back. It's not like you."

Lucas arched dark eyebrows over equally dark eyes, alight with amusement. "No?"

"No." Mike gave an emphatic shake of his head. "You usually know exactly what, when, and how you're going to do whatever it is you want to do."

"Oh, I do know what I'm going to do, Mike," he said. "I won't know the whens and hows of the situation until I get a report and size up the problems, but I know exactly what I'm going to do should the situation prove to be as bad as I suspect."

"So, what is the situation?" Mike asked in exasperation. "You never did tell me."

"I didn't see it as a need to know for you, until I had something concrete." Lucas shrugged. "It concerns The Cutting Edge Surgical Instrument Company."

"We supply their steel," Mike said, looking confused.

"Yes, and as you know, we've had some difficulty collecting from them lately."

"I know that but"—Mike shrugged—"we have this problem from time to time with customers. What can you do?"

"I made an appointment for a meeting tomorrow morning with the company's president."

"Harold Styer?"

"Yes."

"Why?" Mike frowned. "Lucas, it's never been your style to personally visit clients to demand payment."

"That's not why I'm meeting with him."

"Then why?" Mike asked.

"Because for some time now I've been hearing disquieting rumors about Styer."

"What rumors?"

"Mainly that ole good-time Harold is raping that distinguished company."

Mike looked appalled. "You're kidding."

"No."

"But rumors . . ." He frowned again. "Lucas, are you sure there's any validity to them?"

"No. But from the first, I've been uneasy about them, primarily *because* Styer has been fudging on payments for the steel shipments this past year or so. I intend to find out the truth of the matter. That's why I can't give you a definite schedule."

Mike frowned and lowered his eyes to the briefcase. "And those documents you stuffed into your case pertain to The Cutting Edge?"

"Yes."

"I'm afraid I still don't get it," Mike said, sounding more confused than before. "Even if you find the rumors are true, what can you do about it? I mean, other than to refuse to ship them any more steel?"

Lucas's smile held a hint of the marauder, the predator. "I'm going to deball the rapist."

"Christ," Mike breathed, visibly shaken. "It's been so long I'd almost forgotten that look."

"What look?"

"That, that"—Mike paused, as if groping for the perfect descriptive expression—"that narrow-eyed, cat-on-the-prowl look about you when you're determined to get something—or somebody." He shivered. "It's been a long time since I've seen that hungry look, Lucas."

His brother laughed, a soft, deep-throated, not unpleasant sound of genuine amusement. "Thought I'd mellowed with success and approaching middle age, had you?"

"I suppose," Mike said wryly. "Bad assumption, huh?"

"Yes, but then, most assumptions are." Lucas's eyes gleamed with a teasing light. "You do know what they say about assumptions, don't you?"

"Say?" Mike shook his head. "No. What?"

Picking up his case, Lucas walked to the door, grasped the knob, then turned to grin at his brother.

"To assume anything makes an *ass* of *u* and *me.*"

Mike groaned.

Lucas exited laughing.

* * *

He wasn't laughing a couple of hours later; he was cursing. To himself, but aloud. He was "turning the air blue" inside the car.

Driving east on the 422 by-pass around Pottstown through a raging spring thunderstorm was proving to be a bitch. The storm had overtaken him soon after he had driven away from his suburban Reading townhouse, and had kept pace with him up to now, as he approached the exit onto 202 just past Valley Forge, which subsequently gave access to the Schuylkill Expressway into Philadelphia.

Lightning streaks jaggedly rent the churning greenish black clouds. Thunder shook the ground with its angry-sounding roars. Sheeting rain slashed the windshield, diminishing visibility to just about zilch.

"Stupid son of a bitch," Lucas muttered as a low-slung sports car tore past and pulled in front of him as he neared the Valley Forge exit ramp, spewing a spray of water over the windshield; a flash flood of anger raced through him. "Jerk probably doesn't believe there's a hell."

Lucas knew too well there was a hell, if not after death, then right here on earth. He had lived through it, survived hell-on-earth situations from his late teens through his mid twenties.

A grim smile touched his lips. And now he was on his way to administer a portion of that earthly hell to Harold Styer, if the information he had received about the man, and his fast and loose business practices proved correct.

Lucas had a gut feeling that everything he had heard about the man was true. A nasty feeling that went deeper than the sporadic payments for steel deliveries. The feeling burned inside him like an acid, eating away at his patience. If there was one thing guaranteed to enrage him, it was the careless decimation of an old and respected business firm.

"Damn the man," he snarled, peering narrow-eyed through the windshield at the barely discernible highway. Driving the Schuylkill Expressway, which some disgruntled motorists had reportedly referred to as the sure-kill, at any time was a chore.

Under adverse weather conditions, it was a real challenge. Lucas vented his disgruntlement by aiming his ire at his quarry.

He had not been impressed by Harold Styer from the day he met him. He didn't dislike the man, for Styer was both charming and affable. But he hadn't been impressed. The man simply didn't possess the character traits Lucas deemed admirable in a man—those being a strong moral and ethical code and a sharp business acumen.

Charming and pleasant just didn't cut it as far as Lucas was concerned. He was even less impressed by what he discerned in Styer as a flaw, a weakness for the good, easy-come, easy-go type lifestyle.

But then, being brutally honest, Lucas admitted that he measured people by a much more stringent yardstick than did society in general.

Nothing had ever come easily to him; from the time he was old enough to do chores, at the advanced age of eight, his life had consisted of a constant series of battles.

Lucas was the first of three sons born to a young couple struggling for mere survival. Both of his parents were first generation Americans, the progeny of pre-World War II immigrants. His mother's parents had fled their German homeland in the aftermath of World War I. His father's parents had set out as newlyweds from Scotland at about the same time. They had settled on small, neighboring farms in Pennsylvania, north of Reading. At the time, the land was cheap, because it turned out to be poor farming land.

On both sides, Lucas's grandparents were simple, unassuming folk, conditioned by the hardships they had endured in their homelands. Each couple had distanced themselves from the rest of the community. It was inevitable, he supposed, that the son of one pair and the daughter of the other should marry.

Raised as they had been, his mother and father were both undereducated, unassuming people, ill equipped to deal with a society racing to embrace the advance of technology. Not only could they not keep up, they could not compete.

Lucas had witnessed the long, hard days his father had put

into the land just to eke from it a living below subsistence level, only to leave later in the evening to work the third shift, from eleven P.M. to seven A.M. in a hosiery factory located nearly ten miles from home. And he had watched his mother exhaust herself in keeping house and seeing that her children were decently dressed, clean and neat, though she was helping her husband with the farm work and was also doing housework for other women in the area.

At age thirteen, grown tall, his body strong from physical labor on the farm, Lucas hired himself out after school and during the summer to neighbors, doing yard work, house painting, and general all-around repairs. The pay was minimal, but every extra dollar helped.

Then, just as he was about to finish high school, his parents died, within six months of one another; his father of a massive coronary suffered in the field while harvesting, his mother near the end of that winter. Lucas had just turned eighteen. The official cause of his mother's death was listed as influenza. Lucas knew better. He knew that his parents were simply worn out and had simply given up the fight.

But he wasn't about to give up—which was a good thing since for him the bigger battles had just begun.

The first turned out to be the one to complete his education. Though he had earned a scholarship to Franklin and Marshall University, he had his younger brothers, Michael, who was then eleven, and Robert, who was not quite nine, to consider. Life would have been much simpler for Lucas if he had surrendered his brothers into the care of the authorities, allowing them to place the boys in foster homes.

But Lucas, showing signs of the mature man he would become, settled on an alternative resolution.

His grandparents lived nearby and were willing to look after the boys while he attended the university. But they were getting on in years, and were no longer in the best of health, so he commuted to classes every day, driving back and forth in his father's twelve-year-old Chevrolet. In addition, he worked nights and some weekends in a Reading steel mill to supplement his grandparents' meager income.

Through sheer perseverance, Lucas managed to get his degree while supporting two growing brothers, who could eat their way through most of his pay.

No, nothing had come easily for Lucas. He had worked his rump off throughout the intervening years, and he had learned a lot along the way, made some friends and a few enemies, before achieving the success he currently enjoyed.

And for him, "enjoy" was the operative word. He had enjoyed every minute of working his rump off, as he now fully enjoyed the satisfying rewards of his endeavors. He had paid his dues in sweat, fatigue, frustration, and self-denial, paid for his success, his education, and the subsequent education of his brothers, for every dollar of his now considerable wealth, and for the respect afforded him by friend and foe alike. If he had not been victorious in every battle, he had won most of them.

In the business world, Lucas MacCanna was now a power to be reckoned with—no mean feat for a man still several months away from celebrating his fortieth birthday.

But though he was held in high regard and respect by many of his contemporaries, Lucas knew he was feared by some and rightly so. He not only didn't suffer fools, he considered them not worth his notice. And he didn't play games or lavish time on gamesters. Unless, that is, their foolishness spilled over into his personal or professional life. That he did not tolerate.

Now Harold Styer's foolishness was beginning to have a direct effect on Lucas's steel business. Either that or the man was even more inept than Lucas had originally thought.

In either case, Lucas had months ago set the wheels in motion to correct the situation, if necessary, by instructing his broker to buy as much as possible of Styer's company's stock. Unsurprisingly, in light of the company's financial difficulties over the past year or so, his broker had been able to secure over sixty-five percent of the total forty-five percent of the common shares. The stock, plus the proxy votes he had been granted, in addition to the two Cutting Edge board members he had so far managed to come to a tentative agreement with, gave him a lever he wouldn't hesitate to use, should the rumors about Styer be proved correct.

Well, he'd know, and soon, he reflected, aware without having to glance away from the road when he passed the site of The Cutting Edge Surgical Instrument Company. It was located just beyond the Philadelphia city limits, along the Schuylkill River, next to the railroad tracks—the very same tracks on which he shipped his steel.

Lucas eased his grip on the wheel and released a soft sigh of relief as he exited the expressway onto City Avenue, heading for the Adam's Mark Hotel.

He had placed a man, a C.P.A. "mole," in the accounting office of The Cutting Edge Company some months ago. His mole would be joining him for dinner tonight at the hotel.

It now was only a matter of time.

The worst of the storm's fury had passed, moving east toward the Jersey coast. The slashing rain had subsided to a moderate shower. A wry smile feathered Lucas's taut lips as he braked to a stop at the hotel entrance.

Were he a superstitious man, he might well fear that the storm's pacing him had been a sign of some sort, indicating turbulence ahead.

Fortunately, he was not. Nor did he fear the turbulence of a business confrontation. Despite the belief held by many of his contemporaries, he didn't relish it, either.

He had worked too hard, too long; had sacrificed much and had been forced to compromise too often to get to his present position to change now.

He was tough, and he knew it. But then, life itself was tough. Lucas accepted that; he asked no quarter, and he granted it to few.

He would do what he must to safeguard his own company and a company that, until very recently, had earned its mantle of excellence.

It won't be long now, Lucas thought. Stepping from the car, he handed his keys to the doorman. He would soon know how far that mantle had slipped.

Chapter Four

"Embezzlement!"

Frisco crushed the nap of the forest green plush carpet in her father's equally plush office, leaving a flattened path as she prowled restlessly back and forth. Her arms crossed over her breasts, she rubbed her palms over her upper arms, cringing with each recurring flash of lightning and subsequent deep rumble of thunder.

"I wish you wouldn't call it that," Harold protested plaintively. "It sounds so . . . so . . ."

"Criminal?" she asked, gazing bleakly out of the window that took up most of one wall.

"Well, yes."

Frisco turned away from the plate glass to stare in despair at him. She flinched as another streak of lightning crackled beyond the pane.

Her reaction to the spring storm was unusual; normally, she didn't mind the crash and bang of the elements. In fact, she had always rather liked thunderstorms. But this afternoon, she was not her normal self; she felt harried.

She had left her office at noon, as she'd promised, and had

spent the afternoon in her father's accounting department, reviewing the company's financial records. Of course, there had not been sufficient time for her to do more than skim the computer files, but she had seen enough to know that her father was stealing from the firm, and on a fairly regular basis.

Had he said just yesterday that he was in trouble? Frisco suppressed a shudder. He could go to jail for what he'd done.

Despair washed over her as she stared at the man she had idolized as a young girl. God, growing up was tough.

"Dad, there's no other word for it," Frisco pointed out tiredly. "You've committed embezzlement—it's a criminal offense. It's commonly referred to as white-collar crime. You could go to prison for it."

Harold attempted to speak, cleared his throat, swallowed, then tried again, somewhat more successfully. "I . . . I . . . your mother . . . I can't go to prison! Frisco, what would that do to your mother?"

"Destroy her," she said with brutal honesty.

He shuddered, looked sick and frightened. "I've got to do something. Something. There must be a way." He wet his lips and shifted his eyes, glancing around the room as if looking for a means of escape.

Frisco stared at him helplessly, swamped by the conflicting emotions of pity and disgust. Pity for his weakness, disgust for his inability to rise above it.

"What can I do?" he cried in abject panic. "You're an accountant, tell me what to do. Help me fix it!"

"Fix it! Dad, the only way to fix it is to replace the funds you've taken from the accounts."

"But I don't have it!"

"You gambled it all away, didn't you?"

"Y-yes." His voice was little more than a croak.

"And still you continued to gamble, running up I.O.U.s into the millions to casinos." She nearly choked on the last word. "Didn't you?"

"Yes, yes! I told you all that last night." He looked trapped— and ready to bolt.

"You also told me you had borrowed from the company,"

she shot back relentlessly. "I thought—assumed—you meant you had borrowed against the company, not that you had stolen from it." Fury fired by her disappointment in him flashed through her. "Dammit, Dad, it was never your company to borrow from, let alone steal from. It's Mother's."

"I know. I know." He closed his eyes. "What can I do? Who else can I turn to for help?"

"You have to tell her."

His eyes flew open—and were stark with fear. "Your mother! I can't. I—"

She cut him off harshly. "You have to. You must. I can't help you. All I have is my trust fund and my own savings. You know I can't touch the principal of the trust, and the income isn't nearly enough. But Mother does have enough to replace the amount missing from the company accounts."

"I can't tell her," he protested. "I wouldn't know where to begin. It would hurt her too badly."

"I know, but you've got to do it." Frisco heaved a sigh, hurting inside, not for herself but for her mother, whose only crime was loving unconditionally, without question or doubt. "You have no other option, Dad."

"I just can't do that," Harold said, walking unsteadily to stand next to her at the window. "There's not enough time, anyway. Lucas MacCanna will be here at nine tomorrow morning. And I've heard he's never late."

Lucas MacCanna. Frisco had forgotten all about him. Understandable, she mused, considering the outcome of the day's events.

"Cancel the appointment," she said impatiently. "Reschedule it for a later date."

Harold was shaking his head before she had finished speaking. "I already thought of that. I tried this morning. I called his home and his office at the plant near Reading. I got his brother Michael. He told me Lucas left yesterday for Philadelphia, and that he hadn't mentioned the name of the hotel where he'd be staying."

"Then bluff your way through the meeting," Frisco advised. "Put him off until after you've talked to Mother."

"Bluff MacCanna?" He looked at her as if she had asked
him to sprout wings and fly. "You've got to be joking."

"He's only a man, Dad." She dismissed his obvious awe of
the man with a flick of one hand. "Besides, you have no other
option," she went on to remind him, "because you sure as
hell can't run away from this one."

"All right," he agreed, looking utterly defeated, "but I can't
do it alone. I'll need you here with me."

"Me!" She shook her head, hard. "What can I do?"

"Lend moral support." He grasped her hands and stared
pleadingly into her eyes. "Frisco, please."

What could she say? Right or wrong, good, bad, or just plain
stupid, he was her father. And she loved him.

"Okay, Dad, I'll be here."

Chapter Five

"And there you have it." Tim Jenkins, otherwise known as the C.P.A. mole, gave Lucas a wry look over the rim of the brandy snifter he cradled in his hands.

"Hmmm," Lucas murmured around the sip of cognac he had taken. He savored the taste before swallowing. "So, Styer's not only a lousy businessman, he's a thief as well."

"And possibly a lousy gambler into the bargain, don't forget," Tim said, sniffing the aroma of the hand-warmed brandy.

Lucas smiled. "Oh, I won't. In fact, I'll know the truth about his gambling 'losses' before I step into his office tomorrow morning."

"I don't doubt it." Tim shivered and took a big gulp of his drink. Lucas's feral smile had that effect on most people.

The smile relaxed and gave way to a low chuckle. "You did a good job, Tim. Thanks."

Tim eased up as well, enough to offer his boss a slanted grin. "May I go home now? I mean, before my wife and kids forget what I look like?"

Lucas laughed outright. It was a pleasant sound, low, sultry, and according to more than a few females, sexy as the very devil.

"Yes, you may go home, and don't worry, Tricia and the kids will remember you soon enough when they see the presents you've bought them with the bonus I've instructed accounting to add to your salary."

"Thanks, Lucas." Though Tim was obviously pleased, he was evidently not surprised, which was understandable. He had worked for Lucas MacCanna for a long time. He knew the extent of his employer's generosity when the man was satisfied. He knew as well the depths of MacCanna's anger when he was not.

"If you have no objections, I'd like to start back when we've finished here."

"I had booked a room for you here at the hotel, but"—Lucas shrugged—"I have no objections if you want to leave." His smile was slow, knowing. "It's been a long, dry spell for you since that brief visit home, hasn't it?"

Tim's return smile had a wicked quirk. "Yes, it has. Too long—and too dry. I have an urgent need to be with my family."

Lucas saluted Tim with a tilt of his glass. "Then we're finished. I appreciate all you've done, but get out of here. Go home to Tricia and the kids."

"You're the boss." Tim polished off his drink and stood up. "And thanks again."

"Oh, by the way," Lucas said, halting him in mid stride, "give your lovely wife my regards."

"Will do," Tim promised. "Good night, Lucas."

Watching Tim leave, Lucas knew the night was not yet over for him.

Setting his empty glass on the table, he signed the dinner check, then stood and left the dining room.

He had a call to make—to Atlantic City, to a man well placed in a casino, a man who owed him more than one favor.

A faint smile shadowed Lucas's lips as he stepped off the elevator at his floor, a smile born of the thought that he was about to call in an I.O.U.

* * *

"Styer?" Grim-sounding laughter sang along the telephone wire into Lucas's ear. "I don't suppose there's anyone here who hasn't heard of him."

"Earned himself a reputation, has he?" Lucas asked, enjoying the feel of satisfaction seeping through him.

"In spades. The man's a fool, doesn't know when to quit." Laughter again vibrated Lucas's eardrum. "Hell, the way he plays, he should never start. But don't ever say I said that, because I'll deny it."

"Wouldn't dream of it," Lucas drawled. "How deep has our friend plunged?"

"Over a million here, and a half a mil or so down the boardwalk." After a short pause for another snorting laugh, he continued. "And somewhere around three-quarters of a million to a couple casinos in Vegas."

"In the vicinity of two million?"

"Might even be closer to three. You want me to get you the exact amount?"

"Not necessary. This is close enough for my purposes," Lucas said. "Thanks."

As he replaced the receiver, he chuckled at the whimsical thought that flickered through his mind.

Time to sharpen the gelding knife.

Chapter Six

"Lucas! Come in. Come and meet my daughter."

Frisco's spine, already stiff from anger at her father's confession that he had not confided in his wife, stiffened even more at Harold's overly effusive tone.

Standing at the window, her back to the office, she composed her features into an expressionless mask, and then turned to face the legend.

"Frisco, come say hello to Lucas MacCanna." While Harold's smile was broad, his eyes held a pleading desperation. "Lucas, my daughter, Frisco."

"Hello, Lucas MacCanna," Frisco parroted obediently, shifting her gaze from her father's strained face to the closed expression of the man Harold was ushering into the room.

Damned if he doesn't look like a living, breathing legend, she thought. Then again, what exactly does a legend look like? she impatiently chided herself.

Exactly like Lucas MacCanna, her mind shot back at her; tall, trim, fit, quite like a professional athlete—past his playing years perhaps, but certainly not past his physical prime—and dark . . . hair, eyes, complexion. The overall effect he projected was one of power, self-confidence, and sensuality.

Aware of her immediate response, which she resented, and a twinge of trepidation, which she resented even more, Frisco moved forward, right hand extended.

"Hello." His dark eyebrows arched. "Ms.? Mrs.?"

"Ms. Styer," she said, experiencing a strange, trapped sensation as his strong hand enveloped hers. "But don't stand on ceremony, call me Frisco."

"And I'm Lucas."

You certainly are, she thought, irrelevantly, breathing easier when he released her hand.

"Pleased to meet you," she said, knowing she lied; she wasn't pleased about a thing, most especially the lingering sensation of his hand curled around hers. "I've heard a lot about you." That at least was not a lie. She didn't bother to add that she hadn't liked most of what she'd heard.

"Really?" His dark eyebrows arched, either in query or disbelief. "I've never heard much of anything about you." He turned to her father. "I don't recall you ever mentioning a daughter, Harold."

"Didn't I?" Though Harold gave a quick chuckle, it held a tense, forced note.

"No." Lucas returned his direct gaze to her. "In what capacity are you employed in the firm?"

The sharp, intelligent gleam in his eyes made Frisco uncomfortable and abraded her simmering anger. She had to fight for control, to keep from firing a stinging response at him—and to keep from trembling.

"I'm not employed by the firm, Mr. MacCanna," she replied, her impatience evident.

"No? Then why—"

Anticipating his question, she interrupted, saving him the effort of finishing. "I'm here at my father's request. Merely as an observer, you understand."

"No, I don't." He offered her a hint of a smile; the hint was as pointed as a pig sticker. "But that's all right, I have no objections to your being here."

Big of you. Frisco kept the retort inside her head, along with the assurance that she'd stay whether or not he objected to her presence. Instead, she gave him a patently false, over-bright smile in lieu of a verbal response.

"Why don't we get comfortable over here?" Harold invited heartily, obviously sensing the tension building between his guest and his daughter. He made a sweeping gesture with his hand to indicate the furniture grouping, white leather chairs and a settee placed around a large marble-topped coffee table, to one side of the wide window; Harold surrounded himself with the trappings of success.

"Since it's still early, I've ordered a tray of sweet rolls to go with our coffee."

His expression wry, Lucas MacCanna stepped aside to allow Frisco to precede him.

Determined to keep her cool even if it killed her, she bestowed a condescending smile on her father and strolled to the settee, leaving the chairs to the men.

Her father settled himself in one.

MacCanna did not.

To Frisco's annoyance, he stepped around the remaining chair and lowered his considerable form onto the settee beside her. To make matters worse, he did it gracefully.

"This is all very comfortable, pleasant and civilized, but—" he began, only to be interrupted by a light rap against the door.

"Ah! Here's our coffee!" Harold sprang to his feet, looking and sounding as though the summons had been a last-minute reprieve from the governor.

Irritated by her father's blatant ploy to put off the inevitable, even though she had advised him to play for time, and further agitated by the very nearness of the man seated next to her, Frisco watched in frustration as a serving cart was rolled into the office.

At least the coffee smelled good, she thought. The situation certainly didn't.

"How do you take your coffee, Lucas?" Harold asked, after

politely thanking and then dismissing the cafeteria employee who'd brought the refreshments.

"Black, no sugar."

As unremitting as his demeanor, Frisco decided, sliding a sidelong glance at his sternly set profile.

"And I take cream and sugar, a half-teaspoon."

Harold flashed a genuine smile at her. "I remember. And you prefer a plain croissant over Danish. Right?"

"As a rule." She returned his smile, though it wasn't easy; she was already fed up with this farce, and the meeting hadn't even begun. "I'll pass today."

"Dieting?" Lucas turned his head to rake her body with an interested, and to her mind insulting, once-over.

Bristling, yet still determined to stay calm, Frisco managed a dismissive smile and a succinct reply. "No."

"Glad to hear it."

His response confused her. "Really? Why?"

He smiled, and she hated it, primarily because she hated the sensations his smile created inside her. They were unsettling.

"Why?" His eyebrows went up again. "Why because I'm planning to ask you to have dinner with me this evening," he explained coolly. "And I don't enjoy sitting opposite a woman picking at a salad while I'm savoring a meal."

Have dinner with him? Was the man mad? She didn't want to be in this room with him, let alone . . . Stunned speechless by what she perceived as his sheer arrogance, Frisco could do no more than stare at him for some moments.

Her father stepped into the silent breach. "Will you have a Danish with your coffee, Lucas?"

"No, thank you." His smile had fled, leaving a stern, straight lip-line in its stead. "I think it's time to get down to business."

"Yes, yes, of course," Harold agreed, then went on to further procrastination. "But let's enjoy our coffee while it's still hot." His smile was too wide to be real "And I think I'll indulge in a cheese Danish."

Frisco swallowed a groan with a careful sip of her hot coffee. Her father was laying on the bonhomie a little too heavily for her taste. And for Lucas MacCanna's as well according to his expression.

He looked as though he couldn't decide whether he wanted to laugh or swear. He did neither. Following her example, he raised his cup and sipped the coffee.

When, after an awkward and strained silence, Harold finally finished his Danish, MacCanna shattered the uneasy quiet by going directly to the purpose of the meeting.

"You're in arrears on payment for three shipments of steel, Harold."

"I know, I know," Harold said nervously, his cup clattering against marble as he set it on the table. "And I intend to settle in full soon." He wet his lips. "If you'll allow me just a little more time, I'll—" That was as far as he got before MacCanna cut him off.

"Your time has run out." Lucas's voice was hard, unrelenting. "And so has my patience."

"Now wait just a minute!" Frisco began in protest. That was as far as *she* got.

"No, I've waited long enough." Lucas shifted his hard stare from her father to her. "Are you aware that your father has been systematically stealing from this company?" He grimaced, then continued before she could respond. "Of course you know, that's why you're here, isn't it?"

Frisco wanted to rush to her father's defense, categorically deny his perfidy, but in good conscience she could not. She felt trapped, caught in a snare of her own father's making. She didn't like the feeling.

"Yes," she admitted, her voice tight with tension. "Yes, I knew, but—"

"But, hell!" Lucas again cut her off harshly. "This was a setup, wasn't it?" He indicated the serving cart with an impatient flick of his hand. "This whole scene has been enacted to put me off, to stall for time, hasn't it?"

"But that's all we need," Harold cried out in a pleading tone that made Frisco cringe. "A little time, a few days, a week at most."

"To do what?" Lucas said skeptically. "What can you possibly do in a few days, or even a week?" Apparently the questions were rhetorical, for he charged right ahead. "I'm not a fool, Styer. I do my homework. I know you're financially against the wall—no credit, no resources."

"That's where you're wrong, Mr. MacCanna." Frisco derived a sense of satisfaction from contradicting him. "My father is not out of resources."

Lucas's skeptical look was leveled on her, and his hard-eyed stare was piercing. "You?"

Frisco took offense at his mocking tone, but was forced to admit his disbelief was valid. "No, not me," she said, fervently wishing she did have the funds, just for the pleasure it would give her to put him in his place. Even so, she eked some comfort out of setting him straight. "But my mother is in a position to reimburse the company. And she will do so, I can assure you of that."

"In other words, she doesn't know that her husband has been robbing the firm." A cynical smile curved Lucas's lips. "I can't help but wonder if your mother's pool of resources is deep enough to cover your father's gambling debts."

His remark was met with stark silence. But then, a verbal reply wasn't required. The quick look exchanged by Frisco and her father said it all.

"Uh-huh." This time Lucas only raised one eyebrow. "She doesn't know about the gambling debts, does she?"

"That's hardly any concern of yours," Frisco snapped.

"You . . . you know about that?" Harold asked in a croaking voice.

"I do." Lucas turned a cool look on Frisco. "And I disagree, Ms Styer. Your father's gambling losses are of great concern to me." He gave her a smile that had no warmth. "The way I see it, some of that money he tossed away should have come to my company."

"I swear you'll get all the back payments due you," Harold promised. "I just need a little more time."

"At the risk of repeating myself, you have run out of time," Lucas shot back. "I must now take action to correct the status quo."

"Wh . . ." Harold wet his lips, betraying his fear of Mac-Canna and of having his world crash in. "What form of action?"

"I think you know. You wouldn't have contrived this production number to delay me otherwise."

"You're talking hostile takeover," Frisco said, finally fed up with the farce.

"I'm not hostile." Lucas smiled to prove his assertion, but got the opposite result.

"Friendly, hostile, what's the difference?" Harold cried. "The results are the same."

"No, they are not." Lucas gave a sharp shake of his head. "If I succeed in taking over this company, it won't be to tear it apart."

Harold looked sick. "But I'll be gone."

"Yes."

"This company has been under the control of our family for generations, ever since the beginning over a hundred years ago," Frisco interjected in protest.

"Then perhaps this generation of your family should have taken better care of it," Lucas retorted.

Well, he has me there, Frisco conceded to herself, silenced. Her family should have paid more attention to the business. Frisco had to admit, at least to herself, that her mother never should have turned the reins over to her father. Also, perhaps she herself should have paid closer attention.

"At this stage of the game, don't you think self-flagellation is rather pointless?" Lucas asked not unkindly, breaking into her thoughts.

"I beg your pardon?" The look she gave him was as cold as her tone of voice; damned if she wanted anything from Lucas MacCanna, most especially his understanding of the inner workings of her mind—murky though they might be.

"Never mind." He shrugged. "We can discuss it over dinner tonight."

Dinner indeed! Frisco thought. In your dreams!

She was ready to laugh in his face when reason cautioned her to think it through. If she agreed to having dinner with him, in a one-on-one conversation, maybe, just maybe, she could convince him to allow her father the time he needed to work out the past-due payments to MacCanna.

"I'm sorry, but I have a previous engagement this evening," she said, curious as to whether he'd offer an alternative invitation.

He would, and he did.

"Tomorrow night, then?"

Frisco was well aware of her father, a worried frown scoring his face as he shifted his gaze between her and MacCanna. Poor Dad, he believes I've decided to become the sacrificial lamb to save his unworthy hide, she mused, once again containing the urge to laugh.

On the other hand, perhaps she had. Not liking the unsettling idea of appearing to offer herself, her company, to this legend on a dinner platter, she rushed to agree before she could change her mind.

"Yes, I'm free tomorrow evening."

"Good. Is seven all right with you?"

"Frisco, baby, you don't have to do this," Harold jumped in to protest before she could respond. "Your mother and I can handle this without you having to—"

"She doesn't *have* to do a damn thing," Lucas cut him off brusquely.

"And I know that." Frisco gave him a look which she hoped conveyed her utter lack of concern. It was a false expression, of course, but she also hoped he couldn't penetrate it.

Jumping to his feet, her father came to stand in front of her. "Are you certain you want to do this?"

Now Frisco couldn't decide whether she wanted to laugh or cry. Harold's assuming the role of protective father at this late date was both amusing and sad.

That reflection reactivated her feelings of guilt, for in all fairness, he had been protective of her, stiflingly so, when she was a little girl.

Reminding herself that she was no longer a little girl but still the same person, Frisco smiled with tender understanding of his past efforts and his present dilemma.

"It's only a dinner date, Dad."

"In a public restaurant," Lucas tacked on dryly.

Harold shifted his worried gaze to the man seated next to Frisco. MacCanna smiled. Frisco could have sworn she saw a fine tremor of intimidation ripple through her father.

This is getting ridiculous, she thought, deciding to grasp control of the situation.

"Yes, Dad, in a public restaurant. And I am a grown woman, you know, perfectly capable of taking care of myself." She slanted a wry glance at MacCanna. "I promise, if he gets out of hand, I'll scream for the law."

Lucas let out a roar of appreciative laughter.

Frisco's eyes narrowed; his laughter sounded good, too good, completely masculine, utterly sexy.

Oh, boy, was she out of her mind, or what?

Impatient, with herself, with her father, but most of all with MacCanna, she stood, walked to the center of the room, then turned to confront the two men.

"Can we get on with the purpose of this meeting now?" She looked pointedly at the ornate clock on her father's desk. "I have an appointment in town at twelve-thirty for lunch." It was a blatant lie but—she gave a mental shrug—somebody had to move things along here.

"Oh." Harold's voice betrayed unraveling nerves. "You didn't mention it earlier."

"Well"—Frisco really shrugged—"I guess I thought it wouldn't be necessary."

"And it's unnecessary for us to detain you," Lucas said. "Or, for that matter, for us to continue." His smile was too knowing, too wise; it bothered Frisco.

"You mean . . . ?" Harold's relief was so evident it was downright embarrassing.

"I mean, I'm going to allow you the time you've requested," Lucas said distinctly. Then he went on in a steely tone, "But understand this, Styer. I have not changed my mind about a thing. I fully intend to retire you and take control of this company."

Harold blanched.

Frisco blinked.

Lucas, without missing a beat, continued smoothly. "Now, where do I call for you tomorrow evening?"

Chapter Seven

"I've never been here before. It's nice."

Frisco took a small sip of her chilled chardonnay, and sent a leisurely glance around her.

She didn't know why, but Lucas's choice of restaurant had come as something of a surprise. It was a restored old mansion, in a rural setting, located some miles from the usual haute haunts in and about the city. With subdued lighting and muted, nonintrusive background music, this place offered fine dining in a quiet, genteel atmosphere.

The round tables, dressed with starched cloths and napkins, were set with delicate china, the discreet distances separating them allowing for private conversations.

The overall effect was one of subtle elegance, quite like the dark wine-colored car Lucas had driven to convey them to it.

"It fairly reeks of the best money can buy," she observed, letting her drifting gaze wander back to him.

"Yes." He smiled and raised his glass of cabernet in a silent salute to her. "I knew you'd like it."

Frisco wasn't exactly sure how to interpret his remark, still she could no more stem the flow of soft laughter that poured from her throat than she could voluntarily stop breathing at will,

"How did you discover it?" she asked, avoiding a direct confrontation over so small a matter; she was here to advance her father's cause, after all. "An advertisement?"

"No." His smile slipped into a grin, and a rather beguiling grin, at that. "I was entertained here a few months ago by business acquaintances. They were courting, too."

"Too?" She frowned. "I don't understand."

"I know."

Frisco was, and knew she looked, puzzled.

Lucas changed the subject.

"By the way, I liked your home. That's the first house I've been inside, in Radnor."

"Thank you," she said, playing along with the conversational switch. "But it isn't mine. It's my parents' home."

"You don't live there?"

"Not for years. Not since I graduated from college."

"Then where do you live?"

"In the city."

"Where?" he persisted. "Do you live alone?"

The tension she had endured from that first sight of him in her father's office yesterday had just begun to ease a bit. Now his abrupt demand for personal information brought it back. Her spine grew rigid, her eyes grew cautious, her voice grew cold.

"I really don't think that's any of your business."

"That's where you're wrong," he said, in a smooth tone edged with roughness. "This is about business, my business, and your father's business." His expression was sardonic. "Need I remind you that you invited yourself into this business?"

Rotten son of a . . . Frisco kept her mouth shut and worked her stiff lips into a smile.

"So, now that we've cleared that up"—he returned her smile, sort of—"where do you live? And are you currently sharing the place?"

She dearly longed to slug him. She didn't as much as move

her hand, of course. She was angry, not mad in the stark, staring sense.

"I have a condo," she said in a low, gritty voice, providing the exact location. Her voice went lower, got grittier. "And I live alone."

The look he slanted at her was loaded with amusement and teasing. "Now, that wasn't too terrible, was it?"

Frisco's fingers gripped the slender stem of her wine glass; the arrival of the waiter at their table saved her from making a scene . . . and a fool of herself. She fumed in silent frustration as the soup course was served.

It was only as she released her grasp on the glass to pick up her spoon that she was made aware Lucas MacCanna had not missed a thing.

"I'm glad you decided not to toss the wine," he said in a laughter-laced voice. "I am partial to this suit."

"Go to hell, and take your suit with you," she muttered, raising a spoonful of lobster bisque to her lips, certain he hadn't heard her. She was wrong.

"I very likely will," he rejoined with a grin. "And I expect to have a helluva lot of company there."

"All in business suits?" Frisco asked with wide-eyed, patently false innocence. She sipped the soup.

"Umm," he murmured around the soup he'd taken into his mouth. "Some with pants, some with skirts," he said after swallowing. "Good, isn't it?"

"Yes." In truth, the bisque was to die for. She took another sip, a bigger one. "Delicious."

"Uh-huh." Lucas wasn't looking at or tasting the soup; he was staring at her as though he wanted to gobble her down in one big gulp.

The tension threading inside Frisco twanged like a taut guitar string. What was the man thinking? Ha! She was fairly certain she knew. But why? Again hah! She felt even more certain she knew why; the tension simmering inside her was antagonistic in nature, sexual in attraction, and flash point in degree. He was feeling it, too. Feeling it, hell, he was the cause of it.

Heavy stuff. And new to Frisco. Oh, she had been aroused

before, what woman hasn't? But this disorienting heat generated between herself and a man she barely knew was altogether new, and a bit scary.

"So what are we going to do about it?"

The question jolted her. Frisco carefully laid the spoon on
the plate beneath the shallow soup bowl. She wet her lips. She
folded her hands in her lap. She twined her fingers.

"What are we going to do about what?" She despaired over
the crack in her voice.

He smiled.

Damn. Lucas MacCanna could very likely conquer the world
with that smile. If he chose to do so.

"This business about your father's business," he answered
wryly. "He's in trouble, big trouble, and you know it. From
my perspective, I'd say he can't find his ass with both hands,
never mind a way out of the mess he's created."

"Now, wait a minute!" she exclaimed, feeling duty-bound to
protest his assessment of her father, even though she knew it
was accurate.

"No, you wait." He gave a quick, sharp shake of his head.
"I don't deal in niceties. What is, is, and like it or not, your
father is a lousy businessman."

Since there was little point in arguing against the truth,
Frisco conceded by remaining mute.

"Okay." He accepted her silence for what it was, surrender.
"I'll repeat; what are we going to do about untangling this
mess he's created?"

"But, my mother—" she began.

"Join the real world," he interrupted. "My understanding
is that about all your mother can do is replace the funds he
has . . . ah . . . helped himself to." He paused, then added
an aside, "Your mother is a lovely woman, by the way."

Frisco was developing a headache. "Yes, she is, in personality
as well as appearance." Her tone reflected her hard determination. "I will not see her hurt."

"I'm not in the business of hurting women," Lucas responded. "Young or slightly older."

"But, if you persist in your intent to cause trouble for my father . . ." She let her voice fade.

"Oh, I intend to persist. In fact, I have every intention of taking over the company."

"But it's been in my mother's family for over a hundred years!" Her protest had the sound of a strangled plea. "She will be hurt, deeply hurt."

"Then . . ."

The waiter set up a rack next to their table and placed a large serving tray on it. Working swiftly and efficiently, he whisked the soup plates away and replaced them with entrées and side dishes.

"The poached salmon looks good."

Frisco, going along with his polite chatter, forced a smile and a response. "Yes, it does, and your steak looks . . . rare."

MacCanna chuckled.

Frisco sighed; it wasn't easy, disliking a man who possessed such potent qualities as a devastating smile, an engaging laugh, and an exciting grin.

"Now, then, where were we?" The serrated blade sliced through the two-inch steak with the ease of a rapier cutting through cream.

"My mother." Her voice was tight; she couldn't help it. She'd do anything short of mayhem and murder to protect her mother. "You were about to say something about my mother being hurt."

"Yes, your mother." Lucas thoroughly chewed the bite of steak in his mouth before continuing. "What I had been about to say was, we'll have to think of a way to resolve this messy situation in a manner not injurious to your mother."

Frisco nearly choked on the small piece of fish she had slipped between her teeth. "In a manner not injurious . . ." At a loss for words, she simply stared at him. How in the world could this be resolved without hurting her mother?

"Precisely." He popped another chunk of beef into his mouth and chewed with evident enjoyment. He swallowed, took a sip of wine, then went on, "I will not back down on this." His eyes, his tone, his expression were one—hard. "I

am going to take control from your father, because, if I do
not, or someone else doesn't, he will run the company into
the ground."

Frisco lowered her eyes, and voice. "I know."

"All right then." Lucas exhaled, as if relieved. Although why
her agreeing with him in regard to her father's less-than-sterling
business sense should affect him one way or another was beyond
her. "Maybe there's a way."

Frisco couldn't believe her ears. How could he possibly . . . ?
She shook her head, impatient with herself. *Ask, idiot!*

"To go about this without my mother being hurt?"

"Or, perhaps, even knowing."

Oh, come on! Frisco clamped her lips against the incredulous
comment. But . . . honestly.

"How?"

"Well . . ." He made a face, not unpleasant, more uncertain. "I have a glimmer of an idea, I'll have to think about it,
mull it over in my mind awhile." He gave her a crooked smile,
then dug his fork into the center of the baked potato on which
he had slathered butter and sour cream.

Frisco felt certain she was gaining weight just watching him
devour them. She tried to satisfy herself with a bite of her
salad, on which she had drizzled vinaigrette dressing. Somehow the satisfaction wasn't there.

Thirtysome minutes later, she left the restaurant empty, on
all counts. She had eaten less than half of her dinner, she
hadn't garnered one whit of insight into the character of Lucas MacCanna, and she didn't have a clue as to how to proceed
concerning the family business. This last left her both frustrated and empty.

"Back to the house in Radnor or . . . ?" Lucas said, after
seeing her into the car.

"Yes. I'm spending the weekend with my parents."

Frisco didn't bother to expand on the subject. It wasn't any
of MacCanna's business that her visit was unplanned. Nor was
it his concern that she had taken her mother to lunch Friday,
to nullify her lie in the office, or that she had spent the night
with her parents for the very same reason.

The drive back to Radnor was made in near silence. Lucas appeared distracted, in a blue study, and Frisco, still suffering the inner tingles of sexual-attraction tension, was in no mood to draw him out.

"Frisco." His voice was soft, no hint of a question underlying it. Just her name.

A shiver ran through her. "What?" She slanted a wary look at him.

"Hmmm, your name, that's all."

Wonderful. All her life, people had questioned her about her name. By the year she'd turned twenty-one, she had seriously considered having it legally changed. But that, too, would have hurt her mother.

Frisco sighed.

"Why do I get the feeling you've been through this before?" His voice shimmered with amusement.

"Maybe because I have." Her voice was flat with acceptance.

"So, what is it?"

That kind of threw her. "What is what?"

"Your name, Frisco. Short for what?"

"Short for Frisco." She sighed again. "That's it. Get ready for it. My full name is Frisco Bay Styer." She held her breath, waiting for a response; she didn't wait long.

MacCanna roared, actually roared. His laughter filled the interior of the car . . . and aroused her ire.

"I love it!"

"You don't have to live with it."

"True." He tried to look somber and sympathetic; he failed. The light of deviltry blazed from his dark eyes, and his lips had a suspicious twitch. "But if it's any consolation, and I feel sure it isn't, I like the name."

"You're correct," she said, rather acidly. "Not politically, but about it not being a consolation."

Chuckling, Lucas brought the car to a gliding stop on the curved driveway in front of her parents' home. He pulled the hand brake, then turned to face her.

"Testy, aren't you?"

"You were expecting pleasant?"

"Would've been nice." He shrugged. "I gather you are not going to invite me in for a nightcap or coffee."

"You're batting a thousand."

"Uh-huh." He heaved a sigh—bogus, she felt sure. "Can I either see or reach you tomorrow, in the event this idea I'm playing with pans out in my mind?"

Frisco gazed at him for long seconds, in contemplation. She didn't want to see or talk to him again, ever. She didn't want to live in the same state. He bothered her, big time. She was tired, and didn't feel up to the kind of excitement he so effortlessly generated.

But there were her parents to consider, and the family business.

At that moment, Frisco was not inclined to be either kind or forgiving toward her father.

But . . . An image of her mother swam to the forefront of her mind. Gertrude of the soft voice and sweet disposition. The very woman who had appeared to be favorably impressed by Mr. Lucas MacCanna when he had arrived at the house to take out her daughter.

Of course, Gertrude had been chafing at the bit for years, eager to see her daughter married.

Frisco shuddered at the mere idea. Nevertheless, she once again caved in to circumstances.

"I'll be leaving after breakfast tomorrow, and will be at my place in the afternoon," she finally answered. "I have an engagement for dinner." This time her voice held the ring of truth; she was having dinner with her two best friends, as she did at least once a month.

"All right. I may be giving you a call in the afternoon." There was a speculative gleam in his eyes. "Or . . . could I stop by your place?"

"I'd rather you didn't." Frisco regretted her words, her cold tone, at once. She knew she couldn't afford to antagonize this man, and yet . . . She released the door and swung it open. "Don't bother to get out."

"I'll call," he said, strangely amused, not offended by her attitude. "Good night, Frisco Bay."

Determined to hang on to her temper, which did indeed at times reflect her hair color, Frisco stepped from the car, then impulsively advised, "I'd do almost anything for my family, MacCanna, but don't push your luck."

The damnable, exciting sound of his soft laughter rang inside her head all the way into the house, up the wide staircase, and into the bedroom that had been hers for as long as she'd been on the earth.

Chapter Eight

He wanted her.

Standing at the hotel-room window, staring into the hushed, two A.M. streets, Lucas came to a decision.

He was hard, rigidly, painfully erect, harder than he'd been in a long time.

He endured the discomfort; he even savored it. Aching now would make the pleasure that much more intense when he finally relieved the pain by burying himself deep inside Frisco's enticing body.

Heat radiated through him at the tantalizing thought of Frisco, her luscious mouth open, hungry for him, her body spread-eagled on his bed, moist and ready for his.

His sex throbbed and strained against the zipper on his pants.

Oh, yeah. He wanted Frisco Bay Styer, wanted her so badly that, unless he was careful and controlled his imagination, he'd be forced to take himself in hand.

A wry, self-derisive smile slashed his face.

Of course, he had physically wanted other women. And he had had most of them. Lucas was both honest and practical.

He knew the score; when a man attained the status of multi-
millionaire, even if he looked and behaved like a geek or a
gorilla, he could usually have just about any woman he desired,
if the price was right.

By the same token, he knew the reverse was true. Men were
not above selling themselves, for money or position or fame,
or even the illusion of love.

That was the way of it.

But there were exceptions, both male and female. There
were those who were not for sale, and Lucas had a gut feeling
that Frisco was one of them.

He was another.

But there were inducements other than financial. Some
folks would do anything, risk everything, compromise their
lives, out of genuine love of and loyalty to family; Lucas sensed
that Frisco was one of these.

As the old saying went: it takes one to know one.

Pondering whether Frisco had a glimmering of how very
much alike they were, Lucas stared into the night, not seeing
the occasional lone car make its way along the deserted street,
lost to the here and now, even to the discomfort of his own
body, devising plans.

One way or another, he intended to have what he wanted.
And, he wanted Frisco in his bed, her family's company—both
under his control.

It was not yet eleven o'clock in the morning when Frisco
let herself into her condo; yet she felt exhausted, her energy
sapped by frustration and anger.

To begin with, she had slept badly, thanks to the disturbing
encounter she'd had with Lucas MacCanna. The really grating
thing was, the man hadn't actually done anything wrong, other
than tease her about her name.

Then again, his mere presence disturbed her.

Not good, she told herself, listlessly carrying her overnight
case into her bedroom.

Dumping it on the queen-size bed, she walked to the double

dresser and stared at her reflection in the long narrow mirror above it.

Idiot! She silently chastised herself, exasperated. Dark smudges beneath her puffy eyes attested to the restless night she had spent mentally dodging the surfacing urges and needs of her body.

Well, damn, she was an adult, a woman, wasn't she? Frisco defended her right to erotic imaginings. Her body was young and healthy, subject to more than one form of hunger. And it had been a long time, nearly a year now, since her sexual being had been fed.

Hell, it needed a man.

No, it wanted this man.

"Damn."

Swinging away from the mirror, she went to the bed and tore into the suitcase. Impatience ate at her nerves, impatience with herself, impatience with Lucas MacCanna—for being so damned sexy—but most of all, impatience with her father and the can of worms he had opened because of his weakness.

The morning had not gone well.

The understatement of the year.

Harold, coward that he was, had not told his wife about his troubles, damnable as they were.

Frisco had gone to the breakfast table prepared to calm her distraught mother, only to encounter a serene woman presiding over the silver coffee server.

That wasn't the worst of it. Not only had Gertrude taken a shine to Lucas MacCanna, but along with her Sunday best, she had donned the garb of matchmaker. Frisco had the distinct and uncomfortable feeling that her mother was envisioning her only child resplendent in virginal white.

"Ohhh, damn!" she said, recalling the fruitless conversation she had had with her father.

"What the hell do you think you're doing?" Frisco had demanded of Harold the minute her mother left the room to freshen up before leaving for church. "You have to tell her."

"I will, I will, but—"

"Won't you change your mind and come with us?" Gertrude said, pulling on her gloves as she reentered the room. "It's been some time since you've attended services."

"Not this morning, Mother." Frisco excused herself, shooting a chiding glare at her father. "I have things to do at home before meeting Jo and Karla for dinner."

"Well then"—Gertrude gave in, sighing for the soul of her offspring—"give the girls my love."

. . . *the girls* . . .

They'll adore it!

As out of sorts as she felt, Frisco had to smile, anticipating her friends' reaction when she relayed her mother's sentiments.

Of course "the girls" loved Gertrude, as did everyone else who had ever met her.

After dispatching her household chores—quick, between-cleaning-lady dusting and vacuuming, and doing her weekly laundry, Frisco had a long, tension-relieving bath, then a shampoo and overall shower rinse. She was bullying her hair into a semblance of submission when the phone rang. Hoping it was her father calling to tell her the dirty deed was finally done, she ran to answer.

Silly innocent.

"Hello, Frisco Bay."

She ground her teeth.

MacCanna heard it and laughed.

"What do you want?" She was hardly civil, and didn't give one good goddam.

"That's what I'm calling about."

"Huh?" Not exactly eloquent.

"What I want," he replied, oh so nicely.

"I'm falling asleep here, Mr. MacCanna," Frisco snapped, just to move things along.

"Okay," he returned briskly. "I think I've got a solution to our problematic situation."

"And that is?" she prompted, silently cursing her father for causing the mess.

"I won't discuss it over the phone."

"I'm not going to like it." Frisco closed her eyes; the headache was back. "I just know I'm not going to like it. Am I right?"

"Right or wrong, do you want to hear it?"

No! she thought.

"Yes," she said.

Chapter Nine

"You don't like the sole?"

Frisco flicked a puzzled glance at Karla, then looked down to the poached fish she'd been picking into flaky white pieces. "It's fine," she said, spearing a morsel and slipping it into her mouth. It darn near choked her, but she managed to get it down.

"What's with you today?" This from her other friend, Jo. "You seem preoccupied. Problems at work?"

"No." Frisco gave a quick shake of her head. Then she heaved a sigh. "Well, actually, there is a problem," she admitted, reminding herself that these two women were her dearest friends. "But not at work."

"A man?" Jo's voice fairly dripped venom.

Frisco and Karla exchanged knowing smiles; the three of them had known each other forever, and of the three, Jo had always been the most militant feminist, vocal in her disdain of all things male.

"In a way," Frisco said.

"How many ways are there with men?" Jo arched the natural

blond, exquisitely arched brows over her brilliant blue eyes. The features fit perfectly in her beautiful face. "It's always their way, isn't it?"

It's sure beginning to look that way, Frisco conceded, to herself. Aloud, she dared to disagree. "Not always. We females win every so often."

"Right." Jo made a face; it wasn't pretty. "But only when we've backed them to the wall."

"Oh, c'mon," Karla said, dabbing delicately at her lips with her napkin. "They really aren't all monsters." Her smile was serene. "My Danny is a sweetheart."

There speaketh the former militant, Frisco thought, flashing Karla a grin.

"I might throw up right here, all over our dinner," Jo said in deep disgust.

"You'll do no such thing," Frisco admonished, trying to scowl, laughing instead.

Karla laughed, too. "Can't you ever stop playing the gruff, tough detective, Jo?" She rolled her big, brown eyes. "I mean, being a police officer is one thing, but do you have to act the part every minute of every day?"

"I'm not acting, Karla." Jo glared across the table. "I thought you knew better than that."

"Time out," Frisco declared, reaching out to place a hand on the arm of each friend. "We're here to enjoy a meal together, not to have a cat fight."

Karla gave in first, as she always had. She bestowed a contrite look on Jo. "I'm sorry. I know you love your work every bit as much as I love being Danny's wife and the twins' mother."

The mention of the twins brought a soft smile to Jo's stern face; it was a smile not often seen there. "It's very easy to love Josh and Jen, they're great kids."

"Maybe you should have some of your own," Karla suggested, bravely Frisco thought.

"And maybe it'll rain liquid gold tomorrow and we'll all be rich," Jo retorted, good-naturedly.

Karla took on her mother-of-the-world expression. "Well, you could, you know," she persisted. "I truly believe you'd be a wonderful mother, and I just know the perfect man is out there just waiting for you, if you'd only unbend a little and look around."

"No one's perfect . . . trite but true," Jo recited. "And I'm not interested." She dismissed the subject with an elegant toss of her head. "Now, can we get back to more important matters?" She turned her laser blue eyes on Frisco. "What kind of problem are you having with a man, and how can we help?"

"Yes," Karla was at once all seriousness and intent. "How can we help, honey?"

Frisco's throat was suddenly thick, her eyes stingy-hot. God! I'm just tired, she told herself, blinking and swallowing. But it did tug at her emotions to have her friends jump to her defense.

How did that song go? "That's What Friends Are For"?

"Thanks guys," she muttered around the block in her throat. "But I don't think you can help with this one."

"Who is he?" Jo again arched her gold brows. "I could run a check on him through the F.B.I. if you like."

"Heavens no!" Frisco was caught between tears and laughter. "It's not that kind of problem."

"Well, what kind of problem is it, then?" Karla, seemingly scatterbrained, was in fact the practical one.

"Business. My father's," Frisco said. "And the likelihood of a takeover."

"You're kidding!" Karla gaped at her. "I thought the days of that kind of thing were over."

"So did I," Frisco said, recalling her own ideas on the subject a few nights ago.

"There's always a big fish ready, willing, and—most importantly—able to gobble up a little fish." Jo looked world-weary. "Big man, little man, they will play their macho games."

"This is no game, Jo." Frisco sipped her lime-laced Perrier water. "My father could lose the company."

"Who's the raider?" Jo's modulated voice had taken on a professional, interrogative edge.

"He's not a raider," Frisco felt honorbound to clarify that point.

"Who is he, Frisco?" Jo obviously felt obligated to insist.

"Name's Lucas MacCanna. His company provides the steel for The Cutting Edge."

"Never heard of him."

"Well, I have!" Karla piped in. "Even though the man rarely gives interviews, stories abound about his meteoric rise in the business world! And you would have heard of him, too, Jo, if you'd ever bother to read anything but the crime reports in the newspapers."

"Like the social pages?" Jo asked, acerbically.

"Or the business news," Karla rejoined, in a like tone of voice. "Really, Jo."

"Really, my ass. Who gives a flying fuck about all that crap, anyway?"

Karla turned to Frisco with an expression of feigned shock and mouthed: A flying fuck?

"Detective Jo-Lynn Coleman, your language," Frisco inserted, deciding it was time to get the conversation on track. "We are in a public place."

"Screw it." Jo dismissed their surroundings with a toss of her elegant blond head.

"The whole place?" Karla widened her eyes in exaggerated innocence.

Frisco lost it; Karla always had had the ability to break her up. She clapped a hand to her mouth to muffle her burst of laughter.

Karla giggled.

Jo grinned.

It was the same as it had always been between the three, and they loved it.

"Okay, fun's over." Jo, as always, was the first to recover her composure. She once again homed in on Frisco. "Isn't there anything your father can do to stave off this hotshot titan Mac-Canna person?"

Thinking Lucas MacCanna would probably blow a blood ves-

sel if he could hear Jo's disparaging description of him—then
again, perhaps not—Frisco shook her head.

"No, I don't think there's anything Dad can do." She drew
a breath, then rushed on, "But, there may be something I
can do to prevent it."

"You?" Karla's pixie-pretty face puckered in a frown. "But,
Frisco, you're not even connected to the firm. Whatever do
you think you can do?"

"That's part of my problem . . . I don't know." Frisco
shifted a troubled gaze from one woman to the other. "I talked
to him earlier this afternoon. He says he has a solution to the
situation and wants to meet with me later to discuss it." She
glanced at the thin gold watch on her wrist, and sighed. "I
agreed to meet him for drinks at eight."

"An hour from now." Jo consulted her own watch, much
more plain and functional.

"The newspaper photos I've seen were pretty bad," Karla
said, musingly. "Is he good-looking?"

"Now what in hell do his looks have to do with anything?"
Jo snapped impatiently.

Karla was unruffled by her friend's sharp voice. "I'm just
curious."

Jo snorted in a very unladylike manner.

"Good-looking?" Frisco raised a hand to massage a temple;
the ache there was increasing. "No, at least not in the Tom
Cruise, *GQ*-covers model way."

"Well, then, in what way?" Karla was nothing if not persistent.

"Kar-la." Jo shook her head in despair. "Give it a rest, will
you? What difference does it make?"

"I told you, I'm just—"

"Curious." Jo cut her off rudely. "I know. But Christ on a
bike, can't you see Frisco's got more to worry about here than
the man's looks?"

Christ on a bike? Frisco shook her aching head.

"Oh!" Karla looked appalled. "I'm sorry, Frisco."

Frisco smiled at her; she did love this supposed airhead,
who in truth was very bright. And she loved Jo as much, for

all her tough talk and her ability to continue to shock with the gutter language that came out of her aristocratically lovely face.

"It's all right," she assured her. "I don't mind. As to his looks"—she frowned in thought—"well, at first sight, I guess you'd say he's kind of harsh-looking. All tough businessman, very masculine. You know?"

Karla nodded, rather eagerly.

Jo rolled her eyes. "Wonderful. King Kong conquers the corporate world."

Karla gave her a crushing stare.

Jo was serenely unimpressed.

Despite the intensifying pain in her head and the building tension as the time for her meeting with him approached, Frisco had to laugh.

"He does have a nice smile," she went on, chiding herself for the unfair assessment; Lucas MacCanna possessed a disarming, devastating smile.

"That's the first thing I always notice in a man," Karla said. "His smile, I mean."

"I notice his buns."

Frisco and Karla turned stares of utter amazement on their friend, and spoke simultaneously.

"You're kidding!"

"You do?"

"Sure." Jo shrugged. "I like tight buns." This time she arched just one golden brow, at Frisco. "Does your MacCanna have tight buns?"

"I don't know! I didn't notice!" Frisco exclaimed, contriving a weak laugh.

In fact, she had; Lucas MacCanna not only had tight buns, but long, muscular legs, a slim waist, a broad, flatly muscled chest, and satisfyingly wide shoulders. He also had big hands, with long, slender fingers lightly sprinkled with hair.

Oh, yes, she'd noticed. But she wasn't about to admit it, especially not to Jo.

"I was slightly distracted by the circumstances of our first meeting," she said, repressively.

"Testy, testy," Jo chided, grinning.

Frisco exhaled, and returned the grin a bit sheepishly. "Yes, I guess I am. Sorry."

"Gosh, we all sure are sorry a lot this evening," Karla opined, grinning right along with them.

"And not very hungry, I'd say." Jo swept the barely touched food before them with a pointed look. "Whose turn is it to pick up the check?"

"Mine," Frisco said, exhaling again. "This appears to be my day, doesn't it?"

"Are you really worried about this meeting, Frisco?" Karla asked anxiously.

"Well . . ." Frisco moved a hand in a helpless gesture. "I'm just tired, I guess. I keep fantasizing about hot beaches and balmy breezes and foamy ocean waves."

"Oh, that's right! You leave for Hawaii soon. Next Sunday, isn't it?"

"Yes, and I can't wait." Frisco sighed and caught her lower lip between her teeth. "But first I have to get through this worrisome meeting."

"What's to worry about?" Jo demanded. "He's a man—big time C.E.O. or not." Her expression grew fierce. "You go meet the MacCanna, kid, and listen to what he has in mind. And if he gives you grief, let me know."

"And me!" Karla seconded. "We'll make short work of him. There are ways, you know."

Going all misty-eyed once more, Frisco again reached out to grasp their hands. "Thank you, guys. I . . . I . . ." She swallowed. "Thanks for being here . . . for being who you are."

"Mush." Though her tone was hard, Jo's eyes were the soft blue of a baby's blanket.

"Yeah, we are getting pretty soppy, aren't we?" Karla unashamedly wiped her eyes. "Where are you meeting the Mac-Canna, anyway?" she asked, unconsciously picking up on Jo's disdainful designation for him.

The MacCanna. Apt. Frisco suppressed a shiver.

"That neighborhood bar the next street down from my apartment. You know where I mean?"

"Yes." Karla nodded. "We've had drinks there. I thought it was a nice place."

"It is, lots of atmosphere," Jo drawled. Then her voice took on that familiar edge. "Don't sweat it, Frisco. You just go give hell to the bull of the boardroom."

Chapter Ten

Jo's advice was easier given than carried out, Frisco found herself thinking a little over an hour later.

She was five minutes late, and he was waiting for her. Seated at a corner table slightly more secluded than the rest, a full glass of beer in front of him, Lucas MacCanna looked attractive as the devil . . . and bored to death.

As she made her way to him, Frisco noted the glances, some veiled, some blatant, sent his way by a number of the women scattered throughout the large room.

"Hello, Frisco Bay." His voice was low, sexy, exciting, and rife with self-contained laughter.

"A greeting guaranteed to put you at a disadvantage, sir," Frisco said, sliding onto the chair he scraped away from the small round table.

He laughed aloud, softly, close to her ear. His warm breath ruffled her hair—and her equilibrium.

"I'm terrified," he murmured, still laughing as he circled the table and sat down.

"Right." Frisco pulled a sour expression. "Should we cut to the chase? I've got to work tomorrow."

"It's only eight-ten," he said, raising a hand to signal to the waitress. "What'll you have?"

"Nothing, thank you. I just want this over with."

"Frisco Bay." Though his voice was pleasant, it contained a hint of warning, which she decided it would be prudent to heed, like it or not.

She gave in without an argument. "Okay, I'll have a glass of zinfandel, on the rocks, please."

"To dilute it, huh?" He smiled. "Why do I have this nasty suspicion that you don't trust me?"

"Possibly because I don't trust you," she replied with unwise candor.

He laughed.

She gritted her teeth against a responsive shiver. Damn, the man did have a demoralizing laugh.

He ordered her wine from a waitress, who managed to rub her thigh against his arm unobtrusively.

He didn't appear to notice.

Frisco did and contrarily, considering she assured herself she didn't care, was bothered by it.

Musing on her strange reaction to the waitress's obvious bid for his attention, Frisco sat quiet, her hands clasped on her lap, until the young woman delivered the glass of wine, then reluctantly departed.

"Could we get on with it now?" she asked, in a deliberately cool voice.

"You can trust me, you know," he said, answering without really replying to her question.

"Can I?" She raised a skeptical eyebrow, much in the manner of her friend, Jo.

"Yes." His voice held firm conviction. "I don't want to hurt you." An odd little smile curved his lips. "As a matter of fact, hurting you is absolutely the last thing I'd want to do to you."

For some reason, his assurance, coupled with his oddly sensuous smile made her feel uneasy, uncertain, and somewhat breathless.

"Then, what do you want?" she gathered the courage to ask.

"Your father's company," he answered bluntly. "But you already knew that, didn't you?"

"Yes, you certainly didn't so much as try to conceal your intentions in that regard," she conceded.

"Waste of time." He shrugged. "And I don't like wasting time."

"No profit?" she inquired, too gently.

"Not of any kind," he replied, as gently. "Not monetarily, materially, or in personal satisfaction."

"I see."

"I doubt it." His smile turned wry. "But no matter, I told you I've come up with what I believe to be a workable solution to your problem."

"My problem!"

"Well, isn't it?" He didn't wait for an answer. "It sure as hell isn't mine."

"You're that confident of your ability to take over the firm, just like that?" She snapped her fingers.

"Exactly."

She believed him. Why she didn't know, but she did. And, strangely, she was also certain that he had given serious consideration to a solution to her father's problem, which, as he'd said, was hers as well. In giving love, people give of themselves, whether or not it goes against the grain or personal principles.

So again she gave in.

"All right, I'll listen to your solution."

He took a long swallow of beer, hesitating, almost as if gathering courage—yeah, right—then he set his glass back on the table and turned a direct look on her.

"First of all, has your father discussed this with your mother as he said he would?"

"No." She kept herself from shaking her head; it hurt too much for that. "At least, he hadn't as of this morning before I left the house. But he promised me he would."

"There's the phone." He indicated the instrument attached to the wall in the hallway leading to the rest rooms. "Call him and find out."

She opened her mouth to question him; he forestalled her.

"It's important, Frisco Bay. And if he hasn't yet broached the subject, tell him to hold off awhile."

"But that money must be returned to the firm as soon as possible," she protested.

"A day or so won't make much difference," he said. "Now do it. I need to know."

He needs to know. And what the MacCanna needs to know, he needs to know, Frisco recited to herself impatiently as she made her way to the phone. So agitated was she, she didn't even realize that she was thinking of him as Jo had dubbed him.

Fortunately, it was her father who answered the phone; at least Frisco was spared the task of explaining the late call to her mother.

"Not yet, not yet," Harold replied in answer to her question. "But I will, Frisco. I promise."

When, she asked herself, after they were in bed? She shied away from that thought. Like most progeny, Frisco avoided thinking about her parents in the intimacy of the bed. Immature perhaps, but there you have it.

"I want you to wait, Dad," she said. "Don't say anything about this business until you hear further from me."

"But why?" Harold sounded both relieved and baffled. "Just this morning you were insisting I talk to her at once. I don't understand. What are you up to?"

"I'm with Mr. MacCanna now, Dad." Frisco drew a deep breath. "Maybe, hopefully, we can work something out."

"Do you think so? Honestly?" he asked with betraying eagerness.

The near desperation in his voice made Frisco feel at once compassionate and angry. Dammit! He was her father. Why did he have to be so weak willed?

"Yes. Maybe. Possibly." She sighed; her father was her father, after all. Warts and all. But then, hadn't he loved her, even with bony arms and legs and buck teeth? He had. Turn about was fair play. "I'll do my best, Dad."

His relief was palpable. Returning to the table, and the Mac-

Canna, Frisco prayed she could deliver on the expectations she had instilled in him.

"So?" he asked as she slid onto the chair opposite him. "Had he told her?"

"No." Her throat was tight, achy. "He . . . er, he's waiting until they retire for the night," she explained, as delicately as she could.

"Works for me." He grinned.

When? Frisco sealed her lips against the response that sprang to her mind. It was none of her business when, or with whom, pillow talk had worked for him.

When she didn't respond, his grin vanished and he got down to business.

"I believe you are no longer laboring under any illusions as to my ability to take complete control of your family's company, whether or not your mother replaces the money he 'borrowed,' " Lucas said, tilting his glass in a silent salute to her before taking a deep swallow of beer. "Correct?"

As much as it pained her, Frisco agreed with a brief nod.

"Okay, that settled, here's the deal I'm willing to cut with you." He paused to take another, smaller swallow of beer. "I'm prepared to keep your father from going to jail for embezzlement by replacing those missing funds, without your mother ever having to know about them." A half-smile flickered over his mouth as she winced upon his use of the word "jail."

"And?" she prompted in a raw voice, knowing full well that he wasn't finished.

"And I'm prepared to pay off all outstanding invoices," he went on. "In addition, I'm prepared to pour into the business the capital necessary to bring it to parity."

"Are you finished?" Frisco's voice was so dry now she could barely speak. He was scaring the living hell out of her, driving her crazy by making her wonder what he was getting at.

"One more thing," he said gently. "I'm also prepared to cover all his gambling debts."

Oh, Lord, she cried in silent despair. This was going to be a lot worse than she'd imagined.

"And what do we have to do in return for your magnanimity?" she asked in a harsh, bitter whisper. "In other words, what's the catch?"

"You."

"Huh?" Frisco blinked in confusion.

"Your parents don't have to do a thing. Just you." He gave a quick shake of his head. "No, that's not quite correct. Your father has to get the hell out of the way. I'll talk to the board members, get them to provide a golden parachute. All he needs to do is sign his stock over to you."

"But . . . but . . ." Frisco paused to pull her thoughts together. "I don't understand. How will my owning the stock make a difference?"

"We, you and I, will run the firm."

"But I don't even work for the company!" she cried softly. "I have my own work."

"You'll have to give it up, come to work for The Cutting Edge."

"What?" Frisco couldn't believe she'd heard him correctly, nor could she comprehend how her working with him would change things; she'd still hold controlling interest. She proceeded to explain that to him.

"Yes, I know," he said smoothly. "But, you see, I wasn't completely finished. There is a condition."

Wasn't there always? Frisco steeled herself for—what? She couldn't begin to imagine.

"You will also have to give up your condo and move in with me, to live and work with me in equal partnership."

Frisco stared at him in stunned disbelief, as shocked as if he had asked her to strip naked in public.

"But . . . why?" she asked, after she had pulled her wits together enough to speak.

"Because you excite me," he said bluntly. "And I want to sleep with you . . . on a regular basis."

The man was mad, stark, staring, flat-out-of-his-mind mad. A raving lunatic. Maybe worse.

"You're crazy."

Damned if he didn't laugh.

"No, I'm horny," he said when his laughter subsided. "So, that's the deal."

"You can't be serious?"

"I assure you I am. Take it or leave it."

Chapter Eleven

"Live in hope, MacCanna." Quivering with conflicting feelings of anger, shock, and a spark of something she didn't want to contemplate, Frisco shoved back her chair and took one sideways step. "And die in despair."

She considered it a pretty good exit line, thus felt chagrined when she was prevented from sweeping away from him after delivering it. Lucas's droll-sounding voice brought her to an abrupt halt in mid sweep.

"I'd suggest you call your father back as soon as you get home, Frisco Bay," he advised.

"Why?" She pulled her most fearsome expression on him.

"Why, because it would appear he's going to be doing a little pillow-talking to your mother, after all."

"Damn you."

He smiled. "Likely. But that's beside the point. Sit down. Calm down. We have an audience."

Fuming, she glanced around, to find the people at the next table unabashedly staring at her. Resentment flaring, she glared at the nosy foursome, but resumed her seat.

"This is blackmail," she said in a tone designed to relay her disgust.

"Not at all," he contradicted her blandly. "I'm offering you an honest business proposition."

"Honest!" Frisco laughed nastily, in his face. "You're offering to buy sex, nothing more."

"Incorrect, Frisco Bay. I'm offering a lot more than that, and you know it."

Knowing it didn't mean she had to acknowledge that, and she had no intention of doing so.

"Get a life, MacCanna," she said harshly. "And don't call me Frisco Bay."

"I'd rather get a partner—bed and business," he rejoined. "And I will call you Frisco Bay." He smiled again and raised his glass to her. "You may call me MacCanna." His smile curled into a grin. "Or anything else that comes to mind . . . and I can just imagine what that might be."

Frisco decided it really wasn't fair for a man to look so good, so attractive, while being so offensive. "I wouldn't lower myself to use such gutter language," she volleyed back at him.

He laughed again, as if delighted with her wit.

She scowled and cautioned herself against stooping to commit physical violence.

"You're going to wrinkle your brow by frowning like that. Relax, kid." He flicked a hand at her still-full glass. "Drink your wine. It'll help ease the tension."

That was what she was afraid of. Ignoring the drink, Frisco folded her hands on the table, then gazed at him through narrowed eyes.

"You are serious about your outrageous proposition," she muttered. "Aren't you?"

"Dead serious."

"But it can't possibly work!" It was a soft outburst, meant to exclude the curious couples at the next table.

"Why not?"

Impossible. Frisco ground her teeth in frustration. The man was absolutely impossible. Positive she could feel the prying stares of their nearest neighbors burning into the back of her neck, she jerked her head, and winced at the streak of pain the motion caused.

"I can't discuss this here."

"Your place or mine?" He was laughing at her, she knew it, and he obviously knew she knew it.

"I could actively dislike you, MacCanna."

"Pity." He sighed dramatically. "For I could actively make love to you, Frisco Bay, very actively, for long hot nights on cool rumpled sheets."

The images his response conjured didn't bear looking at, or thinking about. Heat seared through her, setting off warning alarms inside her head.

"That kind of talk will get you nowhere with me," she said icily. Yeah, right, she reflected, despairing at the leap of response inside her.

"I was rather enjoying it. Oh, well." He shrugged. "Do we go somewhere and get serious, or do you call your father and tell him the party's over?"

Frisco caved; she had done it so many times over the past few days, she was getting used to it—almost. Resentment a hot, vital presence inside her, she stood, glared at the curious foursome at the next table; then, head held at a regal angle, she made an exit worthy of one of the royals.

MacCanna was right at her heels . . . not like a lackey to one of the royals, but more like a Scotland Yard bloodhound.

Frisco spun to confront him the minute she stepped onto the sidewalk outside the bar.

"We'll talk at my place," she said in a tone meant to chill. "But I'm giving fair warning, here and now, you make one move out of line and you're toast."

MacCanna, looking solemn, raised one hand in the universal sign of peace. "Scout's honor, I'll behave like a gentleman," he vowed. "My conduct will be above reproach."

"It had better be," she threatened, knowing full well she couldn't back it up. "My apartment complex provides security," she tacked on, omitting to enlighten him as to the advanced age of the security guard, who, she had long since concluded, would likely faint on the spot if challenged.

Stifling a sigh, Frisco turned and walked to her car, parked along the curb. "The complex is right up . . ."

"I know," MacCanna interrupted her. "That's where I left my car." He smiled. "Just in case."

This guy was really starting to get to her. It required every ounce of Frisco's control to keep her hand from flying at his smiling face. Instead, she put it to work unlocking her car.

"I'll drive you there," she said tightly, begrudging the courtesy of offering him a lift.

"Thanks." Keeping a straight face with blatant difficulty, he circled the car to the passenger's side.

They made the short run in dead silence, as they did the subsequent elevator ride up to her floor, as they did the trek along the corridor to her apartment. Silence prevailed until he shut the door behind him, closing them alone together, inside her spacious apartment which suddenly seemed small and cramped and cell-like.

Telling herself to get a grip on her jangling nerves, Frisco walked into the living room and motioned to the blue-and-beige-striped sofa and chairs.

"Have a seat," she invited, less than graciously. "And start talking."

"What's left to say?" There was a vague, inattentive ring to his voice, and his interest was focused on the interior of the room. His sharp gaze inventoried every piece of furniture, every decorative knickknack, the plush carpeting, the window treatments of sheer balloon curtains, draped with valanced swags.

"Very nice," he pronounced, shifting his eyes back to her. "Did you do this yourself, or did you have a professional pick and choose?"

"I did it." She smiled wryly. "Not the actual sewing of the curtains and draperies, of course, but . . ."—she shrugged—"I selected every item." Even as Frisco answered, she asked herself why she was bothering, what, if anything, had her taste in home décor to do with the subject at hand. In her usual straightforward way, she put the question to him. "Is it important to the discussion at hand?"

"Could be." MacCanna's response was laconic, dry. "Depending upon your answer."

He had lost her. "Answer to what?"

"My proposition, of course."

Frisco was furious, and more than a little scared. He was in command, and he knew it.

Or was he? she mused, startled by the glimmer of an idea that sprang into her mind. It was a gamble but . . .

"So it's take it or leave it, is it?" she said, acting on the idea before she could change her mind:

"Yes." His answer came fast, final-sounding.

"I see," she murmured, gathering her courage. "And here was I, convinced you were an old-fashioned traditionalist." She smiled; it was twenty-four-carat plastic. "Surprise, surprise. For here you are, proposing a very modern relationship." She arched her brows. "What do you have in mind, exchanging blood-test workups, instead of blood tests of commitment?"

"Premarital, you mean?"

"Yes," she said, thinking she certainly couldn't accuse MacCanna of being slow on the uptake. "As opposed to preco-habitation, that is."

Lucas narrowed his eyes. "You want marriage?"

"Yes," she said, ignoring a sick, sinking sensation in her stomach. "I'm not a business moron, MacCanna. I'm fully aware that if you eventually gain control of the outstanding stock, and the majority of the board, you'll be in a position to call the shots." She paused for breath; he was quick to fill the momentary lull.

"I never thought you were a business moron," he said. "I wouldn't allow you near the place if you were one, regardless of how much I wanted you in my bed."

She pounced. "Exactly. That's why I insist on a commitment from you, a guarantee against being kicked out of the business when you've had your fill of me."

Having tossed the dice, Frisco held her breath, waiting to see if she had won or lost her gamble. Fortunately, or unfortunately, as she discovered to her dismay, she didn't have to wait long.

"All right, if you insist," he said, placing the responsibility squarely upon her head. "We'll make the partnership legal and binding."

Oh, hell! The bottom seemed to drop out of Frisco's stomach, and she had a nasty feeling that she had only succeeded in trapping herself. But who would have figured that he'd agree to marriage?

Now what was she supposed to do? she asked herself, raking her mind for an out.

It went blank.

"Want to renege?"

"Yes!" Frisco said at once. Then, "No!" She shook her head, and sighed. "I don't know."

"It's up to you." He shrugged. "One way or the other, it makes no difference to me. Which one will it be?"

"I'd just as soon forget the whole thing." She absently rubbed her temple.

"And your mother? And your father? And the business that has been in the family for over a hundred years?"

Excellent points. Cruel, but excellently chosen, Frisco acknowledged, staring bleakly at her tormentor. How to respond? she wondered. How could one respond to such ludicrousness? His and her own. If it weren't so serious, it would be funny.

Far from feeling like laughing, she ached to curse him, then send him packing. Yet all common sense told her she could do nothing of the sort. It was utterly galling. Her expression revealed her feelings.

"A bitter pill, perhaps," MacCanna conceded. "But don't lay the blame at my feet. Your father mixed the concoction. I'm simply writing a new prescription."

"I would hardly call either option a drug of choice," Frisco retaliated angrily.

"Both have their highs," he suggested.

She stared at him, in despair for a moment; then she sighed. "Jo's right," she muttered. "Men are bastards."

"The nature of the beast." Lucas shrugged, then demanded, "Who's Jo?"

"My friend."

"And he considers his own sex bastards?"

Frisco gave an impatient shake of her head, and brushed aside the fiery strands of hair that whipped her cheek. "Jo is a woman. A feminist. A police officer."

"And not necessarily in that order, I'd bet," he retorted, disparagingly.

Frisco bristled. "Did I mention that Jo is one of my very dearest friends?"

"Good for her, and you." There was an edge to his tone that conveyed dwindling patience. "Could we possibly get back to the point? I'm getting tired of standing here."

"So sit down."

"I don't want to sit down." He dropped his hands to his sides and flexed his fingers, making her feel he wished they were around her throat. "Dammit, woman, I want an answer. Which one will it be?"

Suddenly, Frisco's head was pounding, and she felt so exhausted she wasn't sure she could remain upright. "I can't give you an answer now. I need time to think." She was babbling, she knew it, but couldn't stop. "And I can't think now. My head hurts, I'm tired. And I've got plans. Dammit, I'm going on vacation next week!"

"Where?" he fired the question at her.

She blinked, and blurted out, "Hawaii."

"Perfect."

"Huh?" She felt lost, and knew it showed. She didn't care. "What's perfect?"

"Hawaii." The look he gave her said it should have been obvious. "How long?"

Still lost, she answered automatically. "Two weeks."

"I'll fly out. We can be married there."

"That's crazy!" She was appalled.

"Why?" He was serene. "You're the one who demanded marriage. I'm willing to accede to your demand. So why shouldn't we get married in Hawaii?"

"Why? Why?" she chattered. "We don't even know each other, that's why."

"So?" He shrugged. "I know people who have been married for thirty years and they still don't know each other." Then he smiled—that inside-melting smile. "Anyway we'll have the rest of our lives to get to know each other. But, believe me, Frisco Bay, after six months of marriage, you and I will know each other, in every way there is."

MacCanna's assurance sounded ominous—and enticingly exciting. Frisco couldn't handle the inner conflict. Her fortitude deserted her. She dropped like a stone onto the edge of the nearest chair.

"I don't believe this."

"Why not?" The expression that swept his strong features was strangely tender.

"Things like this just don't happen." She gazed up at him in unknowing wistful appeal. "Not in real life."

"That's where you're wrong, Frisco Bay." To her amazement, he dropped to one knee on the carpet before her. "Things like this happen all the time in real life, For varied and sundry reasons, contractual arrangements are a common occurrence, that apparently work quite well."

"But . . . but . . ." Frisco raked her mind for a delaying tactic, something, anything to put him off, give her breathing space. Then, forgetting that she had initiated the idea of marriage in the first place, she voiced the first thought to pop into her rattled brain. "But suppose, later, afterward, I meet someone else and want to be free to be with him?"

MacCanna was still and quiet for a moment, a long moment. "There's someone in particular?" he finally asked, in a steely tone that sent chills dancing up her spine.

"No." She shook her head. "I told you there was no one. But, just suppose I did meet somebody?"

"We'd talk about it then."

So much for that delaying tactic, which in retrospect Frisco realized was perfectly logical. Now what? Her racing mind tossed out the next question.

"Well then, suppose you meet someone and fall in love, want your freedom?"

He favored her with a dry look. "I'm going to turn forty

this year, Frisco Bay. If the love bug hasn't speared me with its stinger up to now, I don't expect it's going to get to me anytime soon, if ever."

"But that's no guarantee!"

"True." He nodded. "On the other hand, I must tell you that I'm driven. I've set goals. And I've reached some of them. But I'm not through yet. I don't have time to indulge my emotions, or a woman, in the courting game. I prefer board-room games."

"And one of the boardrooms you now want to play in is the one at my father's company," she said, her voice mirroring the weariness pressing down on her.

"Yes," he admitted without a second's hesitation.

"And you need me to do that."

"Yes." He smiled and took her hand in his. "That, and to warm my bed after the boardroom battles."

"You're nothing if not blunt, MacCanna."

"I'm honest, Frisco Bay." His smile vanished, leaving his expression taut and stern. "If I give you my word, you can take it to the bank. And, here and now, I give you my word that if we marry you will never have reason to question my fidelity. If I make my vows to you, I will keep them."

Frisco was still, reluctantly impressed by the sincerity in his expression, his low voice.

"I will protect you, care for you, in sickness and in health," he went on. "And I'll support you, in any endeavor you choose to undertake. In return, I will expect no less than your full commitment to me." He drew a breath, and laced his fingers through hers. "So, that said, will you marry me, Frisco Bay Styer?" He smiled. "Or will you live with me and be my . . . partner?"

What could she say? What should she do? He scared the hell out of her, primarily because he excited the hell out of her. But excitement, generated by sexual attraction, was hardly her conception of a reason to join her life with his.

But what were her choices? she cried mutely. Unless she agreed to one of the options, he'd simply set in motion the wheels of her father's, and subsequently her mother's, destruction. And there was a very real possibility that her father might go to prison.

Frisco shuddered at the mere consideration.

"It's getting late, Frisco Bay," MacCanna pressed his advantage. "Close to pillow-talking time."

Her string had played out, and she knew it. She had no other choices. If she cared to be able to live with her conscience, she would have to live with him. And, if she did, it would damn well be within the protective bonds of marriage.

"All right. All right," she cried, caving in once again. "Damn you, all right! I'll marry you."

"Don't panic. You'll see, everything will work out," he said soothingly. "You won't be sorry."

"I already am," she snapped, pulling her hand from his. "If you'll let me up, please, I'll call my father." Beginning to feel smothered, closed in, and afraid she'd hyperventilate, she drew in long, deep breaths before going on. "What should I say to him?" She again dragged in a couple of breaths. "How can I explain?"

His eyes probed her face: her wide eyes, her flaring nostrils, her trembling lips. Exhaling sharply, he stood, clasped her hand to pull her up, and glanced around.

"Where's the kitchen?"

"Kitchen?" Frisco blinked. "Why?"

"Because you need a drink, coffee, water, something, before you spin off into space."

She tugged against his grip; he held firm.

"The kitchen, Frisco Bay."

Past making a stand now, or even a show of one, she once again caved in to him. "Through that archway," she said, motioning with her free hand.

"Let's go." He took off with long strides, leaving her no option but to stride right along with him.

She didn't resist. What would be the point? she asked herself, trotting beside him. The MacCanna was obviously in no mood to be thwarted, or even trifled with. She'd only lose anyway—and be embarrassed in the process.

"Nice," he remarked, after entering the bright yellow and white room. "What will it be, coffee or . . . ?"

"I wish I had the glass of wine I left on the table back at the bar," she muttered, feeling decidedly faint. "I think I could use a shot of alcohol."

He laughed, not mockingly, but in sympathy. "You have no wine in the place?"

"Just a bottle of champagne I received as a gift last Christmas." She lifted her shoulders in a half-shrug. "I don't know if it's still good."

"Has it been opened?"

"No." She frowned. "I had no reason to celebrate."

"You do now, and it is still good." His expression turned serious. "You make your phone call. I'll open the champagne. We'll seal our bargain with a toast to the future."

Wonderful. Frisco didn't voice her less than enthusiastic response. Playing it cool—or more correctly, numb—she gave another tug of her arm.

"If you'll let go, I'll call Dad."

Releasing his hold, Lucas stepped away from her. "The wine in the fridge?"

"Yes," she answered vaguely, moving to the yellow wall phone, distracted by mulling how in the world she could begin to explain a decision of such magnitude to her father.

Her mind came up blank. Lord, she was tired. She admitted defeat—was this getting to be a habit?—and she turned to the oh-so-confident MacCanna for help.

"I don't know what to say to him." She was forced to address his backside, as he was bent over, reaching into the fridge for the dark, foil-capped bottle.

"Well, it's not the best, but it ain't vinegar, either," he said in an evident bid to ease the strain. Backing away from the gleaming white appliance, he turned to her with an encouraging smile. "As to your father, for now simply tell him not to say anything about this business to your mother. Tell him we have a solution to present to him—and that we'll meet with him tomorrow to discuss it."

"Tomorrow?" Frisco gave a hard shake of her head; her

hair flew in a tangled mass around her neck and shoulders. She absently raised a hand to swat at the swirling strands. "Tomorrow's Monday. I work on Mondays," she said sarcastically. "My employer frowns if I don't."

"Screw your employer," he retorted. "You're going to be leaving the company, to work with me—in our company," he reminded her. "Remember?"

"But I've got to give notice!" Even as she protested, she asked herself why she bothered. She knew she couldn't win; he'd just keep at her until she gave in—again.

"It's getting later by the minute. Do you really want him to dump this into your mother's lap?"

See, I told you so, Frisco said to herself. To him, she answered, "No"; then she lifted the receiver from the hook and punched in the memory button for her parents' number.

Fortunately, her father again answered.

Frisco dutifully repeated MacCanna's instructions. Harold was both relieved and mystified.

"I can't explain over the phone, Dad," she told him. "Just, please, don't say anything to Mother, at least not until you've heard . . . er, our proposition." She nearly choked on the last two words.

The champagne cork popped behind her.

Harold was making noises in her ear.

"Frisco, can't you give me some idea of what you've got in mind?" His voice lowered to a mere murmur. "It would kill your mother if I was charged with embezzlement."

"That's not going to happen, Dad," she assured him, keeping to herself the brutal fact that she was buying his freedom with her own. "Could we meet very early tomorrow morning?" she asked, in token defiance of the man she knew was listening to her every word. "I don't want to lose the entire day at work."

"Of course, of course," he replied, anxious now to accommodate. "Seven, eight?"

"Eight will be fine." She turned to smile oversweetly at MacCanna. "See you then. 'Night, Dad."

"Feel better for your little display of independence?" Mac-Canna arched his dark brows.

"Not much, no," Frisco confessed. "Is eight o'clock inconvenient for you?" She hoped.

"Not at all," he said, strolling to her, a filled flute in each hand. "But you will give notice tomorrow," he continued, handing a glass to her. "Won't you?"

"Yes," she said, then qualified her response, "if my father agrees to your demand that he step out of the picture."

He flashed her a chiding smile. "I'd say the chances are slim to none that he won't agree. Your father has run out of options, and he knows it."

He's not the only one out of options, Frisco mused, eyeing him warily and wearily.

The MacCanna didn't miss a thing. "You really are beat, aren't you, Frisco Bay?"

"Yes, I am." She heaved a sigh and frowned at the pale gold liquid in her glass. "Could we get on with this toasting business now, please? I need this drink."

"Certainly." He was suddenly brisk, no nonsense. He raised his flute; the wine shimmered. "To us, and to The Cutting Edge Surgical Instrument Company, a long and prosperous future."

"Hear, hear," Frisco said, unable to force herself to repeat the words "to us."

Chapter Twelve

Seven A.M. came early, too early for Frisco. The bedside alarm jolted her from a half-doze—the closest thing to sleep she had had all night.

Groaning, she dragged her tired body from the bed and into the bathroom.

A shower and shampoo helped, but not a lot.

Yawning, wet hair dripping onto the terry robe she pulled on, she padded into the kitchen to fix coffee. The stale odor of wine assaulted her senses, and stomach, as she crossed the threshold.

Although the MacCanna had finished his glass of champagne, Frisco had lost her thirst after choking down a token sip to mark her endorsing his toast to their future.

He had left her to her own devices moments later. They had proved few in number. Too tired to care, she had hit the bed immediately after closing the door behind him, leaving the champagne bottle open on the kitchen countertop.

Wrinkling her nose, Frisco now grabbed the bottle, poured the contents down the drain, then dropped the container into the recycle bin.

The lingering odor of champagne wafted to her from the drain as she filled the glass coffee carafe with cold water. After dumping the water into the automatic maker, she opened the small window above the sink. Chill, moisture-laden air swept inside to smack her on the face.

So much for spring.

Shivering in the nippy air, she thought longingly of her planned vacation in balmy Hawaii, then stared in resentment at the slowly brewing coffee.

Life just wasn't fair, Frisco told herself. In fact, at times it outright sucked.

She didn't want to get married. Most particularly, she didn't want to get married to Lucas MacCanna.

A long sigh blended with the sound of trickling coffee. To all appearances, life didn't give a damn what she did or didn't want.

So much for independence, she mused. Save it for the Fourth of July.

Her mind was rambling, and she knew it. She recognized as well that it was her way of avoiding thinking about the future, both immediate—the meeting with her father—and the extended—her acquiescence to MacCanna's blackmail cloaked within a business proposal.

Bastard.

Feeling somewhat better for having defined his character to ease her sense of self-betrayal, Frisco poured herself a cup of coffee and carried it back to her bedroom. Time was marching on, and unless she wished to make a statement by showing up late at her father's office, she needed to get her act together, unprofessional as it appeared to be.

Thirty minutes later, Frisco strode purposefully from her apartment, dressed to impress in her most severely cut, navy pin-striped suit.

If MacCanna chose to pursue his blackmail ploy under the guise of business, she felt pride-bound to meet his challenge at her professional best.

She had already lost this business maneuver, of course, but that didn't mean she had to roll over and play dead for him.

MacCanna should live that long.

* * *

He looked like hell.

Lucas grimaced at his reflection in the mirror, and rammed the knot of his silk tie into the vee at the base of his white shirt's collar.

What he looked like was a man who hadn't slept worth a damn, which made sense, he figured, since he hadn't. He had spent the long night asking himself if he'd taken a detour in the intelligence corridor.

What madness had attacked his gray matter, causing deterioration to the point of his agreeing to the idiotic contracting of marriage between him and Frisco to resolve the question of Harold Styer and his cavalier looting of The Cutting Edge Surgical Instrument Company?

Lucas readily admitted to himself that he had wanted Frisco from the moment she had turned away from the window in her father's office to scorch him with a heated, drilling stare. That look had gone directly to the most vulnerable part of his body.

Who knew why? Fools gave you answers, and all that . . .

But, even so, having the hots for a woman and being willing to shackle himself to her to scratch the itch were two entirely different things.

Problem was, at too close to forty to make much difference, Lucas had had the hots before, for a variety of women, yet never before had he desired any one of them quite so intensely as he desired Frisco Bay.

Her name alone intrigued him. Honestly. Frisco Bay? Thing was, Lucas loved the name. For some strange reason, he thought it fit her perfectly.

And, possibly for the very same strange reason, he found that she fit him perfectly, too.

Which, if followed to its rational conclusion, probably explained why he hadn't hesitated long enough to think before accepting her demand.

A marriage of convenience? he had spent the night asking himself. This was rational?

Slipping his billfold, loose change, and keys into their proper pockets, Lucas strode to the door. He was tired of his own thoughts. Besides, *tempus* was *fugiting*, he reminded himself wryly. Get on with it.

He had presented his proposition, and Frisco, in turn, had presented hers. A deal had been made, then sealed with a toast, instead of a kiss. And, although he'd have preferred a kiss, a deal was a deal. He could either go through with the agreement or he could back down.

Lucas was a stranger to the art of backing down.

A semihopeful thought struck him as he pulled the hotel room door shut behind him.

Maybe Harold would surprise both his daughter and his would-be son-in-law and successor by refusing the offer.

The noble part of Lucas almost wished he would. The natural part of him prayed he wouldn't.

He surely did want Frisco Bay for his own.

"Are you absolutely certain you want to go through with this, baby?"

Frisco cringed inwardly at the childhood endearment, but somehow managed to lie to her father in a calm and steady voice. "Yes, Dad, I'm certain."

There was a brief silence, during which she caught Mac-Canna mouthing the word "baby" and raising one eyebrow in a mocking arch.

She ignored him. It wasn't easy. He was too attractive not to look at. If she had dressed to impress, and she had, Mac-Canna had dressed to demolish.

And that was more than passing strange, she mused, for generally she barely noticed a man's attire, unless it was really bizarre or extraordinarily classy. And yet, although the white shirt and dark suit he was wearing were similar to those donned every day by thousands of businessmen, on MacCanna they were devastating.

Now that was truly bizarre.

"Well, in that case I most certainly agree to the terms, Lucas," Harold said, the relief in his voice corralling her wandering thoughts.

Frisco felt embarrassed, for both her father and herself. He was obviously so eager for the opportunity to slide from beneath the onus of his own making, it was pathetic. Aching for him, for herself, she watched bleakly as he crossed the room to grasp the hand MacCanna extended.

"Welcome to the company," he literally gushed. "And the family." He slanted a sly grin at Frisco, as if positive she had pulled off this amazing coup. "And, I can assure you, my wife will be delighted." He laughed; it carried the sound of strain. "Gertrude's been plotting to get Frisco into the family business, and into a solid marriage, ever since our daughter graduated from college."

Frisco wasn't paying close attention. She was distracted, feeling hot and uncomfortable and pressured. She didn't appreciate her position—in effect, that of the proverbial sacrificial lamb. Or was it scapegoat? Or dupe? Dope?

Her father's last remark registered. "No, wait," she said. "We can't tell Mother, at least, not right away."

MacCanna shot a suspicious look at her.

"Really, Frisco," Harold protested. "You can't get married without telling your mother."

"I know that." Frisco heard the impatience, the sharpness in her voice, but for once didn't feel guilty for it. "But we simply can't spring it on her out of the blue," she went on to explain. "Mother knows I only just met Mr.—Lucas—last Friday." She made a face. "Now, I know Mother is a starry-eyed romantic, but not even she would believe that we fell head over heels in love at first sight."

Harold gnawed on his lower lip and nodded in agreement. "Yes, of course." He frowned and, true to form, lobbed the ball back into her court. "What do you suggest?"

"Well," she began, determined to put off the day of reckoning as long as possible, most definitely past her Hawaii trip. "We could—"

"Start by inviting me to dinner," MacCanna interrupted

smoothly, volleying the ball for her. "In that way giving her a hint that Frisco and I are attracted to each other."

"That's a wonderful idea," Harold said, acting on it at once by striding to his desk and snatching up the telephone receiver. "I'll call her now and set it up."

"Set her up," Frisco muttered, she thought to herself. She thought wrong.

MacCanna leveled a contemplative look at her. "You've got a better idea?" His voice was pitched to reach her ears alone. "Let's hear it."

He had her, right there in the clichéd spot between a rock and a hard place. Frisco sighed in defeat; it was becoming a familiar position.

"I . . . ah . . ." She paused to draw a breath; backpedalling had never been her thing.

"It's all set," her father called out jubilantly, sparing her the humiliation of retreat. "Gertrude was thrilled." He grinned at MacCanna, evidently already into his role of companionable father-in-law. "It appears that you made a very good impression on her on Saturday evening."

"And she on me," MacCanna responded genially. "Your wife is a lovely woman."

Frisco had heard enough. "If you don't mind," she inserted, just a tad sarcastically, "I'd appreciate it if we could adjourn this mutual admiration society meeting. I really would like to get to my office."

"But I've ordered coffee," Harold objected, sounding quite like a thwarted child.

Again? Frisco swallowed the query. "Sorry, Dad, but I'll pass." She glanced at her wristwatch. "It's after nine now. I have to go." She rose from the settee, then raised her hand as a sign to stop when MacCanna stood up. "It's not necessary for you to leave. Stay and have coffee with Dad. I'm sure he's bursting to know the details of your plans for the firm."

"Yes, yes, do stay, Lucas," Harold said, rather anxiously. "I want to hear all about it, especially this golden umbrella plan you mentioned."

Frisco turned away, ostensibly to collect her handbag, in reality to hide the expression of saddened acceptance on her face.

She had almost made good her escape, her hand twisting the doorknob, when her father's voice halted her.

"Your mother said we'll have dinner at seven, baby," he said.

Baby. She grimaced, already at the door.

"But come around six-thirty for drinks before dinner."

"All right, Dad." Hard as she tried, she couldn't suppress the note of weariness in her voice.

"I'll pick you up at your place at six," MacCanna inserted, in a flat, don't-argue tone. "See you then, baby."

Frisco's spine went rigid. Damn him! She was turning to hurl the epithet at him, when she paused and gathered her control. No, she thought, swinging open the door and exiting, head held high. She would not give him the satisfaction of seeing her rattled by his gibe.

Chapter Thirteen

After such an inauspicious beginning, it was a very long day for Frisco. Murphy's Law was in full force; everything that possibly could go wrong, did.

Even so, by the time MacCanna arrived at her door, she decided the day hadn't been quite long enough, and the early evening had rushed in on her. Aggravated by the screwups of the day, she was edgy about the coming dinner, and was in no mood to be patronized.

"You look lovely," were MacCanna's first words when she opened the door.

"If you ever again dare to call me baby, I swear I'll slap you silly," Frisco snarled, finally relieving her anger over his effrontery that morning.

"Hello to you, too," he said, his lips quivering with amusement. "Bad day?"

Frisco ignored his question to fire one of her own. "Did you understand me?"

"Oh, yes, I got the message."

"I meant it."

"I believe you." He tried on a soothing smile for size; it fit perfectly. "Bites, does it?"

"To the bone," she admitted. "It wasn't so bad when I was five, or even ten." She heaved an anger-releasing sigh and allowed him to usher her from the apartment to the elevator. "But I haven't been ten for over twenty years, so it grates on my nerves to hear my father say it, even as a term of endearment." She leveled a hard stare on him as she stepped into the lift. "Hearing it from another man is insulting, and I will not tolerate it."

"Okay, the word's eradicated from my vocabulary. You won't hear it from me again," he vowed, then qualified, "that is, other than in reference to an actual infant."

Well, she couldn't fault him for not being accommodating, Frisco mused, glancing sidelong at his benign expression. Maybe, just maybe, if they were both willing to make small concessions and compromises, they could make this ridiculous business/personal arrangement work.

But she doubted it. To her way of thinking, while Mac-Canna had made one small concession, she was making large, life-altering compromises.

Hardly a balance on her scales of justice.

"But I am going to continue calling you Frisco Bay," he said a few minutes later. "And threats of bodily injury will avail you not one iota."

Frisco could not see his face, because she was leading the way, striding—marching actually—toward his car. But he was laughing at her, she knew it.

"You can go to—" she began in a gritty mutter, teeth clenched in disgust.

"Now, now." He'd cut her off, daring to laugh aloud. "That is no way to speak to your future husband."

Husband! Yech. It took every ounce of control she could muster to keep from voicing the strangled sound.

"You're not my husband yet," she retorted, emphasizing the word husband with heavy sarcasm. She halted next to his car and tilted her head to give him a warning glare. "If you persist in laughing at me, you might not live to see the day you're any woman's mate."

"Gonna do me in, are you?" MacCanna cocked a brow at her, and reached in front of her to unlock the passenger-side door and swing it open.

"You see?" Frisco exploded. "That's exactly what I mean." Even as she berated him, she felt diminished, childish and nitpicky. Yet she couldn't seem to stop herself; he simply brought out the worst in her. "You laugh at me, all the time. And it makes me furious."

"Perhaps you'd better get into the car," he said, quite seriously. "Before you draw a crowd."

Mortified, both by her bratlike behavior, and by having him point it out to her, Frisco did a quick, head-turning scope of the area. There was not a soul in sight. Fuming, she slid onto the plush contoured seat and sat staring stony-eyed, straight ahead. She didn't deign to acknowledge his presence when he settled behind the wheel next to her.

"I'm sorry if I've upset you."

A reactive fission of something jolted through her. Whether the sensation was caused by his quiet, conciliatory tone or by the startling fact that he'd apologized, Frisco didn't know. She wasn't inclined to delve into the depths of her emotions to find out, either.

"You've been upsetting me since you walked into my father's office," she told him frankly, but in a softer, more reasonable tone. "In fact, from the beginning, you've come across as being hellbent on belittling me."

"Never that." His denial came swift and sharp. "Belittling you has never entered my mind." He smiled, somewhat wistfully she thought. "And I'm honestly not laughing at you, not in any demeaning way. I had hoped to laugh with you." He gave a loose shrug, and twisted the ignition key to fire the engine. "I still have hopes in that regard."

Frisco was struck speechless by his last remark. What had he meant by the statement? Pensive beside him as he drove in silence, she pondered the intent of his admission. Could he, she wondered, possibly be hoping for a congenial rather than a contentious relationship between them, that they should be friends, as well as . . . lovers?

Would it be possible?

She worried the question all the way to her parents' home. A firm, reassuring answer evaded her. Doubts assailed her. They concerned not so much MacCanna's aspirations for them as a pair, but her ability to set aside the deep resentment and anger instilled in her by what she deemed her father's betrayal, and heightened by MacCanna's implacable proposition.

"We're here."

MacCanna's soft voice jerked her from the realm of what-if, into the world of what-now?

"Yes." She sighed, and didn't care if he heard it. He had started this, after all.

"Are you going to make the effort to appear attracted to me?" His tone hadn't changed; it was still quiet, surprisingly gentle. "For your mother's benefit?"

He could afford to be quiet and gentle, she decided, uncharitably. He had her and he knew it.

"Yes, I'll go the extra mile," she said, pushing the door open. "I really haven't a choice, do I?"

He stepped from the car and stared at her over the roof. "Life's a series of compromises."

"Right." Disgruntled, she turned away and headed for the house, her mind railing against the unfairness of everything in general and life in particular.

As life would have it, from the time she had begun reasoning for herself, Frisco had subscribed to the concept of compromise, believing that without the parties involved being willing to give ground, progress would never be made, thus nothing would ever be accomplished.

But now, in her present position, she was reconsidering that premise, mainly because, from her perspective, she appeared to be the only one giving—and giving and . . .

To all intents and purposes, her father would emerge from the mess of his own making free of debt, free of responsibility, and free to enjoy his retirement, sheltered beneath the luxurious benefits of a golden umbrella.

By the same token, Lucas MacCanna would emerge from

the deal with a company he coveted metaphorically in his back pocket and the woman he coveted literally in his bed.

While she, on the other hand, wound up surrendering her freedom, her chosen career, and taking on a partner-cum-husband she neither needed nor wanted.

If this was the end result of compromise, Frisco reflected, they could have it.

But that was all beside the point. She was out of options, other than abandoning her father and in turn, her mother. That she could not do.

Frisco approached the front door of her parents' house, in a dark, fatalistic funk. She heard the distinctive sound of her mother's tinkling laughter as she entered the foyer, and a faint reciprocal smile shadowed her lips.

Even though she herself found little to laugh about, she was glad her mother sounded so happy.

The quiet, yet ominous sound of the door closing behind her, shutting her inside the house, and inside the bargain she had agreed to honor with the man who now called the shots, struck a note of finality in her mind. She had the blackly humorous thought that she should be wearing a sign on her back reading: Compromises "R" Me.

It was so funny, it made her want to cry.

"Did I hear the door?" Gertrude rose gracefully from her chair, an expression of eager expectation glowing on her lovely, unlined face.

"Yes, they're here." Basking in the warmth of his wife's loving smile, Harold breathed a silent sigh of relief, and stood to greet his guests.

"Do you really think there may be a romance budding between Frisco and Mr. MacCanna, Harold?" Gertrude murmured, excitement flushing her cheeks, her bright gaze fixed on the open French doors separating the foyer from the elegantly appointed formal living room.

"I . . . er, feel certain there is," he replied, clearing his throat of its tightness. He could endure the nervousness; he just thanked heaven the panic had subsided.

"He is very attractive, isn't he?" His wife's voice had dropped to a mere whisper.

"Yes." In more ways than physically, Harold silently added, still slightly amazed at MacCanna's offer. "And, from all indications he has an excellent reputation."

That last was not the exact truth. What Harold had really heard was that MacCanna was considered honest but ruthless in his business dealings. That bit of information now gave him pause in regard to his daughter's future.

Harold loved Frisco, had doted on her when she was a child. And he was assailed by some doubt concerning the arrangement she had made with Lucas MacCanna.

If the man hurt his baby in any way, he'd . . . He'd what? Harold asked himself, silently acknowledging his own limitations. He was powerless, and he knew it.

But Frisco had appeared satisfied with the arrangement, he told himself, soothing his conscience—an exercise he had performed since his teens and had become adept at executing.

"Is he very wealthy?"

Harold barely heard Gertrude's sotto voce.

"I think he is." MacCanna must be, he reflected, if the man was prepared to invest the funds needed to reimburse the amount he had borrowed from the firm, to upgrade the business, and to pay off his outstanding gambling debts.

Recalling those made Harold sweat. What a damned fool he had been to get in that deep. Well, never, never again, he told himself, pulling a handkerchief from his pocket to dab his brow and upper lip.

As God was his witness, he would not overextend himself in the future, he vowed fervently.

Of course, this wasn't the first time Harold had made that exact same vow.

"Here they are!" Gertrude trilled, her beautiful, small hands outstretched as she moved forward, toward the couple entering the room.

Chapter Fourteen

"I think the evening went well," MacCanna said as he pulled away from the house. "Don't you?"

"Yes, I suppose so," Frisco agreed wearily. Sighing softly, she settled back against the headrest and closed her eyes; she was so darn tired.

"You suppose so?" His voice now had a bit of an edge. "Aren't you sure?"

She sighed again, louder, and pried her eyes open to flash an impatient look at him. "I said yes, can't you let it go at that?"

"Okay, okay, calm down." His tone now held a soothing note. "I was just trying to find out if you thought your mother bought our performance and got the idea that we're attracted to each other."

"Oh, yeah, she got it," Frisco closed her eyes again. "She didn't miss a trick."

"Good." His voice was laced with satisfaction.

Good for whom? Frisco clamped her teeth together to keep from blurting out the retort. To her relief, he fell silent.

But her reprieve was short-lived, for as soon as he grew quiet, she was bombarded by noisy thoughts.

To the background sound of the engine's purring, her mind spun out quick, isolated scenes from the previous hours, scenes she would have preferred to forget. Nevertheless, her brain persisted in cranking them out, replaying them for her like reruns on a classic film TV channel.

Once again she viewed her mother, Gertrude's lovely face alight with expectation, her hands outstretched in greeting, her voice lilting pleasantly as she came to meet them at the doorway into the living room.

And her father, playing his role to the hilt, charming and urbane as he casually dropped little asides, hinting at not being able to miss how his daughter and his guest had seemed to be immediately drawn to one another at their first meeting in his office on Friday morning.

And, of course, MacCanna, his expression doting, his smile indulgent, making an obvious show of deferring to her, blatantly sitting too close to her, lightly touching her, as if unable to keep his hands off her.

And she herself, going along with her father's and Mac-Canna's every ploy, straining her facial muscles with each successive smile she bestowed upon him, straining her eyes with each beguiled look she cast at him, straining her throat with the effort needed to give her voice a breathless, enthralled tone each time she was called upon to respond to him.

It was enough to make her cringe.

Well, that wasn't quite accurate, Frisco reflected, moving uneasily in the plush seat.

In actual fact it wasn't deception.

The plain truth was, she had felt drawn to MacCanna from the beginning, and she hadn't had to strain at all. Her smiles had been spontaneous; her eyes had mirrored her true feelings; her breathlessness had been a genuine response to his every soft look and light touch.

And that was enough to scare her silly.

Frisco didn't want to be attracted to MacCanna. She didn't want to be enthralled by him. And she most certainly did not want to be legally shackled to him as a result of a business deal.

A business deal, for heaven's sake!

There were mergers, and then there were mergers, but a merger by contractual marriage she could live without! To her way of thinking, sex for sex's sake was much too impersonal an act. Too cold. Too animalistic.

Then why should the mere sight of him, his every glance, his most casual touch, excite her so, overwhelming her sense of outrage and resentment against him?

In self-defense against the scenes and thoughts flooding her mind, Frisco made a concentrated effort to stem the mental flow. When her mind was free of the disturbing flotsam, she let it drift into the fringes of sleep.

The sudden cessation of motion disturbed her rest.

"Your parents appear to be devoted to each other." MacCanna's voice now invaded her doziness.

"They are." Only half-awake, Frisco didn't bother to lift her head from the headrest or to open her eyes. "They've known each other since they were children, and have been in love almost as long."

"They grew up together?" MacCanna's tone held interest, not interrogation.

"Uh-huh." Frisco stifled a yawn, and made the supreme sacrifice of opening her eyes, only then realizing that he had come to a stop in front of her apartment building and not at a red light as she had supposed. MacCanna had shifted in his seat to look at her. "Their families were neighbors."

"Your father's family was well off?"

"At the time, yes," she answered without thinking, raising a hand to cover another yawn that wouldn't be stifled.

"But they're not now?"

Suddenly wide-awake and aware of her lack of reticence, Frisco lifted her head from the headrest and turned to look at him. "They're not anything now," she said disingenuously. "Except for my father, they're all gone. Dad's the last of his line."

"Very interesting," he drawled. "But you haven't answered my question."

"I thought I had." Frisco assumed an expression of innocence. "You asked if his family were—"

"I know what I asked." He cut her off in a tone of impatience. "And you knew what I meant." He smiled wryly. "Don't tell me there was another inept businessman or embezzler in the family?"

"No, another gambler," she said, deciding to be candid, since he'd probably learn the truth eventually anyway. "My grandfather spent more time at the racetrack than in his office." She returned his wry smile. "Obviously, he was as unsuccessful at picking winning horses as my father is at the casino tables."

"Lost the family fortune, did he?"

"And the family business."

"History repeating itself," he said, his smile tilting quirkily. "Or, almost so. Please don't tell me you have a secret gambling habit."

"I don't," she assured him.

"Not even bingo?" he asked, evidently teasing.

"No, not even bingo." Despite the seriousness of the discussion, Frisco could see the thread of humor running through it, and her lips quirked in response. "I have only played the game a few times, yet each time I found it slow and boring." She shrugged. "I must take after my mother's side of the family."

"They're slow and boring?" He smiled.

"No." She resisted an impulse to smile back. "They're careful and thrifty."

"No gamblers, hmmm?"

"Nary a one."

"Good," he said emphatically.

"On the other hand," she mused aloud, "isn't conducting business, or even life itself, a game, a gamble?"

MacCanna laughed.

Frisco shivered, and told herself it was caused by the cool night air.

"To a degree, I suppose you're right," he conceded. "Since you mentioned conducting business," he went on, becoming serious again, "did you give notice today?"

"No," she answered bluntly. "The place was a zoo all day, and I simply didn't have the time." Which wasn't exactly the truth, but . . . She dismissed her blatant excuse with a half-shrug. "It's always like this with the approach of the income-tax deadline. Everybody in the firm is busy." That was the exact truth, everyone was not only busy but stressed.

Frisco knew her constant tiredness was primarily due to stress, and the events of the past few days had only exacerbated the condition.

The absolutely last thing she needed was more pressure, but of course, that was what she got from MacCanna.

"When do you think you will have the time?"

"On April fifteenth."

"The end of this week."

"Yes."

"And you leave on Sunday for two weeks' vacation in Hawaii." His tone was dry as dust.

"I'm not stupid," she drawled, matching his tone.

"Oh, I am well aware of that, Frisco Bay." The glow from the apartment-complex lobby glittered in the depths of his dark eyes. "If I had thought for an instant that you were stupid, or merely not too bright, I'd have never so much as considered accepting your proposal of marriage."

"My counterproposal." She was quick to correct him.

"Whatever." He shrugged. "Call it what you will, as long as the results are the same."

"Whatever," Frisco mimicked, too tired to argue the finer points of the difference. "But right now I'm going to call it a night."

His glittering gaze probed her face, her eyes. "You really are tired, aren't you?"

"Really, really tired."

"Okay." He turned and opened his door.

"There's no need for you to get out," she said, halting him in the process of doing so. "I only have to cross the sidewalk, and the security guard is just inside the entrance."

"I take it you have no intention of inviting me in." He raised his brows in question.

"Correct." She reached for the door release.

"Dinner tomorrow night?"

Her fingers gripped the cold metal. "I . . ." She hesitated; he didn't.

"Or a movie?"

She wet her lips. "I don't think—"

"Then you'd better start," he advised impatiently. "How do you expect to convince your mother we're interested in one another, if we never spend time together?"

"How would she know, either way?" she asked, in what she considered a brilliant ploy to hold him at bay.

He merely gave her a chiding look. "Simple, I'll make certain your father knows. And I'm just as certain that he'll relay the information to your mother."

Like it or not, Frisco was forced to concede his point. "All right, dinner." She activated the door's release.

"And a movie Wednesday night?"

He was pushing his luck, but then, she reminded herself, he was holding all the trump cards. She heaved an audible sigh. "I suppose so."

"Again you suppose. And aren't sure?"

On second thought, she could only be pushed so far. "Give me a break, MacCanna," she lashed out. "I'm damn near asleep sitting here, so no I'm not sure of anything." Shoving the door wide, she stepped out, then turned back to add, scathingly, "I'll be sure tomorrow, *if* I ever get to bed tonight."

"I hear you." He smiled, and held up his right hand in the sign of peace. "What time tomorrow?"

"Oh, I don't know," she said, anxious to put distance between herself and him . . . and that resistance-melting smile. "I don't care."

"Seven?"

"Yes, fine." She moved to shut the door.

"Good night, Frisco Bay." His voice was low, sexy, and loaded with constrained laughter. "Sleep well."

She slammed the door and fled.

Chapter Fifteen

Frisco spent every night of the remainder of that week with MacCanna. To her chagrin, she even enjoyed herself.

He arrived at her door at exactly seven o'clock Tuesday evening looking cool and remote in a light gray suit, white shirt, and striped tie.

He soon proved to be anything but remote.

"I like your hair like that, all loose and wild-looking," he said, his voice low, intimate. "And I like that dress, it makes a refreshing change from the suits you usually wear."

And, as if his compliments weren't disarming enough, he took her to Bookbinder's for dinner . . . the Old Original Bookbinder's on Walnut Street.

She concluded that he had already talked to her father.

On Wednesday, instead of a movie, he took her to the Forrest Theater to see a touring company's performance of a musical show that had been a smash hit on Broadway.

The show was in turn upbeat and sad. The first time Frisco surreptitiously dabbed at her eyes with a tissue, he offered silent comfort by curling his hand around hers.

Frisco felt both comforted and excited by the sensations caused by the friction of his skin against hers.

She didn't appreciate her reaction, because she liked it much too much.

On Thursday it rained.

Undaunted by the stormy weather, MacCanna showed up at Frisco's with a large golf umbrella. Huddled together beneath the nylon protection, they dashed through the spattering rain to a nearby pub and for dinner ate Philadelphia cheese steaks with side orders of salad and French fries.

She thought she could feel every gram of fat gathering in cellulite at her thighs.

Friday morning, Frisco typed a formal letter of resignation, then hand delivered it to her superior, Chester, the younger of the two Manning brothers.

"You can't be serious," he said, after skimming it and noting her request that her two-week vacation be counted as her period of notice. "Are you?"

"Yes, I am," she replied simply.

"But, Frisco," he shook his head, as if unable to believe what he was hearing, "I thought you were happy here."

"I was. I am." She lifted her shoulders in a helpless shrug. "As I stated in the letter, I'm going to be working in the family business."

"But," he began, still shaking his head, "you've always maintained that you didn't want to work for your family."

"My father needs me, Chet," she said with finality. "I can't refuse him."

"Is your father ill?"

He sounded genuinely concerned, and although Frisco appreciated the note of caring, she could not reveal the extent of her father's problem. "Not physically, no, but he is . . . burned out," she hedged. "He wants to retire." Her tone betrayed her acceptance. "If I don't take over, someone else will." An image of Lucas MacCanna formed in her mind, sharpened her tone. "I can't, I won't allow that to happen."

"The business has been in the family too long to let it go?"

Though he posed it as a question, it was in reality a statement of fact.

"Precisely."

"Then there's nothing more to say." He smiled. "We'll all miss you."

"And I'll miss all of you."

Her throat tight, tears threatening, Frisco spent the rest of the day clearing out her desk.

She left the office early and indulged in a good crying spell as soon as she was alone in her apartment. The spate of weeping accomplished nothing except making her eyes puffy; it certainly hadn't lifted her spirits.

Feeling depressed, and not at all in the mood to go out, most especially with the man directly responsible for her condition, Frisco rang Lucas's hotel, intending to plead a headache and beg off for the evening. The phone in his room rang and rang and rang, then the hotel operator broke in to ask if she'd like to leave a message, since Mr. MacCanna apparently was not in.

A quick glance at her watch jolted her into the realization that he had very likely already left to come pick her up, and Frisco thanked the woman politely, but declined. Then she dashed into the bathroom to bathe her eyes with cold water before attempting to set an Olympian record in showering, dressing, and camouflaging the ravages of her tears with makeup. She was feeling rather proud of herself when he arrived; she had made it with twenty-eight seconds to spare.

That evening MacCanna drove them to Penn's Landing where they boarded the *Spirit of Philadelphia* for a leisurely dinner cruise on the Delaware River.

Subdued, still feeling down, Frisco ate sparingly.

Lucas noticed.

"Something wrong with your food?" He lowered his gaze to her plate, then returned it to her.

"No," she denied softly. "The food is delicious. I'm not very hungry."

"Uh-huh," he murmured, and let it go at that . . . until the meal was over.

"Okay, let's have it out," he said over an afterdinner coffee laced with brandy.

Startled out of her moody funk by this sudden, if quietly voiced, demand, Frisco blinked and sputtered, "I don't know what you mean. Have what out?"

He smiled chidingly. "I could probably count on one hand the words you've said this evening. Something's bothering you. What is it?"

Frisco hesitated, then said, "I had a rather . . . emotionally fraught day." She intended to explain, but he was way ahead of her.

"Handed in your notice, did you?" he asked shrewdly, but not unkindly.

She lowered her eyes to hide the quick rush of tears. Impatient with herself, and unsure whether the renewed flow was caused by her situation or his unexpected gentleness, as well as unwilling to probe into the reason for the waterworks, she blinked back the tears, then raised her eyes to squarely meet his.

"Yes."

"Figured." He smiled. "Tough, huh?"

"Very." She didn't smile; she couldn't. She swallowed against the tight feeling in her throat. "It was almost as hard as leaving home."

"I'd have thought it'd be harder." His smile took on a wry curve. "Most young people are eager to leave home, strike out on their own."

He was right, of course. As much as she loved her parents, the home she'd grown up in, Frisco had been too excited about getting her own place, having her independence, to get all maudlin and teary about moving away. Conceding his point, she graciously agreed with him.

"Yes, it was harder."

"But now it's done."

She sighed, and toyed with the delicate stem of her wine glass. "Yes."

"Don't be sad, Frisco Bay," he said, surprising her by reaching across the table to slip his long fingers around hers. "You'll enjoy running your own company." He grinned, causing the tightness in her throat to expand, but for a different reason. "I'll probably work your enticing little tush off until we whip the firm into shape, but I have a hunch you'll relish every aspect of it."

"We'll see," she muttered, too distracted by the sensations the touch of his hand aroused to challenge his assurance.

For the remainder of the evening, MacCanna was attentive and charming, as indeed he had been on every evening that week.

Other than that brief, serious interlude, their conversations were all general and light, with little substance.

On Tuesday they had chatted about the history of the landmark Bookbinder's restaurant.

On Wednesday they discussed the book and music of the Broadway show.

On Thursday their discourse centered on the merits of the famous cheese steaks.

And after that one lapse, while cruising the river, they discussed the success of the restored riverfront area.

During the short drive back to her complex, Frisco reflected that she certainly hadn't needed a life jacket, metaphorical or otherwise, on any one of those evenings, since there hadn't been a lot of depth to their conversational waters.

But did she want depth from this man?

Recalling the quivery way she'd felt from the mere touch of his hand against hers, Frisco mentally dodged the inner probe, and actually was grateful when MacCanna ended her fruitless introspection.

"What would you like to do tomorrow night?" he asked as he brought the car to a stop at her building.

"Go to bed early," she said, reaching for the door release. "I still have most of my packing to do, and I have an early flight Sunday."

"I'll drive you to the airport," he offered. "What time should I be here?"

"Thank you, but that's not necessary. I arranged for a car to pick me up." Certain he was about to argue, she hurried on, "I enjoyed the cruise. Thank you, and good night." She turned away, then froze as his hand curled around her neck.

"Don't rush off, Frisco Bay," he said softly, drawing her slowly, inexorably closer to him.

She could smell him, the intoxicating scent of cologne and man. The aromas filled her senses as he drew her closer, closer to their source.

"Wh-what are you doing?" Her body was stiff, her insides felt mushy.

He laughed.

She trembled.

"I'm going to kiss you."

"No." Her protest lacked authority.

"Yes." His voice did not.

He applied gentle pressure to the back of her head, bringing her mouth ever closer to his.

"A good-bye kiss."

"No, MacCanna. I really don't think . . ." Her voice failed her; he was so close, nearly touching her.

His breath bathed her lips, and then his mouth brushed hers, once, twice before settling delicately upon it, his lips slanted over hers.

When his mouth moved against hers, it was not out of urgency or demand, but in careful exploration.

Frisco felt that she should pull back, away from him, that she should push him away from her; but she could not. Resisting the impulse to respond to him required every bit of inner fortitude she possessed.

There was sweet seduction in the lightest contact of his mouth against hers; seduction of her mind, her senses, her entire being.

Other than the gentle pressure of his lips on hers, his hand against the back of her head, he didn't touch her. But then, he didn't have to.

Frisco was undone by the power of that most innocent of kisses.

She saw no bursting rockets or shooting stars behind her closed eyelids. The earth did not move around her.

The quake was inside her, shaking up and undermining every preconception, every principle she'd previously embraced.

It was nuts.

It couldn't be real.

Yet it was happening, and it scared her silly.

When MacCanna lifted his mouth from hers, she knew an instant of abandonment, was bereft and lost.

Frisco opened her eyes and stared into his intense, solemn expression, and was comforted by the certain knowledge that he had not escaped unscathed by the experience.

"Think about that while you're away," he said, his tone low, emotion-frayed. "And think about me, Frisco Bay."

Chapter Sixteen

Think about me, Frisco Bay.

His charge to her echoing inside his head, Lucas watched as Frisco crossed the sidewalk and entered the well-lit lobby of the apartment complex.

What he hadn't added—and perhaps should have—was that he knew with certainty he'd be thinking about her.

When he lost sight of her, he pulled away from the curb, into the sparse, late-night traffic.

As he picked up speed, and the building receded behind him, Lucas experienced an uncomfortable feeling that he was leaving a part of himself behind.

Most assuredly not a physical part of him, he mused, with self-deprecating humor. At least, not the most vulnerable physical part of him.

He was aroused, fiercely aroused, disproportionately aroused in relation to that brief, almost innocuous touch of his mouth to hers.

Innocuous?

Lucas shattered the stillness inside the car with the sound of his laughter.

Maybe for Frisco the kiss had been innocuous, because she sure as hell hadn't responded to it, but for him, that mere touch of mouths had been devastating.

What in hell would making love with her be like?

The thought was exciting . . . and sobering.

His long fingers gripped the cool steering wheel. He wanted to make love with Frisco so much the wanting caused a pain in his gut.

But, for Lucas, the crucial phrase was *with Frisco*. He definitely did not want to make love to a passive body surrendered to him out of a sense of duty and compliance with the terms of their arrangement.

The very thought of taking his satisfaction from Frisco's unresponsive body seared his mind and chilled his flesh. Hell, he'd seek release from a prostitute first, and that he had never so much as considered, let alone done.

But would he ever see the day Frisco willingly shared a bed, and herself, with him?

The thought intensified the pain in his stomach, while subtly changing it to a hollow, empty ache.

Lucas's teeth were clenched by the time he arrived at the Adam's Mark.

Inside his room, he paced like a caged animal, railing at himself for putting them both in such an untenable position.

But how could he have foreseen that an idea spawned by his determination to take over and salvage her father's faltering company would accelerate, gathering speed and volume like a snowball rolling down a steep hill?

Hell, not in his wildest dreams would he have conceived the idea of Frisco demanding marriage.

Naturally, he had immediately understood why she had made the demand. Her stated reason—protecting herself from being forced out of the company at some future time—while probably valid was not the primary reason. Lucas was positive that she had made her demand hoping he'd refuse.

In all decency, he should have.

Shit.

Now he was feeling like a real heel, and all because he
wanted to go to bed with a woman.

Wrong, Lucas chided himself. He knew full well that he now
found himself in this position because of his strong desire to
go to bed with Frisco.

If someone—anyone—had told him mere weeks ago that he
would go to such extremes simply to sleep with a woman, Lucas would have laughed in that person's face.

He was a businessman for God's sake, not a lover. Besides,
the world revolved around money, not emotions.

Didn't it?

Lucas frowned, recalling the men—and kingdoms—
throughout history brought down by the power of emotions,
the driving forces of greed, physical desire, and perhaps the
strongest of all emotions, love.

Deep in thought, he wasn't aware that he had come to a
stop at the window, nor did he see the artificially lighted view
beyond the pane.

Love.

His mind pounced on the word. Fortunately, that particular
emotion did not come into play in regard to his present situation, he assured himself. While he would readily admit that
he had come to genuinely like Frisco during the hours they
had spent together since their initial meeting, and that that
liking had enhanced his desire for her, his emotions definitely
were not engaged.

Were they?

A fissure of uncertainty invaded his mind.

Lucas was unaccustomed to uncertainty, and he didn't appreciate experiencing it.

Maybe, he mused, he should just call the whole deal off.

But could he at this late date?

He shook his head in silent answer to the inner question.
It was too late. Things had gone too far. The wheels were
already in motion.

In addition to picking up more of the company stock, some
from employees beginning to get nervous about the declining
value of their shares, he had transferred enough funds from

his personal account to cover the firm's outstanding past-due bills. He also had begun negotiations with the authorities of the casinos Harold was indebted to, and arrangements were moving forward on a method of reimbursement of those funds.

Then there was Harold himself, happily making plans to grab his golden umbrella and skip away into retirement.

The gutless bastard.

Lucas sighed, and reminded himself that he and he alone had devised the plan for Harold's escape. And all because he had been determined to take over The Cutting Edge.

No, that wasn't true, he admitted to himself with scrupulous honesty. He could have taken over the company without indulging in elaborate machinations.

The bottom line was, he now found himself in a box of his own devising, because he had experienced an immediate and overpowering sexual itch for Frisco Bay Styer.

Dumb name.

A smile quirked his compressed lips. Dumb perhaps, no, definitely. But he liked it. And he liked her, which made it tough to carry out the real crunchy element of the deal they had finally settled upon.

Marriage.

Enforced marriage.

The quirk of a smile on his lips fled before a curl of self-disgust. For whatever name he put on it, a business arrangement or a marriage of convenience, the simple truth was, he had used coercion to force Frisco's compliance.

Had he taken momentary leave of his senses?

Lucas scowled into the night.

Christ, he had never before employed force or coercion or even monetary reward to gain a woman's sexual favors. He had employed seduction, but nothing else.

Frisco had every right not only to resent but to actively hate him, and for all he knew she did, despite her attempts to remain reasonably pleasant throughout the past week.

Lucas closed his eyes, shutting out the night, if not his persistent thoughts.

Above and beyond anything and everything else, he did not want Frisco to hate or even resent him.

Despite the cost in time, effort, and a sizable amount of money, he had to call this farce off.

That decision made, Lucas felt somewhat better—for all of twenty seconds.

Frisco had resigned her position with the accounting firm at his insistence. And she would be off to Hawaii within several hours.

Lucas had always been credited with the ability to think fast on his feet. Well, he was on his feet at the moment, he told himself. So think.

Perhaps he could call off a portion of the deal, the most contentious portion.

His tightly closed eyes opened to thoughtful slits.

If he were to alter the proposition, changing the condition of partnership by marriage to a more acceptable no-strings equal partnership, they just might be able to make it work.

And then maybe Frisco wouldn't hate him. In time she might even come to like him.

Yes. It was worth a shot, because right or wrong, he still wanted her. And eventually, working so closely together, who knew what would happen?

Which proved the old adage that hope burns eternal.

That settled in his mind, Lucas turned away from the window and began to undress. It was too late to call and disturb Frisco with a discussion of his revised plan. He'd have to wait, call her first thing in the morning, before she left for the airport.

The phone on the bedside table rang before first light. It didn't wake Lucas; his racing mind had denied him the luxury of even sporadic moments of sleep.

"MacCanna," he answered before the end of the second ring, hoping against hope the caller was Frisco, knowing it probably wasn't.

Probability proved correct.

"We've got trouble, Lucas," his brother Michael said without preamble.

"What kind?" he snapped, sitting up on the edge of the bed.

"I just had a call from the local authorities," Michael said tensely. "Rob's been arrested for drunk driving and possession of an illegal substance."

"What!" Lucas shot to his feet, to stand, legs apart and braced, as if to absorb a hard body blow. "Rob? There's got to be some mistake here."

"Not according to the Reading Police," Michael said. "I was informed that, responding to an accident report, the patrol officers found Rob slumped behind the wheel of his car. He apparently ran off the road and into a tree. He—"

"Was he injured?" Lucas broke in anxiously.

"The officer I talked to said that other than a few minor scrapes and bruises, Rob wasn't hurt." Michael sighed audibly. "The bad news is he was intoxicated, and he had marijuana in his possession. I—"

"Have you seen him, talked to him?" Lucas again sharply interrupted.

"No, I wanted to let you know first. But I've already called Ben. His advice was, since he's a corporate attorney, he thought it best to contact a criminal lawyer. He said he'd take care of it."

"Jesus H. Christ . . . a criminal lawyer." Lucas exhaled harshly as an image of his youngest brother formed in his mind. Rob, handsome as hell and devilish, his carefree, happy-go-lucky persona concealing the hard-nosed businessman beneath the teasing facade.

Something was very wrong here, Lucas decided. Booze and illegal substances were not Rob's style.

Or were they?

Damn, did anyone ever really know anyone else?

He had believed he knew both of his brothers, and he had, when they were young and growing up. But Michael and Rob were no longer boys, they were men, in their thirties, mature and independent.

At any rate, he had thought so. Although both his brothers had chosen to come into the company to work with him, Lucas no longer monitored their activities, their personal, private pursuits.

He frowned, suddenly uncertain, a condition that was most definitely not usual for him.

"Lucas?" Michael said, breaking into his reverie, sounding even more uncertain than Lucas himself.

"I'm on my way," Lucas replied, dismissing speculation for action. "I'll be there as soon as possible."

He hung up, then hesitated, his hand still on the receiver, mulling over the feasibility of ringing Frisco. He shot a quick glance at the hotel's bedside clock. It would soon be dawn. She was probably up, or would be getting up soon, since she had an early flight.

But, no. Lucas shook his head and released his grip on the receiver. He didn't have time to explain his decision to change the parameters of their agreement. The news would keep until after she returned from Hawaii.

First things first, he thought, striding to the closet to pull out his suitcase. And, since Lucas was eighteen, if push came to shove, concern for his brothers came first.

Chapter Seventeen

"Do you believe this? Snow in the middle of April!" The grousing cab driver flicked his hand, indicating the wind-driven flurry of flakes spattering the windshield. "What the heck happened to spring, anyway?"

Yeah, anyway, Frisco thought, consoled by the knowledge that it was warm where she was going.

"I don't know," she replied, turning to glance out the side window. The streets were deserted, as they usually were early on Sunday mornings.

"Goin' somewhere interesting," the friendly cabbie chatted on, "or are you heading out on a business trip?"

As if any location for a business trip couldn't possibly be interesting, she thought wryly.

"I'm officially on vacation," she answered, turning to smile at his reflection in the rear-view mirror. "And I'm off to Hawaii for two weeks in the sun."

"Lucky lady," he said ruefully, returning her smile with a cocky grin. "Soak up some sun for me, will ya?"

"Sure." She frowned at the thickening snowfall. "That is, if my plane can take off."

"Ah, this ain't gonna amount to nothin'," he said, with sublime assurance. "Spring snows never do."

"I hope you're right. I wouldn't appreciate a long delay here," she said, as he pulled up to the curb in front of the United Airlines station.

"You'll see," he insisted, jumping out to unload her bags from the trunk. "I bet you take off on time."

He was close.

By flight time the snow had stopped. Frisco's plane took off almost as scheduled.

The only event of note during the flight to San Francisco was breakfast. It was surprisingly good.

When the meal was finished, she reclined the seat, settled in as comfortably as possible, and tried to sleep away the hours. Her attempt was unsuccessful.

Thoughts of the MacCanna, and the kiss he had told her to think about, kept sleep at bay, as they had in fits and starts throughout the previous night.

There was a scheduled three-hour layover in San Francisco. As usual, when one had to sit and wait, the minutes seemed to drag by with frustrating slowness. The plane took off forty-five minutes late.

Feeling rumpled, tired, and in dire need of sleep, longing for the journey to be over, Frisco again tried to drift off to sleep . . . once more unsuccessfully.

Disjointed images and thoughts of MacCanna intruded.

Giving up the pretense, she kept her eyes closed, feigning sleep and allowing her busy mind to have its way.

Contrarily, her fractured thoughts collected, focusing in on one aspect of MacCanna.

His kiss.

Well, what about that kiss? she reflected impatiently, moving restlessly in the confining seat. In point of fact, that brief and feather-light pressure of his mouth to hers could hardly be called a bona fide kiss at all.

But, in that case, why had it affected her the way it had, tangling her emotions into knots, keeping her awake and wondering through most of the night?

Frisco changed position in the seat once again. The evasive action failed to deter her dogged mental activity.

That seemingly ineffectual kiss had not only had a profound effect, her ruminating mind postulated, it had shaken her to the core of her being.

Ridiculous! Frisco dismissed the idea—or tried to. Her subconscious had other intentions, and didn't hesitate in floating them to the surface.

Not only had the kiss shaken her, it had intensified—sharpened—the spear point prick of anticipation she experienced whenever she contemplated the main ingredient of the deal she had made with MacCanna, that of sharing herself in a marriage bed with him.

Frisco swallowed against a sudden tightness in her throat, shifted again in her seat to ease a corresponding tightness and heat between her thighs.

"Can I get you a pillow, miss?"

Grateful for a reprieve from her self-condemning, self-revealing thoughts, Frisco opened her eyes to stare into the solicitous expression of the attractive male flight attendant.

"Or a blanket?"

"Ah . . . no." Frisco smiled. "Thank you."

"You're welcome." The attendant smiled back, displaying a matched set of beautiful, sparkling white teeth. "I'm sorry I disturbed you."

I'm not, Frisco avowed silently. His timely interruption had halted her inner dialogue. The rattle of the meal-tray cart being rolled slowly down the aisle promised further surcease from her mental chatter.

"I wonder what they're serving?"

That question came from the heretofore quiet elderly gentleman seated next to Frisco. Ready to grasp at any straw, she quickly seized the opportunity to keep her errant thoughts in line.

"I can't be certain," she said, inhaling deeply. "But I think I detect the aroma of fish."

Her olfactory sense was right on target. One of the two entrées offered was a Polynesian-style chicken dish, the other a baked fish.

Both Frisco and the elderly gentleman chose the chicken.

"I'm willing to try 'most anything," the man said, appreciatively sniffing the food the flight attendant slid onto his tray. He slanted a sly smile at Frisco. "Anything, that is, except fish." His hazel eyes gleamed with humor. "I love to catch 'em, but I refuse to eat 'em."

Frisco laughed in genuine amusement. "It does smell good, doesn't it?"

"Hmmm," he murmured, taking a tentative sample of the tender white meat. "Tastes good, too." He was quiet while he chewed; then he set his fork aside and extended his right hand to her. "Name's Will Denton." He grinned. "And I'm going to Hawaii to visit my grandchildren."

"Frisco Styer, and I'm on vacation," she said, grasping his hand. "Do your grandchildren live in Hawaii?"

"Yeah, my son's firm transferred him to Honolulu last year." He made a face. "I've been missing the hell out of those two grandkids of mine; they had kinda become the focal point of my life after my wife passed away." He grimaced. "Haven't been fishing since they moved halfway around the world." He sighed. "My wife loved to fish."

Quickly swallowing her food, Frisco murmured, "I'm sorry. About your losing your wife, I mean."

"Thanks, I miss her, but"—he moved his shoulders in a philosophical shrug—"we had forty good years together, and I'm thankful for that."

"Forty years." Frisco smiled. "My parents are married thirty-three years. I had been thinking that was a long time. Forty years somehow sounds like a lot longer for two people to be together."

"I suppose it does to a young person." His return smile held a shadow of sadness, and understanding of her inexperience. "But believe me, Miss Styer, the years slip by so fast, too fast, and each year faster than the last. They add up while you're not looking. So savor every minute."

Frisco chewed on his advice while she finished her meal. It

was good advice, well worth pondering. The years did slip by; Lord, over ten had passed since she had graduated from college. Had she savored them? No, she'd been too busy working, advancing her career. And what did she really have to show for those years?

A small, very expensive condo.

No husband. No children. No prospects of future grandchildren to fulfill and delight her in her more sedentary retirement years. She had thought she wanted it that way, earlier on, when she was caught up in achieving success in her field. She had been convinced that having a career and a family were contradictory concepts, and so not for her.

Oh sure, there were those who claimed success at both endeavors, but Frisco had secret but serious doubts about that. In her opinion, a woman had either a career or a family . . . or eventually a nervous breakdown.

Eschewing marriage as slavery by voluntary vows, even of the self-created variety, she had chosen to pursue her own agenda, unencumbered by mate or offspring. And the one short-lived liaison she had indulged in had only served to reaffirm her belief that commitment to two so diverse goals was like trying to mix oil and water; it simply didn't work.

How could she have foreseen that after years of struggling to attain professional success and material reward, she would be left with vague dissatisfaction, emptiness, and loneliness instead of the well-earned feeling of achievement she had hoped to realize?

Frisco couldn't help but wonder if there weren't lots of women, other than her friend Jo, and those of her ultramilitant ilk, who at some point or other suffered doubts about the decision to put off having a husband and children in favor of a single-minded pursuit of a career.

There were other alternatives, of course, but . . .

"Are you finished with your tray, miss?"

"What?" Startled, Frisco looked up at the smiling face of the attendant, then quickly back at the meal tray, surprised to discover it empty. "Er . . . yes," she said, handing the plastic container to the woman.

"You were really far away there for a while," Will Denton observed, his smile fatherly.

"Yes, my mind was wandering," Frisco admitted, her own smile wry. "It's been doing that a lot lately."

He chuckled. "Sounds to me like you really need this vacation."

"I do," she agreed, while thinking what she really needed was a break from fruitless introspection.

"Let me buy you a drink," Denton said, indicating the drinks cart moving along the aisle. "We'll toast your vacation and my visit with my grandkids."

Frisco was about to decline, then changed her mind, Why not? she decided. It would pass the time, and hopefully keep her rambling reflections contained.

"Thank you, I'd like that, Mr. Denton."

"Call me Will," he said, as the cart drew even with their row. "What'll you have?"

"White wine, please, Will. And I'm Frisco."

"Okay, Frisco it is." He paid for the two small bottles, one white, one red, then passed the white wine and a clear plastic cup to her.

"Tell me about your grandchildren, Will," she invited after the toast was made and a sip of wine swallowed.

He was more than happy to oblige and immediately launched into anecdotes about the ten- and eight-year-old boys. Though Frisco found his stories both amusing and endearing, her eyes were drooping before she'd finished the wine.

"Please excuse me," she apologized, raising a hand to cover a yawn.

Will laughed. "Not to worry. Feel free to nod off at any time. I'll shut up when you do."

He continued on as if uninterrupted, and in so doing accomplished what all her previous efforts had not; in effect, he literally talked her to sleep.

Will woke her as the plane made its approach to the airport. Smiling muzzily, she thanked him, then turned to look out the window.

From the air, Honolulu was breathtaking.

The flower leis they received upon deplaning were the perfect welcome to the beautiful island.

Frisco delicately stroked the brightly colored blossoms in hers as she walked beside Will to the luggage area. His family was waiting there for him. Spotting him, they waved and called out and started toward him.

"It was nice meeting you, Will," she said sincerely, extending her hand to him. "I hope you have a wonderful visit with your family."

"And it was nice meeting you." He grasped her hand and lightly squeezed it. "You're a lovely young woman. But you look tired, Frisco. Enjoy your vacation, by all means"—he hurried on as his grandsons ran to him—"but get some rest, too." He released her hand and turned to open his arms to the boys, then slanted a quick, happy smile at her over his shoulder. "By the way, I like your name."

"Thank you, Will," she said softly. "I like you."

In the next moment his family enveloped him. The happy reunion brought a misty sting to Frisco's eyes.

Sighing, she turned away to collect her bags.

Chapter Eighteen

"Frisco called." Gertrude gave Harold the news, along with her usual greeting kiss, when he came home from the office Monday afternoon.

"Good, good." He smiled tenderly at the woman he had loved for almost as long as he could remember. "Everything all right? Flight go okay?"

"Yes, fine. She said the island is absolutely gorgeous, and she can't wait to see more of it." A soft, motherly smile curved her lips. "She also said she was so tired from the long flight that after she checked into the hotel, she unpacked, had room service deliver a snack to her room, then went to bed as soon as she'd finished eating."

"She must have been exhausted if she wasn't up to even a bit of sight-seeing." A worried frown wrinkled Harold's brow. "Are you sure she's all right?"

"Yes . . . At least she sounded fine." Gertrude's frown mirrored his for an instant; then she brightened. "I believe she was so tired because she had an annoying delay in San Francisco." Her expression softened again, grew dreamy. "I do love San

Francisco." Her eyes twinkled. "I have fond memories of our visits to that beautiful city."

Chuckling, her husband gathered her into a tight embrace, and kissed her again. "If I remember correctly, we saw precious little of the city during our first visit there."

Gertrude delighted him by blushing in exactly the same way she had as a bride. "Yes, it was wonderful," she murmured, snuggling closer to him. "Oh, and I so hope that someday Frisco will find the same kind of happiness you and I experienced there."

"Only there?" he teased.

She gazed misty-eyed at him. "You know what I mean."

"Yes, dear heart, I do." He gave her another warm kiss. "And perhaps, before too long she will."

"Lucas?" The hope Gertrude had been cherishing was revealed in her eyes.

Harold nodded.

"Oh . . ." She sighed. "I do wish . . ."

"Well, you just hold on to that wish," he said, deliberately fostering her ardent dream. "From what I've observed, and from what little Lucas has said to me, I have a strong suspicion he is becoming very attached to Frisco."

"Do you really think so?" his wife asked eagerly.

"Yes, I do." His expression grew speculative. "As a matter of fact, I wouldn't be at all surprised if he should decide to fly to Hawaii himself."

"Oh!" Her eyes widened, and then she laughed. "Oh, my. That does sound like he's getting serious." Her eyes glowed with expectation. "Lucas MacCanna and Frisco. Imagine! I think he's very attractive and rather exciting, if a bit intimidating. Wouldn't you say?"

He smiled, but didn't say anything. So far as the man being attractive and exciting, Harold couldn't say, simply because he had never thought about it. But what he had thought about, often, was MacCanna's seemingly effortless ability to intimidate.

He certainly intimidates the hell out of me, Harold thought.

Suppressing a reflexive shudder, he sought comfort—and a sense of protection—in his wife's embrace.

"What in hell were you thinking?" Lucas demanded, staring at Rob, furious and hard-eyed. "Or weren't you thinking at all?" He charged on before his brother could respond.

"Lucas, I was tired. I—"

"Tired?" Lucas impatiently cut him off. "Tired! Being tired excuses being soused and high?"

"Dammit, Lucas, I wasn't either of those," Rob denied in angry self-defense. "I had had a couple drinks and two joints, that's all."

"That's all?" Lucas repeated, shaking his head in sheer disbelief. "Jesus H. Christ, man, it was more than enough to get you arrested. You ran your car into a tree, for God's sake. You had marijuana in your possession. And all you can say is, that's all?"

Rob tried again. "Lucas, I—"

"I don't understand any of this." Lucas's harsh voice cut him off once more. "I believed you were smarter than this. Goddammit, Rob, now you've got a police record, and for all I know you may be facing a jail sentence." Frustrated, he rubbed his palm over the back of his neck. "The only thing missing is trouble with a woman."

Rob visibly swallowed. "I had just dropped her off."

"What!" Lucas exploded. "I'll be a son of—"

"Calm down, Lucas." This time it was Michael who interrupted. "Let Rob explain."

"Oh, by all means," Lucas shot back, sarcastically. "Be my guest, Rob. I can't wait to hear it."

Rob grew rigid, his expression stark, resentful. "There really was no trouble," he snapped. "I had a woman with me, that's all."

"What woman?" Lucas snapped back.

"None of your damned business," Rob exploded. "Next you'll be demanding a detailed report on my love life."

"Love?" Lucas arched his brows.

"I've had enough of this shit." Shaking, pale, Rob turned and headed for the door.

"Where do you think you're going?" Lucas's voice cracked through the room like a snapped whip.

"Home."

"Rob, come back here." The very quietness of the command brought the younger man to an abrupt halt mere steps from the door.

Rob hesitated a moment, then heaved a sigh. "Lucas, please, cut me some slack." He turned, and his face was drawn with weariness. "I'm so tired."

Staring at his brother, his youngest brother, tore a hole in the fabric of Lucas's determination. Rob appeared to be on the verge of collapse. He did not cave in, but Lucas's will to hear a full account of his brother's folly did.

"All right. Go home and get some sleep," he said, relenting. "But I want to see you in my office tomorrow morning, prepared to give me a complete explanation." Though his tone was soft, his eyes were hard. "Now, get out of here. Michael will drive you home."

Neither one of the brothers reacted to being summarily dismissed, at least not verbally. Rob's shoulders slumped, while Michael merely smiled wryly in response to having his services offered without being consulted.

Lucas didn't notice; he had already turned away to pick up the phone. He still had work to do, people to talk to, strings to pull. Lucas actively hated throwing his weight around, but he didn't so much as pause now. He'd do what he had to do—anything—to keep his brother out of prison.

When the distasteful chore was finished, he poured himself some Scotch, then dropped heavily into a chair.

Sipping the whiskey, Lucas sent a slow, critical gaze around the room. He had bought the townhouse years ago, more for its location in relation to his steel mill than for its design or aesthetic appeal.

The place had served his purposes, for then. But for now? Lucas frowned. What about now? he asked himself. What was different now?

For a while there he had thought he'd have reason to look around for a better, roomier place . . . perhaps a home in the mainline Philadelphia area.

But with his decision to free Frisco from her commitment to marriage with him . . .

Lucas downed the remaining whiskey in one deep swallow, grimacing as it burned down his throat.

What did he need a bigger house for, if there was to be no marriage, no wife, no Frisco?

"Goddam."

Pushing up, out of the chair, Lucas carried the empty glass to the tiny, utilitarian kitchen, rinsed it, and set it in the gleaming stainless steel sink.

Go to bed, MacCanna, he told himself. You know where that is, don't you? he ruminated, heading for the master bedroom. It's where you sleep—that luxury you haven't indulged in in too many hours.

You'll feel better, think clearer about Rob and Frisco in the morning, after a solid night's sleep.

Although he undressed and slid into bed, acting on his own advice, Lucas didn't believe it for a minute.

"Where the hell is he?"

"It's only eleven-fifteen, Lucas," Michael said, glancing at his watch. "And Rob was pretty beat last night."

Tell me about it, Lucas thought, eyeing Michael with visible impatience.

Since he hadn't enjoyed a solid night's sleep, he wasn't feeling better, or thinking much clearer about either Rob or Frisco. In fact, this morning, he wasn't feeling any too charitable toward Michael, either.

Hell, maybe he needed a vacation. He hadn't had one in . . . Lucas frowned. He couldn't recall the last time he had taken time out for himself.

Hawaii sprang into his mind.

He immediately banished the vision of tall, slender palm trees and a tall, slender woman.

"He should have been here hours ago," he said, dragging his thoughts back to the business at hand.

"I'm sure he'll be . . ." Michael let his assurance die as his brother walked into the office.

"It's about time you put in an appearance," Lucas rapped out in a near snarl.

"Oh, screw you and the white horse you rode in on," Rob retorted, obviously rested and ready to fight.

"What's that supposed to mean?"

"You!" Rob said. "Dammit, Lucas, why must you always ride to the rescue like the good guy? The only thing missing is the legendary white hat."

Taken aback by his brother's attack, Lucas was speechless for several moments. Then, to his utter amazement and confusion, Michael joined forces with Rob.

"He has a point, Lucas."

"What?" Lucas demanded, finding his voice with a vengeance.

"You ride herd on us," Michael explained.

"Ride herd, hell!" Rob said. "Lucas, you gallop all over us, trample us in the dust."

"How?" Lucas was mad now, really mad, and he let it show. He was hurt, as well; he concealed that. "How have I trampled the two of you into the dust?" he asked in retaliation. "By fighting to keep you with me after Mom died? By working my ass off to educate you? By building a failing, run-down mill into one of the best steel companies in the world?" He snorted. "Or maybe you both felt trampled by my audacity at investing the profit from the land we inherited when Grandmother died?" He sneered. "I can see how you would have resented that deal, since our return on it only made us millions instead of billions."

"You were already a millionaire by then, Lucas," Michael reminded him, his tone revealing his pride in his brother, something Lucas never seemed to note.

"What does that have to do with it?" Lucas said, once again deaf and blind to his brother's admiration.

"You treat us like mushrooms," Rob complained.

That statement stopped Lucas cold.

"What?"

"Mushrooms," Rob repeated, succinctly. "You keep us in the dark about all the important details of the business, and dump all the unimportant shit on us."

"Mushrooms, huh?" Lucas was hard put not to laugh. He had never heard the expression before, and it was a pretty good analogy. But, though he contained the urge to laugh, something about him betrayed his feelings, because Michael's somber expression gave way to a smile.

"Mushrooms, Lucas," he said. "In other words, you never confide in either of us."

"I never confide in anyone."

"Yeah, we know," Rob said. "But we're your brothers, not just anyone."

Although Lucas reluctantly admitted to himself that they did have a point, it was not germane to the purpose of this particular meeting. Deciding to get the discussion back on track, he fixed a hard stare on Rob.

"What does all this have to do with your stupid performance late Saturday night?"

"I told you, I was tired."

"That's not an answer," Lucas pointed out, not very pleasantly. "That's an excuse. And a piss-poor one for substance abuse."

"Dammit, Lucas, I told you—"

"No, you didn't," Lucas cut him off harshly. "You didn't tell me a damn thing. You made a lot of noises last night—and accusations this morning. I have yet to hear exactly what you were doing and why you were doing it."

"Okay." Rob sighed. "As I said last night, I was not drunk or drugged. I was tired."

"Jesus Christ!" Lucas exclaimed. "If I hear you say you were tired one more time, I'll—"

"You'll what?" Rob interrupted. "Fire me? I *was* tired, damn you! I was bone tired from working *my* ass off at the motivational conference you shipped me off to Chicago to attend."

"I ship you off to those conferences because you are one of the best motivational consultants around."

"Thank you for that, at least."

Lucas frowned, wondering if he had been too demanding of his brothers.

"Anyway," Rob went on when Lucas failed to respond, "I got into A.B.E. late Saturday afternoon. And my ass was dragging. So on my way home, I picked up my, er . . . friend, then went on to have dinner and a few drinks." He sighed and shrugged. "I fell asleep driving home afterward, and wound up wrapped around a tree."

"You left out the part about the marijuana."

"Look, Lucas, I only smoke it occasionally for recreational purposes," Rob said irritably.

"It's risky," Lucas said flatly. "Especially if you're caught with it in your possession."

"So I'll avoid trees."

"That's very funny." Lucas wasn't laughing. "But you'd do better to avoid the pot."

"Dammit, Lucas, I'm thirty-one years old," Rob protested. "Michael's thirty-three. Don't you think it's time you let us do our own thinking?"

Lucas sliced a look at Michael. "You believe I've been doing your thinking for you?"

Michael hesitated a moment, then slowly nodded. "Yes, to a degree."

"So I've misused the both of you, huh?" Lucas suddenly felt as tired as Rob claimed he had been.

"Not misused, Lucas," Michael corrected.

"Underused," Rob clarified.

Lucas had a nasty suspicion it was going to be a very long day.

Chapter Nineteen

"Hi. You come here often?"

Frisco stiffened at hearing a male voice drawling the overused line. Slowly turning away from the poolside bar, prepared to deliver a cool brush-off, she found herself facing a pleasant-looking, grinning young man.

"Pitiful, wasn't it?" he asked jovially. "But I wanted to meet you, and I couldn't think of a thing to say that didn't sound trite and stupid."

Conceding that his approach was at least a little different, and his smile engaging, Frisco hesitated in issuing a crushing putdown. He immediately took advantage of her delay.

"My name's Ken Rhyan," he said, extending his right hand. "I noticed you when you checked into the hotel on Sunday." He gave her a somewhat self-mocking, but quite disarming, smile. "I've been trying to think of a way to meet you ever since."

"Frisco Styer," she said, taking his hand. "Are you staying here in the hotel?"

"No." He laughed; it had a nice, friendly sound, not in the least sensuous or disturbingly exciting. "I work here. I was behind the registration desk when you checked in."

"I didn't notice," she admitted.

"I know." He shrugged, as if to say not being noticed was part of his job description.

"You're one of the desk clerks?"

He shook his head. "Day manager."

"I see."

He smiled.

She smiled.

There ensued a brief moment of awkward silence; then he laughed again.

"May I join you?" He gestured at the empty stool next to hers. "Buy you another drink?"

Frisco hesitated again, then thought, why not? She had only been at the bar for a few minutes, and she was already bored with the uninspired come-on the blond, pumped-up bartender was dishing out.

"Well, I was about to escape the sun by sheltering beneath a table umbrella," she said, which was true, except that it wasn't the sun she wanted to escape so much as the bartender, who obviously believed he was irresistible to the entire female gender. "You're welcome to join me *there* if you'd like."

"That's even better," he said, exhaling as if he'd been holding his breath. "Just give me a minute to get us a drink and I'll—"

"None for me, thanks," she said, holding her nearly full glass aloft. "This is enough for me until dinner."

He got a drink for himself, then trotted beside her to the table like an eager puppy.

"About dinner," he said slowly, offering her a shy smile. "Will you have it with me?"

Taking a sip of the coconut-flavored drink, she gave him a considering look. And she liked what she saw. Besides, despite her original intention of spending her vacation alone, doing nothing but resting and soaking up sun, after just three days she was tired of her own company, and fed up with lying on the beach. It should be safe enough, if he was a hotel employee, which he probably was, considering how easy it was to confirm his assertion.

"I know a place where they serve genuine native food," Ken said as an added inducement.

A sharp, clear image of Lucas MacCanna flashed into her mind, deciding the issue for Frisco.

"How could I possibly refuse to try the genuine article?" she wondered aloud, smiling at him. "Yes, Ken, I'd love to have dinner with you."

"What time?" he asked, every bit as eagerly as he had trotted beside her to the table.

"I left my watch in my room." She raised her left hand, displaying her bare wrist. "What time is it now?"

He glanced at his watch. "Five-fifty."

"What time do you go off duty?"

"I'm off duty now." He smiled in that shy, self-effacing way. "I saw you heading for the pool area as I was getting ready to leave. I followed you out here," he confessed, actually blushing.

Frisco laughed, she couldn't help herself; he was so appealing and boyishly cute.

Ken made a whooshing sound with his breath. "You're not angry about my following you out here?" he asked in a tone of relief.

"No." She smiled. "Matter of fact, I'm rather flattered," she admitted, "since I think I'm somewhat older than you are."

"I doubt it." He gave a quick shake of his head. "How old are you, twenty-six, seven?"

"Oh, you are the diplomat," she said, laughing. "You're off by four years."

"C'mon," he jeered. "You're not thirty-two."

"I'm afraid so." She pulled a rueful expression. "I celebrated my thirty-second birthday last month."

"Aha! I'm older by two months," he crowed, flashing a teasing grin. "I celebrated my thirty-second birthday last January."

Frisco was skeptical, and let it show. "I don't believe you," she said bluntly. "You don't look a day over twenty-five."

"Yeah, I know." He heaved a sigh. "My young appearance has been the bane of my existence."

"Looking young is a bane?"

"Well, hell," he groused, "I was still being carded in bars until about two years ago."

"Oh, please stop," she cried in exaggerated despair. "You're breaking my heart."

His burst of laughter was infectious, and Frisco caught a case of the giggles.

"So, what do you think?" Ken asked when they had both calmed down enough to speak. "Seven for dinner?"

"You want to bring five friends?" she asked in seeming innocence, batting her eyelashes at him.

"Five friends?" he repeated, frowning. Then her quip registered, and he was off again in an eruption of lighthearted laughter.

"Now look, Ken, we've got to get serious here," she reproved him, trying unsuccessfully to look stern. "It must be after six, and if we're meeting at seven, I've got to get moving."

"Why? I'm having a great time right here."

"So am I," she said, surprised by the realization. "But I have to change."

"I wish you didn't," he murmured, running a quick, appreciative, yet not insulting, glance over her body, which was barely concealed by the skimpy bikini and the coordinated, thigh-length sheer coverup she was wearing. "You're breathtaking, just the way you are," he said with complimentary sincerity.

"Thank you," she murmured. "But I don't think beachwear is the 'in' thing for dinner."

"Well, it should be." He paused, appearing to contemplate his assertion, then shook his head. "On the other hand, maybe not. I've seen the . . . er, shall I say larger guests, in their beachwear." He shuddered. "It is not a pretty sight."

"That is an unkind remark," Frisco scolded, fighting a bubble of laughter.

"But true."

Sipping the last drops of her drink through a straw, she set her glass on the table and stood. "What time is it now?"

Ken glanced at his watch. "Six-fifteen."

"I'm hitting the shower." She took one step away from the

table, then turned back to him. "Should we meet in the lobby . . . say, seven-thirty?"

"Okay, seven-thirty."

"Right." She began to move.

"And dress casually," he called after her. "This restaurant isn't fancy."

Frisco waved in answer and kept moving.

"So, what did you really think?"

Frisco laughed, but continued walking toward Ken's car. "I already told you I enjoyed it, and I meant it. I thought the food was delicious, whatever it was."

"I'm not sure what all is in it myself," Ken said, grinning as he unlocked the car. "I do know that the main ingredient is fish."

"I had figured that out for myself." She laughed again at his exaggerated expression of consternation. "But don't worry about it, Ken," she consoled him. "The meal was very good, and that's all that matters." She hesitated before getting into the car. "On consideration, perhaps I'm better off not knowing all the ingredients."

"You know, I never thought of it that way," he said, sliding behind the wheel. "You're probably right." He slanted a shy smile at her as he started the car. "If I knew what the concoction consisted of, I might never order it again."

They exchanged grins, and it struck Frisco that she had smiled, grinned, and laughed frequently in the few hours she had known him.

Although she had suffered some doubts about the wisdom of accepting his invitation to dinner, she was now not in the least sorry she had decided to go out with him.

Ken was very good company. He was polite, considerate, charming, and amusing. Not once had he made an off-color or even suggestive remark.

Initially tense and uncertain, she had found herself relaxing during dinner, her tension easing as he regaled her with his life story.

* * *

"How did you ever discover this place?" was all Frisco had had to ask, indicating the unimpressive, out-of-the-tourist-section restaurant.

"My folks brought me here for the first time when I was around eleven or twelve." Glancing around the small, jam-packed room, Ken smiled reminiscently. "I'm a native Hawaiian, you know."

"Really?" She had been unable to hide her surprise. "You don't look like a native."

"Oh, we come in all shapes, sizes, and colors—and from many different backgrounds and cultures," he said, his eyes bright with humor. "Much the same as the citizens of the rest of the U.S."

"I'm sorry." Frisco was afraid she had insulted him, despite his show of humor. "I didn't mean—"

"I know you didn't," he interrupted, brushing her apology away with a flick of his hand. "I'm used to it. Most tourists expect Hawaiians to be . . . native, for want of a better word." He grinned. "Just natural, I suppose. People expect Hawaiians to look Polynesian, and quite a lot of us don't."

"You were born here in Honolulu?"

"Yep, and my father before me. His father, my grandfather, was of Irish descent, originally from Idaho. He was stationed here for a while during World War II, and fell in love with the beauty and the climate of the islands. After the war ended, he and his wife came back here to live." Ken chuckled. "She was British. He met her when he was stationed in England near the end of the war."

"So you're a multinational family," she said teasingly.

"More than you know," Ken responded. "My father was with the group of advisers sent to Vietnam in the early sixties. He met and married my mother there. She's French."

"I feel almost inbred." Frisco laughed. "As far I as know, every one of my antecedents was German. Not an Irish or British or French person in the lot."

"And where are you from?"

"Philadelphia." She gave him a teasing smile. "That's in Pennsylvania, you know."

"So I'd heard," he replied, quite seriously. "The famous Pennsylvania Dutch country, and all that."

"Settled by Germans," she informed him.

"So where does the Dutch come from?"

"It's a corruption of the word Deutsch, which is German for 'German.' "

"Hmmm."

His expression was so comical, Frisco had to laugh, as she had many times throughout dinner.

All in all, she mused, as they drove back to the hotel, she had had a delightful evening.

"Penny for them," Ken said, turning to give her a quick smile when he stopped for a red light.

"A penny!" Frisco exclaimed huffily. "I'll have you know my thoughts do not come that cheaply."

"Two pennies?" He wiggled his eyebrows at her before returning his attention to the road.

"Sold." She shifted in the seat to smile at him. "I was thinking about how much I enjoyed this evening . . . and the company."

"Yeah?" He shot another swift look at her. "Wanna do it again tomorrow night?"

"Well . . ." She hesitated, making a show of playing hard to get even though she knew she'd accept.

"We could go to one of the touristy places," he inserted into the pause.

"Since I haven't done any of the touristy things yet," she replied, "I'd love to, thank you."

Ken brought the car to a stop in the hotel parking lot, then turned to stare at her in astonishment.

"You haven't done any sight-seeing at all?"

"No." Frisco shook her head. "I came here to rest," she explained. "So far, all I've done is lie on the beach, splash in the ocean, and swim in the hotel pool. I haven't ventured very far from the hotel's grounds."

"Would you like to do some sight-seeing, or do you feel you still need to rest?"

Frisco was touched by the concern and consideration in his expression and his tone.

"Actually, I'd love to see some of the sights." She smiled as relief swept over his face. "I'm getting pretty tired of the solitude."

"Great!" he fairly hooted. "If you'd like, tomorrow evening we could go to a luau. It's very touristy, but fun just the same . . . the hula and all that, you know."

"Fine," she said, laughing. "I'm in the mood for some fun—maybe even the hula."

"Terrific! And I have Friday and Saturday off," he went on eagerly. "I'd be honored if you'd allow me to escort you to some of the many and beautiful attractions of my home city."

"Thank you, kind sir." She inclined her head in lieu of a curtsy. "That sounds wonderful. I accept your invitation, but only on the condition that you allow me to return the compliment if you ever visit Philly."

"You've got a deal." He flashed the grin she was coming to think of as endearing, and thrust out his hand.

Keeping her expression solemn, Frisco took it, then had to smile when he gave hers a hard, businesslike shake.

"We need to leave earlier tomorrow evening," he said, as he opened his door and stepped out. He circled to meet her as she got out her side. "We should leave here no later than six."

"All right, six it is." She walked beside him into the hotel. "Casual dress?"

"Yes. May I see you to your room?"

"No." Frisco smiled to remove any sting from the refusal. "I'll meet you here in the lobby tomorrow evening at six."

"I'll be waiting with bated breath." He grinned, then added, "Pant, pant."

"Good night, Ken." Chuckling, Frisco turned and headed for the elevators.

"Good night, Frisco."

Chapter Twenty

"Have you spoken to Frisco lately, Lucas?" Harold asked abruptly, not bothering with the courtesy of the usual telephone greeting.

Lucas frowned at the note of anxiety in the older man's voice. "I haven't talked to her at all," he answered, quelling a corresponding curl of unease. "Why, is something wrong? Is she all right?"

"Yes, she's fine, it's just . . ."

"Just what?" he demanded, the unease unwinding and expanding inside him.

"She called last night . . . of course it wasn't night there, you understand . . . but—"

"Harold, get to the point," Lucas interrupted impatiently. "It's obvious that something has you upset. What is it?"

"Well, it seems she's met a young man."

The curl flared inside Lucas, sending shards of tension to every nerve ending in his body. He was still, speechless, for a moment, shocked by the intensity of the sensation.

"So?" he asked with deceptive calm.

"So? So!" Harold sputtered. "Suppose she really likes him."

He paused, then said in evident alarm, "Lucas, suppose she does something really stupid like thinking she's in love with this man?"

"Oh, get a grip, Harold," he scoffed, while the echo of Frisco's voice rang inside his head.

What if I should meet someone and fall in love?

Goddammit.

Stay cool, MacCanna, he told himself. She is only a woman. But, dammit, she is *my* woman.

The thought shocked Lucas more than the jolt to his nervous system.

"I think that's highly unlikely," he assured Harold, slightly surprised at the lack of emotion in his own voice. "Frisco's a levelheaded woman, not the type to fall in love at first sight."

"But you never know," Harold insisted. "And apparently, she's been spending all her time with him since Wednesday."

This is Sunday.

Shit!

In that instant, all of Lucas's lofty plans to release Frisco from her promise to marry him went by the boards. They had made a deal, he decided. She had agreed. And, fair or not, he was going to see to it that she lived up to her end of the bargain.

"Okay, Harold, I'll fly to Hawaii and make sure she doesn't do anything foolish."

"I think that's best." Harold's voice was rife with relief.

For you, Lucas thought cynically, under no illusions as to the root cause of Harold's concern. The man might love his daughter, but in Lucas's opinion, Harold's main concern at present was Harold.

After ending the conversation with him, Lucas flipped through the phone directory for the number of United Airlines.

He replaced the receiver moments later, a thin smile of satisfaction shadowing his lips.

The reservations operator had been very accommodating; he was booked onto a flight out of Philadelphia that afternoon. Lucas had not so much as winced when the operator had informed him that he would have a short layover in Chicago and in San Francisco.

His reservations secured, Lucas again picked up the phone, this time to call his brother Michael. There was no answer.

He smiled wryly as he depressed the disconnect button; it was Sunday morning. Michael was playing handball or golf.

That left Rob.

And after the previous week, Rob was not too happy with his eldest brother.

Lucas grimaced as he recalled the on-again, off-again arguments he and Rob had had throughout the past week, each one a replay of their original confrontation exactly one week ago.

Heaving a tired sigh, he punched in Rob's number.

"Hello?"

Lucas swallowed another sigh; the voice was definitely not Rob's.

"Who are you?" he demanded.

"Melanie," she blurted out in reaction to the note of command in his voice. Then, as if pulling herself together, she shot back, "Who are you, and what do you want?"

"Lucas MacCanna," he snapped. "And I want to talk to Rob."

"Oh!" Melanie said in a subdued voice. "Just a minute, Mr. MacCanna, I'll get him."

From where, the bed? Though the question sprang to Lucas's lips, he didn't voice it; after the weeklong battle with his brother, he had finally conceded that maybe he had been holding the reins too tightly on both his brothers.

Besides, he had more important and pressing matters to think about at the moment than the identity of Rob's current bedmate. Matters like his own relationship, or lack of same, with his promised bride.

And, dammit, if Frisco was screwing around with—

"Lucas?" Rob's sleep-slurred voice cut across Lucas's fury-arousing thought. "What's up?"

"Apparently you are, but that's beside the point," Lucas drawled.

"Clever, but incorrect," Rob drawled right back. "I was deep in sleep, not in Melanie."

"Melanie the girl you were with last week?"

"Yes."

"Is this affair getting serious?"

Rob didn't respond for a moment, then he said, "Could be, I don't know yet. Ask me again in another coupla months or so."

"I will."

"I know." Rob chuckled, evidently more than ready to call a halt to the hostilities between them.

In truth, Lucas was just as ready to agree to a truce. After a week of giving due consideration to Rob's explanations and complaints, he was willing to try to deal with at least a few of them. Something Rob had said in the office on Friday afternoon had been the deciding factor in Lucas's thinking.

"You can't imagine what it's been like for me, and Mike, too, I guess, trying to emulate you!" Rob had suddenly declared in the middle of their on-going argument.

"Emulate me?" Lucas repeated, caught off guard and taken aback by what sounded to him like an accusation. "I never expected either one of you to emulate me. Why did you think you should?"

"Because of who you are, what you've accomplished." Rob speared his fingers through his hair in evident frustration. "You're so goddam successful at everything you do. Take the investment of the money we got for the sale of the land. Jesus Christ, Lucas, you gambled several hundred thousand dollars on the market, and damned if we haven't realized millions!"

"I would hardly call investing in Microsoft when it went public much of a gamble," Lucas drawled.

"But . . . who knew?"

"I did."

"That's what I mean!" Rob exclaimed. "You got in on the ground floor, because you knew."

"Only because I was fascinated by what I'd heard about

Gates's work," Lucas explained. "There was nothing mysteri-
ous or anything about it." He had smiled. "I'm not omnipo-
tent, you know."

"Well, you could'a fooled me," Rob muttered. "Having you
for a lifelong example, with your iron will and uncompromis-
ing dedication can get pretty damned daunting at times."

Rob's words had replayed inside Lucas's mind, and they'd
echoed inside his heart, ever since. Oh, yes, he was long over-
due in making concessions to his brothers. Maybe he'd even
go so far as replacing himself in the company, hire a new man
as C.E.O.—someone not so *damned daunting* to his brothers.

But he had no intention of discussing that now; he had
more pressing business.

Consequently, he inadvertently said the one thing guaranteed to disarm his brother.

"Rob, I need your help."

He frowned at what sounded to him like a sharply indrawn
breath, followed by a slow exhalation.

"Anything, Lucas. What can I do for you?" The slurred
sleepiness had disappeared from Rob's voice, to be replaced
by a brisk, businesslike tone.

Recalling that not only Rob but Michael as well had complained about his never taking either of them into his confidence, Lucas decided to compromise a bit with his tendency
toward self-containment.

Then again, maybe his preoccupation with a particular
woman was making him soft in the head.

Lucas mentally shrugged off that consideration and focused
on the business at hand.

"I have to go out of town for a while on personal business,
and I need you and Michael to take care of things for me
while I'm away."

"It's done." Rob laughed, then said, "That is, if I'm not in
stir."

"You're not going to jail, Rob," Lucas said with absolute
certainty.

"If you say so, I believe it." His brother's tone held absolute certainty.

"But I want your word that you'll find another—legal—way to unwind, because I sure as hell will not interfere for you again." Lucas's voice was hard, adamant.

"You'd trust my word?" There was a vulnerable, uncertain yet hopeful, note in Rob's voice.

"Yes," Lucas said at once, and with conviction.

Rob heaved a sigh of relief. "Thank you," he murmured, then went on quickly, once again all business, "have you talked to Mike?"

"No, and I'm not going to. I've got a plane to catch. You can fill Mike in."

"Will do. He's probably on the golf course by this time Sunday morning, anyway."

"Probably," Lucas agreed, smiling to himself.

"Yeah, well, you just go do whatever it is you have to settle. We'll mind the store."

"Thanks, Rob. I appreciate it."

There was a pause, just long enough for Lucas to wonder how long it had been since he had thanked his brothers or voiced his appreciation for their dedication to him and his company.

"You're welcome," Rob said, his voice emotion-thickened. "May I ask a question?"

"You may always ask."

"Does your personal business concern a woman?"

It was now Lucas's turn to pause; he was unaccustomed to confiding in either one of his brothers—or anyone else, come to that. But, on reflection, he had never chased after a woman, either.

Oh, well. What the hell.

"Yes, it does," he finally answered. "And that's all I'm going to say on the subject."

Rob laughed; it sounded lighthearted.

"Go get her, Lucas," he advised. "A true MacCanna never loses his woman."

"Yeah, right. Good-bye, Rob. I'll see you when I see you."

Rob laughed. "Good luck, Lucas."

Chuckling softly, Lucas hung up the phone.

Moonlight skipped in a silvery path across the night-dark ocean, and a soft breeze whispered through swaying palm fronds, ruffling spiral curls into a fiery dance around Frisco's face and on her shoulders.

"You're an excellent guide, Ken," she said, coming to a halt near the wavelets swishing against the water-cooled sand. "Thank you for these past few days. I've had a wonderful time exploring with you."

A clear note of sincerity rang in her soft voice; Frisco had had a really enjoyable time with Ken.

Although she had avoided the poi after one taste, she had indulged liberally in the other foods offered at the luau, then had allowed Ken to talk her into joining the tourists in trying the hula.

The itinerary Ken had worked out for them for his two days off had proven both fun and exhausting. They had visited the state capital and the governor's mansion. They had strolled through the Bernice Pauahi Bishop Museum, the oldest museum in Hawaii, which had opened in 1889. They had laughed and clapped along with the crush of other enthralled tourists while watching a performance by Polynesian dancers. And they had stood in silent reverence at the U.S.S. *Arizona* Memorial in Pearl Harbor.

And these were only a few of the diversions they had crammed into those two days. Frisco's mind whirled with memories of many sights and sounds, and with the utter beauty she had glimpsed.

This evening, Ken had escorted her to another out-of-the-way restaurant. They had dined on tender filets of steamed fish, rice, crisp salads, and fruit, accompanied by a delicate white wine. On returning to the hotel, he had suggested a stroll on the beach.

Every minute had truly been wonderful.

"Thank you," Frisco repeated, on a soft sigh.

"You're welcome." Ken turned to her, his face pale in the moonglow. "But it's not over yet." Smiling, he slowly bent his head to hers.

Frisco's fingers tightened their grip on the narrow leather heel straps of the sandals she was holding. He was going to kiss her, she knew it. Actually, she had expected it, had been expecting it at the end of every evening they had spent together.

"Ken, I . . ." Her voice trailed away, and she raised her free hand and placed it on his chest.

His motion ceased. His lips hovered inches above hers. His eyes were dark, intent.

"I want to kiss you, Frisco," he murmured. "I've been wanting to since the day you checked into the hotel, looking tired and wan, and deliciously kissable." His hovering lips curved into a teasing smile. "Besides, it would be a sin to waste this romantic setting."

Frisco gazed up at him through eyes shadowed by uncertainty. She was tempted, sorely tempted. Ken was genuinely nice, so much fun to be with, and yet . . .

An image sharp and clean formed in her mind, giving her pause.

Lucas MacCanna.

She could see him, almost feel his presence, the essence of him, tall and lean, attractively tough looking . . . and stern.

She shivered.

"Are you chilly?" Ken's voice contained a note of hope, a betraying eagerness to supply warmth.

"No, it's just . . ." She let her voice drift away on the ocean breeze; there was no way she could explain Lucas MacCanna to Ken.

The two men were as different as sea and fresh water. One as light and bubbly as a harmless stream; the other as strong and potentially dangerous as the ocean.

"Just a kiss," he finished for her. "What harm could there be in just a kiss?"

What harm? She had made an agreement with Lucas, a deal.

They had sealed their bargain, not with a kiss but a sip of wine and a binding handshake.

Still, Ken was right. What harm could come from a kiss, a flirtation, an innocent holiday romance?

Less than a week remained of her vacation. Then she had to go home to face a contractual alliance. And just as Mac-Canna had promised to be faithful to his vows, once given, she would honor hers.

"Do you think you might decide anytime soon?" Ken asked, ending her reverie. "I want to kiss you so bad it hurts." He laughed. "And I mean literally hurts. I'm getting a crick in my neck bent over like this."

Oh, what the hell! Frisco laughed and raised her face to his.

Breathing a murmured, "Thank the gods," Ken drew her into his arms and lowered his mouth to hers.

His kiss was exactly like Ken himself, warm and pleasant and enjoyable. And Frisco did enjoy the taste of his mouth, flavored with the dinner wine and afterdinner coffee.

His kiss was nice, sweet, not in the least disturbing. Frisco didn't feel at all shaken or sexually aroused, as she had by the mere touch of Lucas MacCanna's mouth to hers a little over one week ago.

Nor did she feel bereft, vaguely lost, when the kiss ended.

"That tasted as delicious as I anticipated it would," Ken said, softly sighing as he lifted his mouth from hers. "It tasted like more."

"No." Frisco shook her head and stepped back, out of his embrace. "You asked for a kiss, and you've had it," she went on, laughing lightly. "Now don't be greedy. Tomorrow is another day."

Ken appeared crestfallen. "Unlike some lucky others, I have to work tomorrow."

"Poor baby," she commiserated, grinning at him. "While I, being one of the lucky others, plan to spend the day lying on the beach, working on my tan, listening to music on my Walkman."

"Life's a beach," he sorrowfully intoned, using the slang phrase of some years back.

"And you're a nut," Frisco rejoined, clasping his hand and striding out, heading for the hotel. "Come along, ill-used one. Time to call it a night."

Hand-in-hand, they strolled through the flower-scented night, from the beach and across the exotically landscaped grounds fronting the brightly lit hotel entrance.

Swinging her sandals in her left hand, a carefree Frisco walked beside Ken. They were crossing the lobby toward the bank of elevators when a call rang out.

"Hey, Ken, can you come here a minute?"

"Oh, hell," Ken muttered, reluctantly turning to look at the desk clerk, who was motioning to him. "Sure," he answered, raising his voice so it would carry to the other man. Keeping a tight hold on her hand, he pivoted and headed for the registration desk.

Frisco tugged against his grip. "Ken, I'll just go on up to my room."

"No." He shook his head. "Come with me. This shouldn't take long."

Not wanting to intrude, and not really caring what the clerk's problem might be, she pulled her hand free of Ken's grasp and stepped to one side.

Yet, Frisco couldn't help but overhear the conversation. The clerk was apparently in a quandary about what to do with an unregistered guest.

"He had no reservation, but he insisted on being accommodated." The man sounded harried, as if he'd been intimidated by a demanding person. "And, as you know, we're completely booked."

"Did you offer to call another hotel to arrange other accommodations for him?" Ken asked.

"Of course, but he insisted on staying here," the agitated clerk said.

"Where is the man?" Ken sent a quick, frowning glance around the nearly deserted lobby.

"He left." The clerk shifted his eyes, following the path of

Ken's survey. "But he said he'd be back, to see the night manager."

"And where is Ralph, by the way?" Ken's frown darkened in disapproval.

"He's dealing with an irate guest. She was raising a fuss about not having her dinner properly served." The man moved his shoulders in a helpless shrug. "It's been one of those nights." He heaved a sigh. "So, if Ralph's not back when that man returns, what'll I tell him?"

"What else can you tell him? He'll simply have to settle for—" Ken's voice was overridden by a stronger, more commanding voice.

"That's all right. I'll stay in Miss Styer's room."

MacCanna! Frisco went cold with shock, then immediately grew hot with embarrassment.

"I beg your pardon, sir?" His expression indignant, Ken whipped around to level a managerial stare on Lucas.

Lucas was unimpressed.

Frisco was too stunned to speak.

"I said," Lucas enunciated clearly, "I will stay in the room with Miss Styer, my fiancée."

Chapter Twenty-one

"Fiancée?" Ken turned his stare on Frisco, his expression a mixture of hurt and accusation. "Is he telling the truth?"

Frisco felt awful, sick inside. Mortified, she was overwhelmed by a desire to cry, to just disappear from the scene, to curl her hand into a fist and punch Lucas MacCanna right in the face.

She did none of those things, of course. Instead, she met Ken's disbelieving stare, drew a deep breath, and dealt him another blow.

"Yes, Ken. Mr. MacCanna is my fiancé." She nearly choked on the last word.

Ken appeared momentarily rocked by the verbal hit, but he quickly recovered, and even managed a commendable, if weak, smile.

"I see." His smile curved into an uncharacteristically cynical angle. "A last fling before the noose is tied. Was that it?"

"Ken, please," Frisco said with soft urgency, feeling sicker by the second. "Please believe that I never meant to hurt you."

Ken gave a short, strangled-sounding laugh. "You know, the funny thing is, I do believe you."

The desk clerk had discreetly moved away, not so Lucas Mac-Canna. He had moved to stand beside Frisco.

His possessive action hadn't been necessary; she hadn't forgotten that he was there. Neither had Ken, nor had he forgotten his professional position.

"Are you willing to share your room with Mr. MacCanna?" His voice had lost all personal interest.

Frisco hesitated, but only for a moment. The damage was done. What difference could it make now? she thought, knowing that sooner or later, she would have to share a bedroom, and a bed, with Lucas.

"Yes." It was harder to get this word out than any she'd ever spoken.

"Very well." Ken motioned to the clerk, who hurried forward.

"Yes, sir?"

"Give Mr. MacCanna a key to Miss Styer's room." Without another word or look, Ken turned and walked away.

"How dare you?" Frisco demanded the instant the door was shut, closing her into the room with her uninvited, unwanted fiancé.

"How dare I . . . what?" Lucas asked in a reasonable, thus further enraging, tone.

"You know damn well what!" Frisco's voice was shrill; she didn't care. She couldn't remember ever being so incensed before.

"How dare I tell the truth?"

Lucas had taken a leisurely looking stance just inside the door. The sight of him, seemingly calm and unaffected by the embarrassing position he had cast her into, merely served to exacerbate Frisco's fury.

"No!" she shouted, trembling with outraged indignation. "How dare you humiliate me like that!"

Other than to slightly raise his eyebrows, Lucas's expression remained unaltered. "Are you, or are you not, in effect, my fiancée?"

"Yes, but . . . but—"

"But what?"

"You humiliated me in public!"

"I see." A cynical smile curved his lips. "You're humiliated by my telling the man that you're my fiancée, but you're not humiliated by having a sneaky little vacation affair with him? Have I got that right?"

Frisco's trembling was intensified by his very soft, controlled tone; though despite his calm and casual appearance, Lucas was not unaffected. She feared that he was cold with anger. The sudden realization troubled her.

She was alone in this room with him, a man she knew relatively little about.

"Well?"

She started at the sharpness of his voice, and made a concentrated effort to control her own.

"I did not have an affair with him," she declared as calmly as she could.

"No?" Lucas smiled again.

Frisco shivered, but managed to keep her voice steady. "No, I did not."

"I feel I must tell you that I caught your romantic performance on the beach a while ago," he informed her, his voice so gentle, it was terrifying. "And what I witnessed certainly had the appearance of a lovers' embrace."

"It was a kiss," she blurted out unthinkingly.

"I know," he said with deliberate calm.

Frisco shook her head, impatient with herself, with him, and with the entire situation. "I meant it was only a kiss," she snapped. "The first one."

"And what's a kiss between friends . . . hmmm?"

That did it. Frisco's feelings of trepidation dissolved in the face of his sarcasm. Indignation flared anew. "It was harmless," she stated emphatically.

"Are you in love with him?"

The question came from left field, so fast and clipped that Frisco, caught off guard, again answered without thinking. "No, I am not in love with him! Ken is a very nice young man, but . . ." She shrugged, damned if she'd admit that Ken's kiss had failed to generate an iota of the excitement she had felt from the light touch of Lucas's mouth to hers.

"Are you still planning to honor the commitment you made to me?"

"Yes. I made a bargain, and I'll stick to it," she answered, with a lot more confidence than she was feeling. "But that still does not give you license to assume you have the right to share my room."

"It has two beds," he pointed out, unnecessarily, as she knew full well the room came equipped with double beds; she had occupied one for a week.

"I had noticed," she said, tossing the sarcasm back at him. "So?"

"So"—he shrugged—"I'll sleep in one, and you'll sleep in the other."

Thinking that something was better than nothing, Frisco heaved a sigh of relief; it caught in her throat, and her craw, when he continued:

"Until after we're married."

"Wh . . . what?" Surely he didn't mean . . . ?

He did, and stated his meaning bluntly.

"We'll be married as soon as is legally possible."

Frisco was stunned for a moment, unable to think, never mind speak. Married! As soon as possible? She could actually feel herself blanch. Stepping back, she sank down to sit on the edge of the bed—the one she had been sleeping on throughout the last week.

"But . . . but . . ." She drew a deep breath, told herself to cease sounding like a motorboat running out of fuel, then tried again.

"I thought we had agreed to wait, play a courting game, for my mother's sake."

"We can still do that." He crossed the room to the other bed, and it was only then that Frisco noticed he was still holding his suitcase in his right hand.

"How?" She watched him nervously as he deposited the case on top of the bed.

He threw her a chiding smile before he flipped the lock on the case. The click sounded loud in the suddenly much too small room.

"We won't tell her."

"Won't tell her?" Frisco stared at him in utter confusion.

"Her, or anyone else." Lucas calmly began unpacking his case. "Is there an empty drawer I can use?"

"Huh?" Frisco wasn't sure which of his remarks elicited her brilliant response.

"A drawer." Lucas paused halfway between the bed and the long double dresser. He turned to display a handful of underwear. "Is there an empty one?"

"Oh, yes." Frisco could feel herself flushing; she detested the feeling. "The left side," she instructed with a wave of her hand. "All those drawers are empty."

"Thank you."

She watched him, growing more nervous with each passing minute as he stashed socks, briefs, and hankies in one of the dresser drawers.

Apparently he slept in the nude or in his briefs, for she detected no sign of pajamas. The realization made her even more nervous.

Lucas returned to the bed to collect outerwear: shirts, jackets, pants. Despite his use of only one drawer, there appeared to be at least a week's supply of changes of everything from the skin out.

This abundance of clothing was a clear indication of his determination to remain in Honolulu with her for the duration of her vacation.

The implication of that made her downright edgy, which in turn made her impatient with herself.

She was an adult. Wasn't she? And she was neither novice nor virgin. She had agreed to the business partnership and marriage. In actual fact, she had proposed the arrangement, she reminded herself.

But, Lord! She'd never dreamed he'd accept her condition! And not in her wildest imaginings had she believed he would follow her to Hawaii to carry out their agreement. The whole scenario was just too Hollywood backlot production to be real.

But it was real, and was happening to her.

Frisco swallowed against the dryness in her throat. Push had now come to shove, and she was very much afraid that she would be the one to give way.

"Would you like to have the bathroom first?"

"What?" Frisco asked, startled out of her fruitless introspection.

"The bathroom," Lucas repeated. "Would you like to use it first, before I go in for a shower?"

Why don't you make yourself at home? Frisco thought peevishly. She didn't say it though. She didn't have to, since he obviously was doing just that.

"Yes," she said.

Practically leaping off the bed, she scurried around, collecting her nightgown and robe, then dashed into the bathroom and locked the door. Although she didn't hear so much as a muffled sound, she felt certain Lucas was laughing his head off at her.

Some sophisticated, with-it, feminist-thinking female I turned out to be, she thought, grimacing in disgust at her image in the vanity mirror. Since meeting Lucas, whenever it came to the crunch she folded.

And, if he was laughing at her . . .

Lucas heaved a sigh at the sound of the bathroom door's lock clicking into place.

Frisco had found the perfect way to make it crystal clear that she didn't trust him.

Then again, he reasoned, why should she? He was the interloper here. He had created the situation, both past and present.

The worst of it was, he had deliberately embarrassed her by laying claim to her in the lobby.

No, even worse. He had deliberately created that embarrassing scene in the lobby because of the jealous rage he had experienced at seeing Frisco in the arms of another man.

The very intensity of his reaction had shocked him. God, never in his life had he felt such an impulse toward violence as he had at the sickening thought that the man was Frisco's lover. Nor, on reflection, had he ever felt such relief, as he had on hearing her unequivocal denial of an affair.

Sighing again, Lucas stared in bleak despair at the seemingly impenetrable barrier of the closed and locked bathroom door.

He had hoped that she could trust him.

No, more. He had hoped that she could like him.

No.

Hell. What he had secretly begun to hope was that she could come to love him.

Why?

Lucas frowned and began to undress.

Why did he want her to come to love him? Eventually . . .

Like he could understand, he mused, absently draping his suit jacket and pants neatly on a hanger and hooking it over the rod in the deep closet, next to his other clothes, next to *her* clothes.

Like made some sense to Lucas. He and Frisco would be working closely together, living together, and the relationship would have a much better chance of succeeding if she could come to like him.

But love?

Mulling over the inner workings of his own mind, Lucas shrugged out of his shirt, tossed it onto a chair, then reached into the closet for the robe he had impulsively folded into his case as an afterthought.

The garment was silk, black shot through with fine threads of silver. It felt cool and sensuous against his skin. He didn't particularly like the thing. It reminded him of an affair that shouldn't have happened.

Lucas had received the robe several years ago. It had been a surprising Christmas gift from a woman who had admittedly lusted after his body—and, he suspected, after his bank account.

She had seemed cool and abrasive emotionally.

But that was only one of the reasons Lucas rarely wore the robe. His primary reason was that he slept in his briefs, and in his opinion, the sight of hairy legs sticking out from under the knee-length robe was pretty damn unappealing.

But now, considering the current conditions, he was glad he had packed the blasted thing.

So much for this rumination, he acknowledged. It was a dodge and not germane to the original question.

Why had he begun hoping Frisco would come to love him?

The answer was simple, of course. All he had to do was face it.

He was very much afraid that he was falling in love with Frisco.

It bothered the hell out of him, but there appeared to be little he could do about it.

Naturally, never having been in love, he couldn't be certain. But if being in love made a man think and do uncharacteristic, not to mention stupid, things, then, yes, he was afraid he was falling in love.

It was a bitch of a situation, but . . .

It hit him then that he had been standing there, Lord knew how long, staring yearningly into the closet at Frisco's clothing. He smiled with wry self-mockery as he pulled on the robe and looped its silken belt around his waist. He was turning away from the closet when the bathroom door opened.

Distracted by the brush she was tugging through her wet hair, Frisco nearly walked into him.

"Oh!" She blinked, and her arm poised, trembling, in mid air.

The sight of her, her face scrubbed clean of makeup and flushed pink from her shower, made his breath catch in his throat. Her hair was a tangled mass around her shoulders; he ached to slide his fingers into the damp strands, to stroke her soft cheek, to taste her tender mouth, to pull her into his arms, to . . .

"You can have your shower now," she murmured, skirting around him.

"Thank you," he said, thinking he needed it to cool down—
now.

Inside the bathroom, with the door shut between them, Lucas paused to take a deep breath, and groaned softly as he inhaled steam laden with the scent of perfumed shampoo, soap, and body lotion.

Lord! He was worse off than he had suspected. How was he going to get through the nights, sleeping so close yet separated from her, when he wanted her so badly that he ached all over?

Lucas felt like a fool, and he was uncomfortable with the feeling. On the spot, his determination to carry out his plans became hard, irrevocable.

Frisco had said she was prepared to honor their agreement. And a deal was a deal.

His decision was made.

First thing in the morning, he would inquire about the legal requirements for marriage in Hawaii.

Chapter Twenty-two

Frisco stood statue-still, staring at the bathroom door, imagining the man inside the room.

Did Lucas have any idea of how very masculine and sexy he looked in that black and silver robe? she wondered, quivering in response to the image.

Well, of course he did, she scoffed. Hadn't he been standing in front of the mirrored closet door? He had to know how arousing he appeared with his muscularly trim body encased by silk and his strong, straight legs revealed below it.

A soft sigh whispered through her slightly parted lips. Had he been nude beneath the robe?

The thought both excited and dismayed her. Conflicting urges tore her in two different directions. A part of her longed to see his unadorned form, to stroke and caress his skin and the muscles under it, to test with her fingertips the firmness of his jaw, his slashing cheekbones, his lips. While another, saner part of her demanded retribution for the humiliation and embarrassment he had caused her, continued to cause her.

How in the world was she to sleep in a bed less than three feet away from him?

Frisco turned to gaze at the beds.

Would he attempt . . . anything?

Sizzling anticipation excited her libido, and shocked her intelligence.

Dammit! She was a woman, not an object! She berated herself, her rioting hormones. She was worthy of being loved, not merely used.

Her feminism rising to the fore, Frisco threw off her robe and slid between the sheets on her bed, determined to repulse Lucas, should he so much as suggest that he join her there.

But, heaven help her, she wanted him so.

Why—why, why?—hadn't she met him under normal, more harmonious circumstances? Perhaps then, the attraction simmering between them could have been explored to their mutual satisfaction. As the situation stood, Frisco could see no way for them to be together, not in any true and real sense of the word.

Sighing for what might have been, she closed her eyes, pretending sleep. Her pretense endured long after Lucas had crawled into bed . . . so near, yet so far away.

"I like it."

"It's too large." Frisco stared in dismay at the marquise-cut diamond solitaire weighing down the third finger of her left hand. In her unstated opinion, the rock was big enough to choke a medium-size animal.

"Oh, it can be sized to your exact fit within twenty-four hours," the clerk, a young, slender man, gushed, obviously having misinterpreted her remark.

Frisco heaved a sigh.

Lucas looked amused.

"The matching wedding band also," the clerk went on, seemingly unaware of their reactions.

"We'll take it."

"But, Lucas, I really don't . . ." She began to protest his preemptive decision.

"And the band, sir?" the clerk twittered, either not hearing her or affecting deafness to her voice.

"No," Frisco said adamantly, sending a challenging look at Lucas; the engagement ring was showy enough, but she could always leave it locked away in a safe. She absolutely would not accept that ostentatious-looking, diamond-encrusted matching wedding band.

"The lady's choice." Lucas moved his shoulders in a light shrug. Then he leveled a hard stare on her. "Choose one."

"None of these," Frisco frowned at the tray of bands, all set with gems of various sizes. She transferred Lucas's hard stare to the clerk. "I want plain, narrow gold."

"Yes, ma'am." Although the man sniffed in disdain, he nevertheless hastened to remove the offending tray and replace it with another.

"That." She pointed to the thinnest band nestled in a slot in the black velvet.

"The pair," Lucas instructed the clerk, indicating the slightly broader man's ring.

Frisco started in surprise. Lucas was going to wear a ring proclaiming his marital status?

"Don't look so stunned," he murmured dryly, watching the clerk who had turned away to get the sizing board. "You'll give the man the wrong impression."

"Who gives a flying f—" Frisco caught herself just in time to prevent Jo's habitual and outrageous remark from escaping her. "Fancy," she finished lamely.

His lips twitched, and his expression said clearly that he had heard the remark in its original form.

Frisco couldn't help herself; as irritated as she was with his arrogant and overriding decision to load her down with a pretentious diamond, her lips mirrored the twitching motion of his.

"Careful," he cautioned, in a low-pitched voice. "You don't want to shock his sensibilities."

"Perish the thought," she muttered, curving her lips into a

charming smile as the clerk turned back to face them, patently anxious to fit them properly.

It was dreadfully unfair, she knew, for them to garner amusement at the poor man's expense, but he was so fussy and precise—persnickety her grandmother would have said—so like the stereotypical bank clerk of old that they were both tickled.

The absolute crowning touch came when, to the man's expressed consternation, he discovered that all his precision in measuring was unnecessary, as it appeared the store had their ring sizes in stock.

Carefully not looking at each other, Frisco and Lucas stood by, rigidly containing their amusement until the details of the purchase were completed.

They'd just made it outside the door and away from the plate-glass display window, when, chancing a quick glance at each other, they burst into laughter.

It was a small thing, but a small *shared* thing, and that eased considerably the tension that had been a constant between them since Lucas's arrival in Hawaii.

Three days had passed. Days of nonstop activity throughout the day and taut tension at night, after they had gone to their room. She'd felt guilty every time she had to pass by the reception desk and see Ken behind it, his expression remote, but Lucas had gone forward single-mindedly, determined to see them married before returning to Philadelphia.

It was now Wednesday.

They were to be wed on Friday, by an ordained minister in a small local chapel.

Frisco found the prospect daunting as hell.

"How about a drink?"

She was relieved by the intrusion of Lucas's voice into her thoughts.

"Coffee, iced tea, something harder?"

"Iced tea sounds lovely." She managed to maintain a smile. "I'm parched."

"And me."

Taking her arm, he guided her through the throng, in the

main tourists, to a small coffee shop. The place was doing a brisk mid-morning business. Lucas snared the last empty table.

"They're coining some change here," he observed, glancing around at the animated patrons, many of whom wore brightly patterned clothing.

"Ever the businessman," she observed, feeling suddenly deflated and slightly depressed.

"Certainly." Lucas returned his sharp-eyed gaze to her. "Is there something wrong with that?"

"No, of course not," she answered, shaking her head in silent denial of the sense of defeat stealing over her, the niggling inner voice asking: What happened to that beautiful moment of shared laughter?

"There's something bothering you," he said softly. "What is it, Frisco?"

Something bothering her? Something! Frisco was hard pressed not to laugh—or cry . . . or something.

"It's nothing." She worked her lips into a parody of a smile. It's everything, she admitted to herself.

Lucas appeared on the point of pursuing the issue, but fortunately, at that moment a harried-looking young waiter came to an abrupt halt at their table.

"May I take your order, sir?"

Lucas turned to face the waiter.

Frisco turned inward to face her dilemma.

She was dissatisfied.

Unhappy.

Scared.

So what else is new? she chided herself. She had been feeling dissatisfied for months, long before Lucas MacCanna strolled over the horizon. And, in retrospect, she acknowledged that, although she hadn't been actively unhappy, she hadn't been actively happy, either. But being scared was new to her, and that could be directly attributed to Lucas.

In all honesty, Frisco knew the situation she found herself in scared the living daylights out of her.

"Hello." The object of her ruminations called out in a low voice. "Is anybody home?"

Frisco glanced up from the hands she hadn't been aware she was gripping in her lap, and found herself staring at the cause of her discontent.

"Someone must be home," he mused aloud, gazing deep into her eyes. "The lights are lit."

"Clever." Frisco was aware of the downside tone to her voice, but she couldn't lift it; her mood was too heavy. "Do you earn extra money on the side doing stand-up comedy?" It was a feeble attempt, but all she could muster.

Lucas frowned and, as the waiter arrived at their table, remained silent until their tea was served.

"What became of the laughing companion I brought in here with me?" he asked, as soon as the waiter departed. "And who are you?"

Not Frisco Bay, apparently.

That thought startled Frisco, because it was so very revealing. Lucas had not called her Frisco Bay since his sudden appearance on the scene at the hotel desk on Sunday night.

"Oh, you must remember me," she retorted, rather cynically. "I'm the sacrificial lamb."

Until then, his manner and expression had remained congenial. Her imprudent reply wrought an immediate change in his demeanor.

"Sacrificial lamb?" Lucas repeated, his tone pitched low, his voice chilling, his expression at once hard and unrelenting. "Explain that remark."

Frisco desperately hung on to her confidence, which was rapidly fraying, and salvaged a tattered bit. Raising her chin, she met his cold stare with open defiance.

"What else would you call it?"

"A business arrangement, or—"

"You would," she interrupted.

"Saving your ass," he finished, coldly.

"Not mine," she objected.

He smiled. "Your father's, then."

She shivered in response to his smile, but nevertheless retaliated. "Exactly. It's my father's ass that's in danger of being singed. And I, as his only child, am left to go to the altar in his place."

"The sacrificial altar being me?"

"Precisely." She lifted her shoulders in a quick, helpless shrug. "I rest my case."

"You are a case." Lucas picked up his tall glass and took a deep swallow of the tea. "A basket case."

"You've got that right." Not to be outdone in appearing casual, Frisco mirrored his actions. She sipped the tea; it was very good. Too bad she was beyond appreciating its delicate flavor.

"I had to be nuts to agree to this farce."

He narrowed his eyes.

She followed suit.

Tension was again palpable, a living entity crackling between them.

"Frisco?"

The sound of her name snapped the charged tension coiling her insides into knots. Startled, she glanced around to find herself staring into the grinning face of her plane seatmate.

"Will!" she exclaimed, smiling with genuine pleasure at seeing the man again. "Speak of serendipity!"

"Were you?" Denton laughed.

"Well, no," Frisco said, laughing with him. "But meeting you like this is . . . I've thought about you often. How are you . . . and your family?"

"I'm fine. So are they." His hazel eyes probed her face. "You look better."

"Better than what?" Lucas asked, his voice edgy and demanding.

"Oh, I'm sorry." Flustered by the impatience underlying his tone, Frisco rushed on, "Will, let me introduce you to Lucas MacCanna. Lucas, Mr. Will Denton. I met him on the plane over."

"Mr. Denton." Lucas was on his feet, right hand extended, and though his voice and tone had smoothed, his eyes held a challenging look.

"Call me Will," the older man said, grasping Lucas's hand. "Everybody does."

"So I noticed." Lucas transferred his riveting gaze to Frisco.

"Please, join us," Frisco said to Denton, avoiding Lucas's disapproving stare.

"Thank you, I'd like that." Will scraped a chair away from the table. "That tea looks good."

"It is delicious." While she responded, Frisco watched from the corner of her eye as Lucas hesitated before resuming his seat. Keeping her smile in place, she turned to him. "Isn't it, Lucas?"

"Delicious," he parroted, in a deceptive drawl.

What's with him? Frisco asked herself; but unable to fathom Lucas's attitude, she mentally shrugged it aside and concentrated on their unexpected table guest.

"How is your visit going?" She glanced around, then went on before he could answer. "And where is the family . . . your grandsons?"

Will laughed; it had a good sound—easy, relaxed—and caused a twinge of longing deep inside Frisco.

Why couldn't her father have been more like Will Denton, a man who found all the joy he required in the company of his family?

Guilt for the thought sprang up immediately, yet even while the pangs stabbed her, Frisco found herself asking why couldn't Lucas be more like Will?

"Ah! There's the waiter."

Will's remark refocused her attention, and made her uncomfortably aware of the vague disapproval in the dark eyes of the man seated opposite her.

Disapproval? Frisco mused. Of Will? Why?

What was Lucas's problem?

For an instant, she entertained the startling notion that he might be a bit jealous, but the idea lasted only for an instant. She rejected it with a self-mocking. Yeah, right.

Will gave his order to the harried waiter, then proceeded to reply to her query.

"I'm doing a little sight-seeing on my own because my son

and daughter-in-law had a meeting to attend," he explained. "And my grandsons are in school."

"Oh, that's right. They would be, wouldn't they?" Frisco smiled at the older man. "It's so much like summer here, I forget it's still spring."

Will smiled in understanding. "I know what you mean. When I left home it still felt like winter."

"And where is home?" Lucas inserted.

"Montana." He grinned. "Spring usually arrives late in the Northwest."

"It was snowing when I left Philadelphia," Frisco said, easing back into the conversation.

"Didn't amount to anything." Lucas made a dismissive gesture.

Will shifted his gaze from one to the other. "You both hail from Pennsylvania?"

"Yes," Frisco answered.

"You retired, Will?"

Feeling Lucas's question was out of line and too personal, Frisco shot a warning look at him; he blithely ignored her.

"Yes," Will replied, then heaved a regretful-sounding sigh.

"From what?" Lucas asked with sudden, inexplicable interest.

Thinking that he had gone too far Frisco took it upon herself to protest. "Lucas, really."

"No, I don't mind." Will chuckled. "Matter of fact, I've been longing to talk business with someone."

"You miss it?"

"Yes, Lucas, I do." Will shrugged. "I miss it more than I ever dreamed I would."

Lucas nodded emphatically. "I know sure as hell I would."

Tell us about it, Frisco retorted in silence. In her estimation, Lucas epitomized the concept of an A-type workaholic. Drive. Drive. Drive.

She suppressed a sigh, wondering if he would eventually drive her to distraction.

"I should have known," Will admitted, the defeated sound

of his voice corralling her wandering attention. "I really should have known."

"What line of business were you in, Will?" Frisco felt impelled to ask.

"Steel," came the surprising answer. "I owned and operated a small steel mill." He heaved a deep, heartfelt sigh. "God, I loved it."

Chapter Twenty-three

Serendipity? Coincidence? Frisco's inner tingle was followed by an urge to cry.

Obviously Will had been cut from the same bolt of corporate broadcloth as Lucas. And here she'd been, wishing her father were more like Will.

Well, you win a few and you lose a lot, she reminded herself. Some days it didn't pay to get out of bed, let alone face the world.

Consigning her fruitless wishes to where they belonged, never-never land, Frisco tuned back in on the world of reality—the world of business.

"You're kidding!" Lucas was saying, sitting forward, alert, and intent. "I own and operate a steel mill, too. Talk about coincidence."

Frisco managed not to sneer.

"You do?" Will laughed, then immediately sobered. "Wait a minute. Pennsylvania." He blinked. "You're *that* Mac-Canna?"

"Guilty," Lucas said.

I'll say, Frisco thought.

"Christ!" Will exclaimed, then he turned to smile sheepishly at Frisco. "Pardon the language."

She dismissed it with a flick of her hand and a wryly murmured, "I've heard worse." She smiled. "I've said worse."

Lucas sliced a sardonic look at her.

She blithely ignored him.

"I never made the connection." Will shook his head. "Shows you how far out of the loop I've become. When I dropped out, I dropped out."

"There's something I don't understand here," Lucas said, frowning. "If you loved the business so much, why did you sell out?"

"I promised my wife we'd travel when I retired." Will's eyes reflected his sadness. "When she was diagnosed with cancer two years ago, I packed it in." His eyes grew bright, filmy. "We had six wonderful months traveling together before . . ." His voice trailed away on a sigh, then he murmured, "She died two months later."

"Oh, Will," Frisco impulsively grasped the older man's hand in an offering of condolence.

"I'm sorry." Lucas was quiet a moment after murmuring these words of sympathy; then he followed them up with a positive offer. "You want a job?"

Will's astonishment was evident in his expression, but he didn't hesitate for more than a second.

"Yes!" he said, laughing. "Doing what?" he asked, as if in afterthought and as if he didn't much care so long as he was back in the swing of things.

Lucas shrugged, and grinned. "Hell, I don't know. We'll think of something, some way to utilize your talent, won't we, Frisco?"

Frisco. Not Frisco Bay. Asking herself why in hell it should bother her, she produced a smile for the excited man who had saved her from herself on the plane.

"Of course."

Will's eager expression changed to one of confusion. "You two run the business together?"

With a sweetly serene smile, Frisco gazed at Lucas, as if to say, you can field the tough questions.

Like a true, red, white, and blue titan of business, Lucas forged straight ahead.

"Not the steel company," he explained, flicking a droll look at her. "We're partners in another firm located in Philadelphia."

"Are the businesses related?" Will looked from one to the other.

"Yes." They answered in unison.

"Would it make any difference which company we slotted you into?" Lucas asked.

"Not at all." Will shook his head. "I may be an old dog, but I'm still able to learn new tricks."

"You're not old!" Frisco objected.

Lucas shot her a look that could only be described as quelling.

Frisco reproduced her sweetly serene smile.

He frowned, but returned to the subject under discussion. "You won't mind pulling up stakes, relocating to the East?"

"No." Will's reply came fast and adamant. "There's nothing for me there anymore."

"Wait a minute," Frisco said, suddenly recalling a remark Will had made during the flight. "Weren't you seriously thinking about moving here to be with your family?"

"I was." He gave her a patient, fatherly smile. "But only because I was at loose ends rattling around on my own in Montana." He slanted a conspiratorial grin at Lucas. "Can you imagine how boring it can get when all your friends are busy working, and all you're doing is making believe you're busy, too?"

"Hell, yes!" Lucas laughed. "I'd go completely nuts if all I had to look forward to was a round of golf with cronies every day or so."

Will nodded, chuckling. "But even then you'd be better off than me," he said, grimacing. "In Montana, I do more snow shoveling than golfing."

Well, hail fellow, well met, Frisco thought, glancing from

one man to the other and feeling decidedly shoved aside, out of the discussion.

"So, how long were you planning on staying in Hawaii?" Lucas asked.

Will shrugged. "I hadn't set a departure date. I have an open-ended plane ticket." He smiled. "If you're wondering when I can arrange to be in Pennsylvania, give me a date and I'll be there."

Lucas laughed. "Will a month give you enough time? I don't want to rush you."

Will was shaking his head. "A month will give me plenty of time." He frowned. "But I don't want to rush you, either. Were you planning to be back by then?"

"Before then." Lucas glanced at Frisco. "We'll be leaving together at the end of this week." He paused for an instant, then said bluntly, "Frisco and I are getting married on Friday."

Stunned speechless by his abrupt announcement, Frisco stared at Lucas in astonishment.

Will appeared every bit as stunned as she, if not as speechless.

"Well, congratulations," he said, thrusting his hand out to Lucas. "You're a lucky man."

"I know." Lucas smiled as he released the older man's hand. Then he switched his smile to her.

Of course, you know, Frisco thought, working her lips into a parody of a smile. You're not only gaining a wife, you're acquiring an old and reputable business.

She scrupulously avoided the nudge from her conscience reminding her the firm's reputation would be shot to hell without his help.

Will again bestowed that fatherly smile on her. "Frisco's a lovely young woman," he complimented, then he frowned. "Look, I know it's none of my concern, but I can't help but wonder why you'd get married one day, then leave this honeymoon paradise so soon afterward?"

"Can't be helped," Lucas said, pulling an expression so rueful she was sorely tempted to kick him under the table. "Business reasons, you understand."

Business. Frisco was becoming convinced that if she heard that blasted word a few more times, she'd start screaming and tearing her hair.

"Oh, yes, I understand completely. I've been there." Will sighed. "But . . ." He hesitated, then said, "I hate people who offer advice where it's not wanted . . ."

"Lay it on me," Lucas invited.

A brick? Rather surprised at herself for the unpleasant thought, Frisco lowered her eyes in contrition.

"Well, being dedicated to your work is fine, as long as you maintain a balance." Will unflinchingly met Lucas's wary stare. "What I'm trying to say is, it doesn't pay to lose sight of other equally important elements of life. You hurt yourself if you hurt the people you love."

Bravo! Frisco could have jumped up and hugged Will for reaffirming her initial opinion of him. He was a genuinely nice man.

Naturally, she didn't jump up and hug him; she did something even more impulsive and startling.

"Will, would you do me the honor of attending our wedding, and of standing in for my father?"

To say Will was surprised would have been a gross understatement. Shocked came closer to the mark. Come to that, Lucas appeared just as jolted by her sudden audacious request.

"You want me to give you away?"

Frisco came close to laughing at the note of near awe in Will's voice. What held her back was that she was even closer to tears.

"In a manner of speaking, yes."

"I don't understand."

"What Frisco is trying to say, Will, is that the wedding will be a small affair," Lucas explained before she could respond. "There will be no pomp or circumstances."

"Why not?" Will frowned his disapproval.

"Because it's only a formality," Frisco answered, before Lucas could respond.

He gave her an annoyed look.

She glared back at him.

"A formality," Will repeated, once again noticing the glances between the two of them.

Keeping her mouth shut, Frisco remained silent, leaving Lucas to clean up after himself.

"Yes."

Will shook his head, obviously baffled. "Damned if I understand young people anymore. When I married my wife, it was the most important step I ever took, and the last thing from a formality."

"I'm not all that young, Will," Lucas observed dryly. "And as a rule, I don't justify my actions to anyone. Nevertheless, perhaps an explanation is called for in this instance."

Frisco was dumbstruck. Lucas was going to clarify the situation? She couldn't wait to hear this.

"You see, Will, there's a reason why Frisco and I have chosen to get married informally."

Frisco was all ears, but Will made his discomfort with the turn of conversation known.

"Ah . . . it's really none of my concern, Lucas," he said uneasily, shifting a worried look to Frisco.

"Oh, but it is," Lucas maintained. "That is, if you're serious about coming to work for me?"

"Of course I'm serious!" Will said. "But I don't see what my working for you has to do with it."

"Simple." Lucas shrugged.

It is? Frisco frowned.

Lucas calmly continued.

"No one back home is to know that we're married."

"Huh?" Will shook his head. "Why not?"

"We don't want to upset Frisco's parents."

"They don't approve of you?"

Lucas laughed.

Knowing the reason for his laughter, Frisco simmered. Not approve of Lucas MacCanna? Ha! Her father couldn't wait to give her away to the legend.

"It isn't that they don't approve," Lucas said, oh so smoothly. "It's just that we've known each other such a short time. Frisco's mother is rather old fashioned, and while we don't want to upset her, we still want to be together. Don't we, darling?"

He turned to gaze at Frisco with such passion and longing, she almost responded to his act.

Will obviously bought it.

"You mean . . ." He paused, cleared his throat, then went on in a discreetly lowered voice. "I think you're saying you want to sleep together. Aren't you?"

"Yes," Lucas replied bluntly.

Frisco had to fight an urge to roll her eyes, as well as a singeing flash of anticipation. A sigh lodged in her throat; if only Lucas meant what he said. But he didn't, and she knew it. The knowledge hurt.

"I think that's commendable," Will said, bestowing a benign smile on them. "For you see, like Frisco's mother, I'm old fashioned." He chuckled. "Young folks might even call me stodgy. But I'm from a different era, before the latest push of the liberation movement." He shook his head. "I don't understand this new open lifestyle—or alternative relationships or whatever the latest buzz term happens to be. I just see it as an excuse to avoid responsibility and commitment."

Frisco felt she should protest, defend the feminist point of view. But she remained silent, because although she hadn't defined her feelings on the subject, and had even once indulged in a no-commitment relationship, lately she had been leaning toward the position Will had taken.

"Then you understand our dilemma?"

"Oh, sure." Will nodded, then frowned. "So when will you tell Frisco's parents?"

Good question, she thought, looking to Lucas for what she felt certain would be an equally good answer. He did not disappoint her.

"That we're already married? We never will."

"But . . ." Will began.

"Wait, let me finish," Lucas interrupted him, holding up a hand, palm out. "When we get home, we'll tell them we're engaged. Then, after a reasonable waiting period, we'll get married . . . or remarried." Once again, he turned that heated look on Frisco; she resisted an immediate impulse to melt. "I feel positive her mother will have some ideas of her own for the wedding."

Oh, will she ever, Frisco silently confirmed, denying a surge of excitement inside.

Will laughed. "Don't all mothers? Lord, I'll never forget my wife's mother's reaction when we set the date. She went completely haywire."

"That's what I figured." Lucas smiled, as if resigned to the coming ordeal.

Frisco sighed, not in resignation, but in acceptance of Lucas's performance in the role he had chosen to play to achieve his goal of acquiring her father's company by acquiring her as his wife.

Though it no longer mattered, she repeated her original request to Will.

"So, now that you know the situation, will you give me away on Friday?"

"And while you're at it," Lucas inserted, "stand up for me as best man?"

Will sent a considering look from Lucas to Frisco. Then he gave a hearty laugh.

"I'd be delighted to assume both duties."

Chapter Twenty-four

It was over.

They were married.

Frisco felt sick.

"You may kiss the bride, young man," the elderly cleric prompted, his smile kind, gentle.

Lucas wasn't smiling. His expression sober, he lowered his head and touched his mouth to hers, exactly as he had the one and only time he had kissed her before.

Frisco's stomach churned, not with excitement, but in dread of the night to come. If this type of almost kiss was what she had to look forward to from Lucas, she wasn't sure she could endure it.

"Congratulations." Will shook Lucas's hand, then turned to her. "May I kiss the bride?"

"Of course," she said, thinking it couldn't be any worse, or less personal, than the passionless peck she had received from her husband.

Her husband. Frisco suppressed a shudder and somehow managed a smile for Will, who had opted to bypass her mouth to kiss her on the cheek instead.

"You are a beautiful bride." Will's voice was raspy with emotion, and his hazel eyes were suspiciously bright. "Isn't she, Lucas?"

"Yes, beautiful." Lucas fixed his somber gaze on Frisco. "Imagine how breathtaking she'll look in bridal white."

Contrarily, Frisco was both thrilled and dismayed by his compliment. The thrill she dismissed at once, knowing full well he was uttering the words for Will's benefit.

But the sinking sensation of dismay had become a given; she had reached the point of expecting it.

Still, all things considered, especially the ordeal of getting dressed that afternoon while Lucas seemed determined on getting in her way, Frisco was both pleased and proud of her appearance.

Eschewing white as too obvious, she had chosen to wear a tailored skirt suit in a muted shade of dusty rose, which should have clashed with her hair, but instead enhanced the red highlights in it. Her blouse and accessories were all a complementing cream.

She had pulled her long hair up and back into a loose coil, allowing shorter tendrils to escape and frame her face or curl against the back of her neck.

Her makeup, as usual, was minimum; a brush of mascara to her eyelashes, a whisper of shadow to her eyelids, a sweep of blush to her cheeks.

In lieu of a bridal bouquet, she wore around her neck a lei of spicy-scented exotic blossoms.

She had worn no other adornment, until Lucas slid the narrow gold wedding band onto her finger and immediately followed it with the large diamond solitaire.

On reflection, Frisco had been right in her assertion that the large stone would weigh down her hand; it not only felt heavy, it instilled in her an unsettling feeling of being bought and paid for.

"That engagement ring sure is beautiful, too."

Will's observation brought Frisco to the realization that she had been staring at the glittering marquise-cut gemstone.

"Yes, it is," she felt compelled to reply, prudently not adding that it was also ostentatious.

"Thank you, Reverend."

Frisco heard Lucas speak at the same instant he tugged on her arm, reminding her of her manners, or her lack of them.

Dutifully smiling, she offered her thanks to the aged minister and to his wife, who had generously agreed to be the second witness. Noting with a twinge of concern that this man of the cloth appeared fatigued by the performance of the brief ceremony, she murmured a farewell, and turned in response to another tug on her arm to depart the tiny, plain yet serene, and somehow comforting chapel.

On the western horizon, the sun was deserting the day, while leaving behind fleeting yet soft golden fingers of light. The breeze was a sweetly scented caress upon Frisco's skin, enhancing the exotic fragrance of the flowers around her neck.

The scene should have been perfect, the ultimate location for a romantic wedding.

To Frisco's beleaguered mind and nerves, it appeared more like a disaster area, devoid of sentiment and joy, unworthy of celebration.

Yet Lucas had decreed a celebration was not only in order but necessary, if only to maintain the illusion of the occasion.

The form it would take, Lucas decided, was a quiet dinner . . . for three: Frisco, Will Denton, and the legend himself.

Upon arrival at the chosen location, Frisco couldn't imagine how Lucas had found the time to discover the place. Much like the very first restaurant he had taken her to, this one was tucked away, out of the mainstream of flashy tourists attractions.

Even the décor was similar to that of the first place, in its subdued elegance, its wall adornments, and fine table linens and silverware.

The food, unobtrusively served, was expertly prepared and a delight to the taste buds, however untutored.

The champagne was the very best the management had to offer—which was the very best there was.

While barely sampling her entrée, Frisco fed her ever-tensing nerves with the shimmering gold liquid. By the time the second cork had popped, she had loosened up considerably . . . as had her tongue.

"What was it like?" she asked Will, in response to a remark he had made about his own wedding some forty years ago.

"Traditional," he said, his eyes taking on a dreamy, faraway expression. "My Betty wore a white tulle and lace gown with a wide, belled skirt, sorta like the pictures you see of the gowns before the Civil War, you know?"

"Yes." Frisco smiled softly. "Antebellum."

"Yeah, that's right. I couldn't recall the word. Sign I'm getting old, I guess." He shrugged. "Anyway, with the gown, she wore a long lace train, been in her family since the Civil War, I think. I still have it."

"It sounds beautiful," Frisco said.

"It was." Will was quiet a moment. Then his dreamy eyes grew clear and bright. "I'd be proud if you'd wear it, Frisco. On the day of your real wedding, I mean."

For a moment, Frisco was too surprised, too overwhelmed by his offer to speak.

Lucas apparently felt no such constraint.

"Believe me, Will, this wedding today was the real thing, however informal."

"Oh, I know that, Lucas," Will was quick to assure him. "And I wasn't inferring anything else. But you said yourself that Frisco's mother would probably want to plan a traditional ceremony sometime in the future."

"Yes, I did," Lucas conceded the point.

"Well then, in that event, I'd be honored to have Frisco wear the heirloom veil and train." He grinned. "Come to that, I'd love to see her wear the gown, too, but"—he chuckled—"my Betty was only a hair over five foot, and the gown wouldn't go much past calf length on your lady's tall frame."

Lucas's lady.

Frisco shivered in response to the many and varied connotations in that small, innocent-sounding phrase. Implications ran through her mind in quick succession: honor, pride, caring, possession. She immediately discounted caring. That left honor, pride, and possession—his.

"Are you chilly?" Lucas frowned. "The air temperature does feel a little low in here."

Caring?

Right.

Denying a sigh, she smiled instead. "No, I'm not. It must be the wine," she improvised.

"Champagne gives you the chills?" His dark eyes gleamed with a teasing glow.

"When it's this cold," she said, taking a sip of her wine, which was in fact very cold, perhaps because she had spooned some ice from her water glass into it.

Had she consumed more of the potent liquid, she might have expanded her statement from cold wine to cool husbands. Fortunately, or maybe unfortunately, she hadn't imbibed enough to be that candid.

Although Lucas's expression grew doubtful, questioning, to her relief he let the subject drop.

Frisco toyed with her dessert for a few more minutes, then relinquished the pretense of eating and gave way to the inner conflict eating at her.

The men were discussing business—what else?

She was left alone with her thoughts.

Feeling tense and on edge, she longed to leave the restaurant. Yet at the same time, she dreaded returning to the hotel, to the privacy of the room, and to the wedding night ritual . . . with Lucas.

What would being intimate with him be like?

Frisco suppressed another shiver as she pondered the big question.

She couldn't wait.

It scared the hell out of her.

Until that moment, she had never realized what an abject coward she really was.

"Are you ready to leave?"

Controlling the urge to bolt from her chair at the soft sound of his voice, Frisco composed herself enough to smile faintly at Lucas.

"Yes," she said, mentally steadying herself for the night ahead of her.

Since Lucas and Will had driven their own rental cars, the threesome parted company in the restaurant's parking lot.

"The best I can wish for you two is that you'll be as happy together as Betty and I were," Will said, after shaking Lucas's hand and kissing Frisco on the cheek.

"Thanks, Will," Lucas replied. "We'll see you in Philadelphia in a month."

"I'll be there."

"Enjoy the rest of your vacation with your family," Frisco said as he turned away.

"I'll enjoy it even more now," Will responded, giving a final wave as he slid behind the wheel of his car. "Now that I know I have something to do after my vacation."

Chuckling in understanding, Lucas unlocked the car and ushered Frisco into it. He seemed so relaxed, so obviously unconcerned, so immune to the nervous trepidation tormenting her that Frisco was hard pressed to keep from hauling off and slugging him.

Of course, she mused, fuming, the indomitable legend was in all probability merely anticipating a long night of hot, steamy sex.

In other words, a satisfying roll in the hay.

While she . . . Frisco's thoughts fractured. What was she anticipating? Romance? Tenderness? Possibly even a hint of loving?

Her stomach lurched, alerting her to the wishful drift of her thinking.

Get a grip, she advised herself, before you lose it altogether. This alliance—or misalliance, as it were—was a business deal, simple and not so pure.

In a bid to avoid conversation, which would have to be stilted on her part, Frisco settled back against the seat's headrest and closed her eyes.

What was she thinking?

Driving automatically, Lucas let his thoughts unwind along with the passing miles.

He could tell by Frisco's breathing pattern that she wasn't asleep. And her withdrawal by feigning sleep made it perfectly clear that she didn't want to talk.

Was she thinking about the two of them together? In bed?
God, he hoped so, for he couldn't seem to think about anything else.

And his imaginings, heated and wild, were driving him to
the brink.

Lucas was unused to muddled thoughts and conflicting emotions. He much preferred his customary clear and concise thinking process. Now, after nearly a week in which his thoughts and
emotions ran rampant through uncharted terrain peppered with
psychological land mines, he no longer knew what to think.

The most destructive of those mental land mines had exploded inside him the very night he had arrived at Frisco's hotel.

Although Lucas had been beat from the long flight to Honolulu, the lengthy delays, the three changes of planes, he had
been feeling pretty good about the decision he had made during the last leg of his journey. Having once again concluded
that his intent to hold her to her own demand for marriage
was unfair, unjustified, and probably unproductive, he had de-
planed prepared to offer her a strictly business proposition.

Not that he had given up his original intention to have her
in his bed; he hadn't. He was just going to change his game
plan from coercion to seduction.

Lucas had never been one to force women. He adhered to
the concept of two willing and consenting adults.

So he had arrived at the hotel tired but with a feeling of
self-satisfaction. Being informed by the desk clerk that there
were no rooms available was a minor annoyance. Being further
informed by the clerk that Frisco was likewise unavailable
abraded his patience. Since he was ready to concede, her ab-
sence irritated him.

Refusing the clerk's offer to call other hotels to secure a
room for him, Lucas had determined to await her return.

Restless and in need of exercise after hours of confinement
in a plane, he stashed his suitcase out of sight behind a potted
plant, then strolled from the hotel to the beach.

The breeze was soft, the moon was bright.

Lucas spotted the couple standing close together near the
water's edge, and identified the woman as Frisco almost im-

mediately. His impatience level rising, he was about to approach the pair just as the man lowered his head to kiss Frisco.

It was at that moment the unforeseen and never before experienced psychological land mine of jealousy went off, tearing a hole inside his mind.

Lucas resisted an overwhelming impulse to run across the beach and knock the man flat on his ass. It was the hardest inner battle he had ever fought.

He had won it, but in the process he had lost the war over his more noble intentions. So far as he was concerned, all other bets were off; the marriage was on once again.

He assuaged his conscience by reasoning, if push came to shove, Frisco could damn well blame her association with Ken Whoever for her current marital status.

But . . . Would she give herself freely? No. Lucas frowned and sliced a glance at Frisco. If he was honest with himself, and he always was, he had to admit that he wanted more than freely given sex from her. He wanted total capitulation.

The admission caused his conscience to trouble him.

Was he willing to offer the same unequivocal surrender to her?

Lucas conducted an evasive battle with his conscience for a moment before conceding.

Yes, he was, willing and quite ready to grant Frisco the ultimate victory. What he had initiated as a tactical maneuver in the hardball game of business, had now become a desperate move in the game of love.

And there it was, finally, out in the open.

God help him, he was in love with Frisco, deeply, irrevocably in love with her.

And she had every right to despise him.

With cool and calculated deliberation, he had pushed her to the wall, then had cut the ground from beneath her by allowing her no choice other than the betrayal of her father and, in turn, her mother.

And now he wanted her to love him.

Arrogant bastard.

Lucas didn't particularly like the left turn his thoughts had taken. Or, more accurately, the *right* turn they had taken.

Then again, perhaps it was time, past time, for him to evaluate the damage caused by his actions, he reflected as he literally made a right onto the wide boulevard leading to the hotel.

His destructive course had been two edged; Frisco had been slashed by one, he by the other.

And now, despite the impossible position he had cast her into, he wanted Frisco to offer her body for his physical possession and to open her heart by loving him.

While he was weighing his chances of achieving both of his desires, a mocking inner voice whispered: *Life ain't that long, MacCanna.*

Pulling the car to a stop at the entrance to the hotel, Lucas decided that it was a damned good thing he had never been a quitter, since this time even he didn't hold out much hope for his success.

Fortunately he had never given up as long as there remained a spark of hope.

And that spark continued to glow.

This night, Lucas determined, he would take whatever Frisco deigned to offer, and tomorrow, indeed in all the tomorrows left to him, he'd dedicate his life to proving himself worthy of her love.

Girding himself for whatever lay ahead, he turned to gaze at Frisco. A sudden tightness invaded his throat, preempting the nearly constant and uncomfortable tightness in his loins.

His bride.

Lucas was suddenly overwhelmed by a new realization of the meaning of the word, and of the trust bestowed upon any man by the woman consenting to join with him in lifetime partnership.

That many partnerships were dissolved long before the lifetimes ended was of little import. The important point was that the commitment was made.

Lucas knew for him it would be for life.

But for Frisco?

He sighed.

She opened her eyes.

She looked so very beautiful, so much younger than her actual years, so very helpless.

That two-edged sword nicked Lucas's heart, exposing vulnerability.

Damn. Merely looking at her hurt, deep inside, in a wrenching way he had not realized it was possible for him to hurt. The pain went deeper even than what he had felt when he'd lost his parents, what he'd suffered every time one of his younger brothers had injured himself.

He wanted to close his eyes, as if by doing so he could shut out the pain along with her image. But he didn't close them, because he knew it would be useless; her beautiful image was imprinted in his mind.

The glorious red mane she had twisted into a knot on top of her head had loosened, circling her face with wispy strands. In the light from the hotel, her eyes regarded him in somber questioning. Her lips were slightly parted, in what he knew was an unintentional invitation to him to taste her mouth.

Her mouth; such a sweet, if unknowing seduction.

Tenderness welled inside him; it was reflected in his soft voice. "We're here."

Chapter Twenty-five

Frisco was as nervous as a high-wire walker halfway along a rapidly fraying cable.

What was Lucas up to now?

The question had been in her mind ever since she'd opened her eyes to find him staring at her in an altogether new and strange way.

She had pondered the possible meaning behind the gentler expression on his usually self-contained visage as they went from the hotel's entrance, across the lobby, where to her relief Ken was not in evidence, and into the elevator to their floor.

What could that gentle expression portend? she wondered, keeping her spine militarily straight, her features composed, as she preceded him into the room.

Gentle persuasion perhaps?

Everyone knew it was easier to catch flies with honey than with vinegar, she reminded herself. Trite, perhaps, but true nonetheless.

Feeling her grip on the little control she had left loosening along with the hair on her head, Frisco set her purse on the dresser, then turned to confront whatever it was he had in mind for her.

Lucas was in the process of removing his jacket.

Frisco swallowed; it wasn't easy. The sight of him so casually undressing before her dried all the moisture in her mouth and throat.

Up until that very afternoon, a mere several hours ago, they had both rigidly adhered to an unstated agreement of allotted privacy while dressing and undressing.

Now, apparently, with the legal and binding words having been spoken, all such previous considerations were nullified. Lucas made that abundantly clear by proceeding to undress without allowing her time to collect herself, or her things, and escape into the questionable privacy of the bathroom.

As he tugged his shirt from his pants, Frisco froze.

His fingers went to work on the shirt's buttons.

Frisco quickly unfroze.

"I . . . er, I'll just get my stuff and . . . ahmmm, change in the bathroom," she said none too coherently, groping for the middle dresser-drawer handle behind her.

"All right." His smile made her even more nervous, simply because it was every bit as gentle as his expression. "I'll open the champagne."

"Champagne?" She frowned. "What champagne?"

He gestured to the other side of the room, to the small table and four chairs grouped to one side of the sliding glass doors which opened onto a balcony overlooking the beach and ocean.

The table was laid for two, with snowy linen, small plates, gleaming silver and narrow champagne flutes. A tray of assorted fruits and cheeses was set in the center of the table, and to one side of it at least a half-dozen white orchids cascaded over the side of a low wide vase. A rack holding a silver bucket was placed next to the table. A dark, long-necked, foil-capped bottle lay in a bed of ice in the bucket.

How had she missed noticing it? Frisco mused. But the very fact that she had missed it was a telling indication of how very distracted she was. And the direct cause of her distraction stood gently smiling in front of her, his chest now bared by his open shirt front.

"I . . . er, didn't see it," she said, feeling ridiculous for stating the obvious.

"I know." His voice was low, and his smile faded as he slowly walked to her.

Frisco's pulses leaped with his first step, and began to thrum when he stopped less than two feet from her.

He raised his hand.

She conquered an urge to step back.

His fingers brushed the curve of her neck.

She held her breath.

They captured an errant tendril of hair.

She felt the feather-light touch to the tips of her fingers and toes.

"You're nervous," he murmured, coiling the strand around his finger. "Aren't you?"

"Me? Nervous?" She tried to laugh; it was an abysmal failure. She lowered her eyes. "Yes."

Lucas sighed. "You have nothing to fear. I won't hurt you, you know."

Frisco's eyelids flew up, and she opened her mouth to remind him that he had already hurt her, but the words were never spoken. He trapped them inside her mouth by pressing his lips to hers.

This time, his kiss was not a mere brush of his mouth against hers. This time, it was all consuming, an unmistakable declaration of intent.

For a moment, Frisco was too startled to move, to think, to react. Resisting the allure of his mouth was not easy, yet she managed to do so for another moment.

She had every reason to resent this man—and to reject him. But she also had an excellent reason to accept his advances.

Put simply, Frisco desired Lucas, wanted to be with him, be a part of him, and she wanted him to be a part of her. To pretend she didn't want him would be yet another compromise for her, a compromise of her feelings, her innermost being.

And such an act of self-betrayal she absolutely would not allow herself.

Frisco surrendered to the inevitable, and with devastating

force, the attraction that had sprung to life between them from their first meeting took her by storm, the winds of passion sweeping away her last lingering bit of resistance.

Gone were all the logical reasons for her to reject her own needs. Gone with the feelings of righteous anger and resentment.

In their place surged a searing desire too intense to be denied an instant longer.

Bowing eagerly to the clamoring dictates of her senses, Frisco curled her arms around Lucas's neck and matched his kiss with a singeing demand of her own.

As if caught off guard by her impassioned response, Lucas went still for an instant, a heartbeat, then his arms coiled around her, pulling her against him in a thrilling, crushing embrace.

The time lapse between crushing embrace and total nudity was pleasurably, excitingly, long.

Frisco initiated the procedure by gliding her hands to Lucas's bared chest and pushing the silky material of his shirt off his shoulders, thereby making a silent, tactile statement of intent.

Lucas reciprocated. His touch delicate, careful, he slid the suit jacket from her shoulders and down her arms.

It fell to the floor unnoticed.

In turn, and with arousal-heightening slowness, each article of their clothing was dispatched and discarded with mutual unconcern.

But there was one item Lucas refused to remove.

His fingers caught, caressed, then crushed a creamy petal of one of the exotic blooms on the lei around her neck, and he shook his head as its spicy scent permeated the air between them.

"Leave it on," he murmured, gently rubbing the petal against her skin. "The fragrance will mingle with our perspiration, and fill our senses."

To Frisco's overheated imagination, the sheer eroticism in his whispered request contained more potency than gallons of champagne.

Shivering in anticipation of feeling his chest press the blossoms to her breast, of inhaling the combined aromas of perfumed petals and raw sex, she granted his request by silent acquiescence. Curling her arms around him, *she* pressed her breasts to his chest.

Lucas was quick to respond. Tightening his arms around her, he lifted her off her feet and carried her to the bed . . . the one *he* had slept in throughout the preceding week.

Freeing one hand, he pulled the coverlet aside, then with infinite gentleness, tenderness, he settled her in the center of the smooth sheet and positioned himself over her on the bed.

Ready, willing, anxious for his possession, Frisco parted her lips, seeking his mouth with her own.

Smiling, Lucas gave a brief shake of his head as he pulled back, denying her his kiss and immediate possession. Then, forestalling her protest, he lowered his head to pay homage to her body with his mouth.

Not an inch of her was overlooked by his lips, his tongue, his stroking hands. Moving sinuously beneath the onslaught of his mouth, Frisco endured the inflaming pleasure inflicted upon her as long as she could. Then, her senses made wild by his sensuous ministrations, she cried out her desperate need for him to end her torment.

"Lucas, please, please," she pleaded, grasping him by the waist to bring him to her, "I can't bear any more. I need you—now."

Betraying his own passionate need, Lucas slipped between her parted thighs and pressed his mouth to her parted lips, thrusting his tongue into her mouth at the exact instant he thrust his body into hers.

Hungry for him, Frisco coiled her legs around his taut thighs, and arched her body up and into the driving rhythm of his. For precious minutes, her senses swimming in the scent of flowers and sex, Frisco held on to the thin essence of tension unwinding inside her.

Then it snapped, unleashing a flood of sensations throughout her, so intense, so electrifying, she again cried out, this time in response to the unbelievable, never-before-imagined pleasure derived from her shattering release.

An instant later, Lucas gave a final thrust, shuddered, and then he too cried out in exultation.

"Good?"

"Hmmm," Frisco murmured, popping the end of the strawberry into her mouth. "Delicious."

Lucas mused that he could have applied the same term to her, but he refrained. Smiling, he gave her a silent salute, then took a swallow of his wine.

It was late, or early, depending on how one looked at time. He had awakened a short time ago from a restorative nap following the most exciting, satisfying sexual experience of his life. And he had awakened hard and ready for a repeat performance.

Surprisingly—or perhaps not so surprisingly after her previous uninhibited response to him—Frisco had willingly, eagerly, accepted his suggestive caresses.

Within moments she was writhing against him, her hands buried in his hair, intermittent gasps and moans torn from deep in her throat by the intensity of pleasure he was giving her with the intimate caresses of his hungry mouth and tongue.

Yes, Frisco is delicious, Lucas reflected. A reminiscent smile quirked his lips.

A delicious tiger.

She had actually clawed at him. Not once, but twice. And he had savored the sensations evoked inside him by her raking fingernails.

The first time he had felt her scoring nails came an instant before he had driven her over the brink of pleasure with his stroking tongue. He had felt, and gloried in, the results of his endeavors when she had shattered around him, crying out with the depths of her release. And though he had not attained his own release, it didn't matter—at least not too much—pleasuring her had sufficed.

He had soothed and calmed her with soft kisses and gentle caresses.

Then she had turned the tables on him.

Never imagining she could regain her strength so quickly, she caught him off guard when she levered herself up, and pushed him flat on his back.

"My turn," she said, giving him a smile so exciting in its insinuation, he nearly lost it right then.

Fortunately, as it turned out, Lucas managed to exert control . . . for a little while.

It didn't take long for him to be thankful that turnabout was fair play. And play was applicable, for Frisco's mouth played a teasing game over all of his body, tormenting him with nips of her teeth followed by laving strokes of her tongue.

And then he was writhing, shivering from the caress of her mouth on the insides of his thighs, arching his body in supplication as her mouth slowly moved up . . . up. His entire body jolted at the first feather-light touch of her mouth to his shaft, shuddered in reaction to the tip of her tongue skipping along its length.

"Frisco!" Lucas had barely recognized the groaning voice as his own.

"What's your pleasure, Lucas?" The purr of a tigress rippled in her voice.

"You . . . know," he ground out between quick gasps for breath—and control. "Get up here."

"And how do you ask?"

"Please." Somewhere on the fringes of what he had left of his mind, Lucas knew she was getting her own back for his having reduced her to pleading for his possession; he knew, and didn't care. "Frisco, please."

Whipping his quivering body with the tip of her tongue, she slowing crawled up and over him. Straddling him, but holding herself away from his arching hips, she exerted her power by tormenting him with her stroking hands.

His utter destruction came when she lowered her head to suckle at his nipple. Near the point of exploding, he cried out another hoarse plea.

"Frisco, please . . ."

She laughed.

He didn't care about that, either. All he did care about, could think about, was being with her, joined to her, riding the wave of their passion. He moaned in exquisite pleasure when, at last, she settled over him, sheathing him within the silkiness of her body.

Their gallop was brief . . . but intensely satisfying.

After that bit of exercise, they both needed another short nap.

Pouring a swallow of champagne into his depleted body, Lucas couldn't help but wonder if Frisco now thought that he was delicious, too.

"Have you tasted the Camembert? It's delicious."

Lucas was hard pressed not to laugh, and not just because of her unintentional remark, either. He simply felt too damn good.

"Not yet." He smiled instead. "I've been too busy working my way down to the strawberry."

Frisco did laugh. "That was a wonderful idea of ,yours, to drop a berry into the flutes." She tilted hers in salute to him. "Gives me an excuse to drink every drop of the wine to get to it."

He arched his brows. "You need an excuse?"

"Well-l-l," she drew the word out. "I feel rather decadent, sitting here in my nightgown and robe, eating cheese and strawberries and drinking champagne at four in the morning."

"You look decadent, too." He swept her body with an appreciative glance, gave her a deliberately lascivious smile. "I like it."

It was a gross understatement; in truth, Lucas loved the way she looked. Even hidden behind the gown and robe, her enticing breasts fired his imagination. And, though she had attempted to tame her hair with a brush, the mane framed her face and curled on her shoulders like flaming strands of silk, inviting the delving of his fingers. Her lips were stained scarlet by the berries, beckoning his mouth to taste the sweetness of the fruit.

God she was beautiful.

And she was his wife.

His.

Staring into her eyes, Lucas raised his glass to quench the thirst that went clear to the depths of his being. He was not a young man anymore. Hell, he was almost forty. And yet he wanted her again, was hard and aching to be inside her.

"What are you thinking?" Though her tone was austere, her lips quivered with a smile.

"I'm thinking you had better get to that strawberry at the bottom of your glass pretty soon," he said, rising to circle the table to her.

A solitary wisp of hair curled against the side of her soft throat. Without conscious direction, his fingers caught it, tangled with it.

Murmuring deep in her throat, she rubbed her cheek against his arm.

"Yes, Frisco Bay, you had better get to that berry pretty damned soon," he muttered, amazed at the steely reaction of his body to her slightest touch.

"Oh?" She looked all wide-eyed and innocent. But the impish light in her eyes betrayed her. "Why?"

"Because I'm about to play Rhett to your Scarlett, and carry you off to bed."

"Well, if that's the case," she murmured, setting the glass down, then raising her arms to him, "who needs food and drink?"

"If we should get hungry," he said, putting words to action by sweeping her off of the chair and into his arms, "we can always feast on each other."

"Suddenly, I'm ravished." She laughed gently and sank her teeth into his neck.

"Not yet, Frisco Bay." Laughing with her, he dumped her onto the bed and stretched his length on top of her. "But you will be very soon."

Chapter Twenty-six

"Yes, Harold, I assure you, the marriage is legal, binding, and consummated." Lucas stared through the sliding glass doors to the sea, a wry smile playing over his mouth. "All that's left for you to do is sign over the shares of stock to Frisco and clean out your desk and office. I'll be taking over when we get back tomorrow."

"Is . . . er, is Frisco all right?"

Thinking it was a trifle late for the older man to start making noises like a father, Lucas answered, "Yes, certainly, she's fine." In his opinion, Frisco was more than fine, she was fantastic, magnificent, the perfect match for him; and he loved her to distraction. But he wasn't about to say that to her father.

"Good, good," Harold said, too heartily. "Then I'll see you both tomorrow."

"Yes. Good-bye." He quietly replaced the receiver so as not to disturb Frisco, then turned to look at the bed, to confirm his own reassurance to her father.

She was awake, and staring at him. Her face was somber. Her eyes were cool and remote. And he knew she had heard at least part of his conversation with Harold.

Hell!

Lucas moved to go to her.

Frisco moved faster.

Shoving the revealingly tangled covers aside, she slid from the bed and headed for the bathroom. The very fact that she was nude said a lot about the time they had spent together. It was now Sunday morning, and except for meals they had eaten at the small metal table on the balcony, they had not been outside the room since returning to it after their wedding dinner Friday evening. In truth, they had spent most of those hours nude, and in bed.

But now there was a decided difference in Frisco, an unmistakable message for him in the stiffness of her spine, the proud lift of her head.

Although Lucas was positive he wasn't going to like hearing that message verbalized, he knew that he had to ask her what it was.

"Frisco?" Though his voice was low, soft, it stopped her cold in the act of collecting her clothing, shoes, and toiletries.

She hesitated a moment, then turned to face him, standing tall and looking regal.

"Yes?" Her voice was as cool and remote as her eyes, devoid of inflection.

Lucas felt a stab of grief and longed for the laughing, passionate, playful woman of the last few days. Due to an ill-timed phone call, that exciting woman had reverted to becoming once again his antagonist.

"Can't we talk about it?"

"What is there to talk about?" Frisco smiled in a way that made him sorry she had bothered, in a way that redefined the word chilling. "You said all that needs to be said to my father."

"But—"

"The marriage is legal, binding, and *consummated*," she cut him off sarcastically, underlying the last word acidly. "My father is to clean out his desk and office, sign over to me his shares of company stock, and then hit the road because you're going back." She paused, her upper lip curling, to rake a contemptuous look over him. "And . . . you're . . . taking . . . over."

"Frisco, listen . . ." he began, sighing when she shook her head and turned away.

"Sorry, don't have time." Her voice was now almost pleasant, impersonally so. "I have a lot to do. Got a plane to catch. But first things first," she went on, her voice growing grimly determined as she slipped the two rings from her finger.

"Leave the engagement ring on . . . please." Though Lucas had made the request in a soft voice, it carried a steely note of command. "I told your father to give your mother the idea that we have become engaged."

Frisco went still for an instant, then she replaced the ring, her anger revealed by her unsteady fingers. Without another word or look, she gathered her things and went into the bathroom.

The sound of the door closing was like a death knell inside Lucas's head.

The honeymoon was definitely over.

"Who was calling, dear?"

Quivering inside with relief, and a touch of anxiety, Harold carefully cradled the receiver, then put a smile on his face for his wife.

"It was Lucas MacCanna," he answered, contriving an amused-sounding chuckle. "Now I understand why I haven't heard from him this past week."

"Really?" Gertrude smiled and raised her brows in inquiry. "Why?"

"Seems he's been visiting Frisco in Honolulu."

Gertrude frowned.

Afraid he'd been too candid, too quickly, Harold hastened to soothe her maternal concern.

"I believe Lucas is getting rather serious about our Frisco, darling. And I mean marriage serious."

"Do you think so, Harold?" his wife fretted. "I do like and admire Lucas, and I'd be thrilled to hear he had marriage with Frisco in mind, but I certainly wouldn't want to see her become involved in another *open-ended* relationship—not even with him."

"Don't worry, darling," Harold soothed, drawing her into his arms. "I feel quite certain Lucas wouldn't dream of making that sort of offer to Frisco." He paused, choosing his words carefully before continuing. "As a matter of fact, I wouldn't be at all surprised if Frisco returns home wearing Lucas's engagement ring."

Gertrude leaned back to stare up at him, her expression one of cautious delight. "Do you really think that is a possibility, dear?"

Harold had no difficulty in infusing absolute confidence into his voice, since he already knew his answer to be an accomplished fact.

"Yes, darling, I really do." He controlled an urge to express his relief with a burst of joyous laughter, and smiled encouragingly at his wife instead. "I will even go so far as to suggest that you might want to start planning an engagement party for, say . . . next weekend?"

"But, my dear," she said, frowning. "Suppose they come home and are not, in fact, engaged?"

"Hmmm," he murmured, mirroring her frown for a moment. Then, as if suddenly inspired, he said, "I know, plan the affair as a welcome-home party, and then, if I'm proved correct, we can make the grand announcement."

"Yes. Oh, yes!" Gertrude exclaimed enthusiastically. "Oh, Harold, you are so clever!"

Harold accepted her accolade with a charming smile.

"Did you suggest this so-called welcome-home party, as well?" Frisco impatiently demanded the instant she and Lucas were alone together in the privacy of his car.

"I did not." Lucas's flat denial held the sound of truth. "I knew nothing about it."

Absently twisting the contentious ring on her finger, Frisco fumed in agitated silence.

She hadn't even been home yet, for heaven's sake! Having prearranged it with a garage, Lucas had had a driver waiting for them with his car at the airport. And, after dropping off the driver, he had driven directly to her parents' home.

The long flight had been a trial for Frisco. She had boarded the plane for the first leg of the journey feeling disappointed, hurt, and more than a little depressed.

After the day and two nights she and Lucas had shared holed up in the hotel room, she had foolishly begun to harbor hope for their future together.

He had been so . . . so wonderful—kind, considerate, fun, and passionate—the most thoughtful lover any woman would fantasize about being with.

But overhearing a part of his conversation with her father had shattered Frisco's budding dreams and brought her down from the clouds to earthly business.

Blaming herself as much, if not even more, than Lucas for her disillusionment, she had nevertheless maintained a stony silence throughout both flights and the layover between, rebuffing with an indifferent stare his every attempt to discuss the issue.

Though she had wanted to rant and rave at him for the pain she was suffering, she had locked her ire and pain inside. Intellectually, Frisco knew she could not fault Lucas for his actions, for in truth, he had done nothing more than he had told her from the beginning he wanted to do—have her in his bed.

And, Lord, had she been had.

But then, she admitted to herself, she had taken as much as she had given. Then again, perhaps not, Frisco had concluded, while on the second flight. She had given her heart, along with her body.

She was in love with Lucas, damn his hide. That truth she also kept locked inside.

And, after another long journey spent primarily with her own conflicting thoughts, she was weary to the very depths of body and soul.

Now, after force-smiling her way through her mother's genuine delight at their engagement, and Gertrude's raptures over the engagement ring, even through the breaking of the news of the party Gertrude was planning for the coming Sunday, Frisco was on the very edge of exhaustion.

. But as they drew near her condo complex, her greatest concern revolved around what Lucas might be assuming. If he thought for an instant that he was moving in with her, he could damn well think again.

To paraphrase Dorothy: they weren't in Hawaii anymore.

"I suppose, for appearance's sake, we had better live apart until after the wedding," Lucas said, as if he had tapped into her train of thought.

"Yes," Frisco quickly agreed, relieved at having been spared an argument.

He sliced a probing look at her.

She met it with a bland expression.

He drove into the complex parking lot, and Frisco practically leaped from the car as soon as he brought it to a stop.

They rode up in the elevator in silence.

Since Lucas was carrying her suitcases, she unlocked her door and preceded him into the apartment.

It seemed she had been away for years instead of a mere two weeks.

"I'll take these into your bedroom," he said.

She didn't argue. She didn't move a step away from just inside the door, either. He frowned when she opened the door as he strode from her bedroom.

"We have to talk about it sooner or later, Frisco."

"It will have to be later." Frisco glanced pointedly at her watch. "I'm tired, and tomorrow is a working day . . . remember?"

"You don't have to go in to the office tomorrow," Lucas decreed. "Take the day, rest, and do whatever needs doing—unpacking, laundry." He shrugged, and repeated, "Whatever. Tuesday's soon enough to begin."

How magnanimous of him, she thought cynically. And how damned autocratic. His voice, speaking the words that had sent her soaring hopes into a tailspin a lifetime ago—that very morning—echoed sickeningly inside Frisco's head:

I'll be taking over when we get back . . .

The words left a bitterness in her, and it spilled over into her voice.

"Correct me if I'm wrong, Mr. MacCanna, but is the company not legally mine now?"

"On paper, yes, *Mrs.* MacCanna," he said, emphasizing the Mrs. "But you know as well as I who will, in fact, be running it."

"Well, I intend to be running right beside you," she said forcefully, ignoring the tiny thrill she experienced upon being called Mrs. MacCanna for the first time. "And I will be at the starting gate early tomorrow morning. So, if you don't mind . . ." She opened the door fully.

His jaw clenched, and for a moment she felt certain he was going to belabor the point. Then, with an impatient shake of his head, he moved to her, only to stop.

"Are you planning to wear running shoes into the office?" he asked, lips twitching with amusement. "Or can I look forward to seeing your gorgeous legs and ankles enhanced by more attractive footwear?"

Lucas thought her legs and ankles were gorgeous? Catching herself tingling with delight, Frisco squashed the reaction. Damn him! Damn his seemingly effortless ability to muddle her mind. Narrowing her eyes, she glared at him.

"Out," she ordered, gesturing to the corridor. "And I'll wear what I damn well please to the office."

No longer bothering to contain his amusement, Lucas laughed aloud. "Your wish is my command, dear wife," he said, stifling another chuckle. "I live to serve." Then, as if his words weren't enough, he caught her face in his hands, lowered his head, and crushed her mouth beneath his own, in a kiss guaranteed to really screw up her thoughts, and singe her eyebrows into the bargain.

And then he was gone, leaving Frisco gasping for breath, hungry for more of the same, and damning him for reminding her of how exciting their being together and making love to each other had been.

As if she'd needed reminding . . .

Sighing for what might have been, Frisco slammed shut the door, fastened the three safety locks, then, with dragging steps, went to her bedroom.

In the quiet of the night, in the emptiness of her bed, hidden away from prying or mocking eyes, and too weary to fight them off any longer, Frisco gave way to the tears that had threatened ever since she had awakened to overhear the tail end of Lucas's conversation with her father early that morning.

Dammit! Dammit! She protested in silent frustration, the memory of his kiss burning her lips even more than the tears burned her eyes. Why had she done something so stupid as falling in love with Lucas MacCanna?

Chapter Twenty-seven

To Frisco's amazement, she and Lucas worked very well together. She was not, however, amazed by the fact that he was a dynamo, a living, breathing, get-it-done-yesterday, workaholic.

His work methods didn't bother Frisco. On the contrary. She had always been something of an A-type, dig-in person herself.

And there was plenty for her to dig into. The accounting department was in deplorable condition, which explained how her father had avoided detection of his liberal finger-dipping into the company's profits. Gritting her teeth, Frisco set about bringing the records up to speed.

Immersed in her own work, she found it easy to get along with Lucas, who was in forward drive on revitalizing the entire company.

It was after the workday ended that Frisco had difficulty dealing with the man.

In his usual autocratic way, Lucas insisted they spend all of their free time together, to convince all and sundry, and most especially her mother, of the validity of their romance and subsequent engagement.

And so on Monday and Tuesday evening Frisco and Lucas

had dinner together, then drove to her parents' home, ostensibly to help with the planning of the welcome home/engagement party on Sunday, but in reality to display their affection for each other.

It didn't take long for Frisco to get fed up with the entire deceitful number. Her father's too jovial, too enthusiastic act was simply too much. Worse still was enduring the smoldering glances, the lingering touches, the smooth endearments Lucas laid on for her mother's benefit.

Every time he smiled tenderly, lovingly touched her, or murmured yet another lying endearment, Frisco had to bite back a protest.

That her mother appeared to be swallowing the performance of both her father and Lucas without question only served to further annoy her.

But though she dreaded the evenings, the absolute worst times for her were the nights following the evenings, the nights alone in her bed.

During that brief, idyllic period they had spent in the hotel room, Lucas had seduced her mind as well as her body. While her mental fogginess had cleared in response to the wake-up call of the conversation between Lucas and her father, her senses had remained thoroughly seduced. In consequence, she had spent Sunday, Monday, and Tuesday night fighting the demands of her body.

On Wednesday afternoon, Frisco was dreading yet another evening of playacting when salvation came in the form of a phone call from Karla.

"Hi! Welcome home," she chirped, in her normal upbeat tone; then, not giving Frisco a chance to reply, continued on, "I know you're busy, and I won't keep you. I only called to ask if you'd like to meet Jo and me for dinner this evening?"

"Well, I . . ." Frisco began, intending to accept the invitation. It would provide an excuse to get out of spending another evening with Lucas, and she genuinely enjoyed the get-togethers with her friends.

"Oh, I know we'll be seeing you at the welcome-home party on Sunday," Karla interrupted, obviously thinking Frisco was about to decline. "But we won't get a chance to talk at the party, and Jo and I want to hear all about your trip to Hawaii. Please say you'll join us."

"I will," Frisco responded obediently, laughing. "Just tell me where and what time."

"Sfuzzi's at six. Okay?"

"Oh, sure," Frisco drawled, mentally picturing the Italian bistro on Market Street. "You don't care if I gorge myself with all their fattening goodies, do you?"

"Nope," Karla said unrepentantly. "I never need to watch what I eat."

"You do know how I'd respond to that remark if I were Jo, don't you?"

Karla giggled. "Of course. You'd tell me to *blank* off and die . . . if you were Jo."

"Correct." Frisco laughed. "But since I'm not, I'll merely say good-bye, Karla."

"See you at six?"

"I'll be there."

"With bells on?" Karla asked in feigned breathless wonderment.

"Good-bye, Karla." Laughing, Frisco shook her head and hung up the receiver.

"An amusing call?"

Frisco's laughter dried in her throat. Lucas's tone was deceptively mild. Tamping down a startling feeling of intimidation, she slowly turned her head to look at him.

He was standing in the office doorway, one shoulder propped against the frame, looking for all intents and purposes as if he owned the place, which in reality, if not legally, he did.

"Yes," she answered, striving to keep her tone as mild as his. "That was Karla. She called to invite me to dinner with her and Jo." She arched her brows. "I believe I mentioned their names to you once. Didn't I?"

Lucas gave a brief nod, then launched into a recitation about the women in question. "Karla, one of your dearest friends. Chose the role of homemaker as a career. Husband's name is Danny—short for Daniel, I suppose. Twins, Josh and Jen."

He paused to acknowledge her look of astonishment with a wry smile, then continued on, "Jo, your other dearest friend. Beautiful, wise-cracking, hard-nosed cop. Militant feminist. Unmarried." His voice turned extremely dry. "Why doesn't her single status surprise me?" He favored her with a teasing smile. "Yes, I believe you mentioned them in passing . . . once."

Stunned speechless, Frisco just sat and stared at him in utter disbelief. What he had said was the simple truth; she had mentioned Karla and Jo in passing, on one of the evenings they had had dinner together during that very first week after she'd met him.

No damned wonder he's so good at what he does, she thought. The man was a walking memory bank!

"And they'd like you to meet them for dinner this evening?" Lucas prompted her when, instead of replying, she continued to stare at him.

"Yes," she said, gathering her inner fortitude to withstand, and win, any argument he might present. Yet once again he confounded her.

"Fine," he said, throwing her off balance with his easy agreement.

"You don't mind?" she asked suspiciously, wondering what game he was now playing.

"Mind?" Lucas frowned and shook his head. "No. Why should I mind if you have dinner with friends?"

Good question. Too bad she didn't have a ready answer. Come to that, a renegade part of her felt slighted by his easy concession to her individual rights. She didn't have a ready answer as to why that was, either.

Avoiding the connotations of commitment inherent in the feeling, she decided it was all too complicated, and let it go at that.

"Beats me," she said, flippantly dismissing the subject. "Have you come to my office for a particular reason?"

He smiled, but allowed her to get away with the change in topic. "I just stopped by to see how you're getting on," he said, pushing away from the doorway and strolling into the room. "Making any headway?"

Frisco grimaced. "As the old saying goes, I'm making haste slowly. These files are an accountant's worst nightmare."

Lucas grinned. "As another old saying goes, don't feel like the Lone Ranger, honey. The state of this entire operation is a businessman's nightmare."

Frisco experienced a twinge of guilt, which was patently ridiculous and she knew it. Nevertheless she apologized. "I'm sorry."

"For what? You didn't screw up the works." Leaning across the desk, he extended his arm and stroked her cheek with 'his index finger. "Don't worry, honey, we'll pull it off together."

Frisco had never appreciated being called honey by anyone other than her mother. Yet coming from Lucas, the casual endearment held an altogether new appeal.

"That's right, we will," she said briskly, moving her head back, away from his touch, her tone and action a denial of the sensations he aroused.

Lucas took it personally. Straightening, he leveled a thoughtful look at her, then, with a barely audible sigh, he turned away.

"Have a good time this evening," he said, as he strode from the office.

Feeling vaguely bereft, hurt, Frisco unknowingly echoed his sigh as she stared at the empty doorway.

Because she had immersed herself in her work to escape her conflicting and confusing feelings, Frisco was the last to arrive at the restaurant.

With her usual sharp eyes Jo spied the engagement ring before Frisco had settled into her seat at the table.

"Would you look at the size of that rock!" she exclaimed, if softly. "What millionaire did you have to bang to earn that as a reward?"

"Jo!" Karla protested in evident shock and dismay. "That was a terrible thing to say—and to Frisco, of all people."

"It's all right, Karla," Frisco said, deflecting the insult. "Jo will be Jo."

Jo merely shrugged, blatantly unrepentant.

"But I must agree with her about the size of the stone,"

Karla said, eyeing the diamond in awe. "It's fantastic. Wherever did you get it?"

Frisco hesitated a moment, then knowing it would be useless to hedge, or even outright lie since they would be hearing the truth in a few days anyway, she thrust her hand forward for their closer inspection.

"Lucas MacCanna gave it to me," she said with as much enthusiasm as she could muster. "We'll be announcing our engagement at the party on Sunday."

"Oh, Frisco!" Karla literally gushed, clasping her friend's hand and giving it a squeeze. "I'm delighted for you."

"Frisco," Jo chimed in, her tone cynical, the complete opposite of Karla's.

Frisco shifted her startled gaze, to find Jo peering at her through narrowed eyes.

"Do I detect the nasty smell of coercion here?" Jo raised her eyebrows. "Blackmail, maybe?"

"For goodness' sake, Jo!" Karla cried, looking appalled. "What are you implying?"

The question hung in the air between them for several minutes as, just then, a waiter appeared at the table to deliver the drinks Jo and Karla had ordered, including one for Frisco.

"Really," Frisco said when the waiter departed after taking their dinner orders. "Coercion? Blackmail?" She managed to hang on to her light tone. "Whatever gave you that idea?"

"You did," Jo said flatly.

"Stop this," Karla ordered. Her fingers picked at the cocktail napkin beneath her wine glass, revealing her agitation. "This isn't funny."

"Bet your ass it isn't," Jo agreed grimly, her stare riveted on Frisco. "Is it, kid?"

The icy look to her friend's blue eyes sent a chill up Frisco's spine. She could almost hear the wheels revolving inside Jo's head. Frisco contained a shiver. She had to put a stop to this before Jo came up with the correct answer.

She said with desperate calm, "Believe me, there's nothing to be concerned about."

"No?" Jo arched her brows. "I think there is. I smell a rat, and the rat is male."

"Oh, is that it?" Karla rolled her eyes at Frisco. "It's the old every man's a villain routine."

"If the black hat fits . . ."

"But for you there are no white hats!" Karla exclaimed. "For you, all men wear black hats."

Frisco remained silent, hoping against hope Karla's argument would distract Jo. She knew better, of course. And she was right. With a flick of her elegant slender hand, Jo literally waved aside Karla's intervention.

"You're wrong," she said, a hint of resignation in her smile. "But that's beside the point." Her laser stare returned to pierce Frisco. "You want me to spell it out for our innocent friend here?"

Oh, hell. Frisco's stomach did flipflops. She had to shut Jo up. "Really, I assure you—"

"Yeah, I know, you already said that." Jo curled her hand into a fist, then extended her index finger. "Fact one: at dinner, just three and a half weeks ago, you told us your father was in danger of losing the family business to a raider."

"No, I—"

"Fact two." Her second finger shot out. "At that time, you also said you were meeting later that evening to discuss a possible solution to your father's problem."

"But—"

"Fact three." She raised her third finger. "The very next week you were off to Hawaii, which doesn't leave a helluva lot of time for a romance to develop."

"Jo, listen. I know the time constraints." Not to mention the constraint now evident in her voice. Frisco moved her shoulders in what she prayed was a helpless-looking shrug. "What can I say? I fell in love." Well, at least that much was true, even if it had been after the fact.

"Bullshit." Jo was obviously not buying.

Karla heaved a long-suffering sigh. "Jo, will you watch your language. We're in a public place."

"Karla, dear friend, get a grip on reality," Jo said, not unkindly, and a lot more softly. "I think our Frisco here is in deep shit." She sliced a probing look at Frisco. "What did this MacCanna person do, blackmail you into marriage to get control of the firm?"

Damn, she's good, Frisco thought, raking her mind for a reasonable-sounding response. Jo's deductive powers were right on target. No wonder she was so well respected in the law-enforcement community.

"Frisco?" Karla murmured when the silence had become palpable. Her soft brown eyes were shadowed with worry. "Please say Jo's mistaken."

Frisco found she could smile at Karla, which came as no surprise; she could always smile for Karla. Then, while the smile was still in place, she turned it on Jo.

"Saying she's mistaken would solve nothing," she said, continuing to smile at Jo. "What I will say is, wait until Sunday, decide for yourself after you've met Lucas."

"Yes, of course!" Karla's smile of relief chased the shadows from her eyes.

"I can't wait," Jo drawled, both her tone and eyes sharp with skepticism.

In that instant, Frisco knew she would have to put on the performance of her life that Sunday. Convincing her mother had been a walk-through; convincing Jo would be something else altogether.

The waiter arrived at their table bearing a tray laden with steaming, aromatic pasta dishes.

Unsurprisingly, the appetites of the three best friends had diminished considerably.

Chapter Twenty-eight

"So when do you expect this Will Denton?"

Lucas sipped tentatively at his hot coffee before responding to Michael's question.

It was Sunday morning. Lucas, Michael, and Rob were seated around a table in the dining room of the Adam's Mark. Since it was still a bit early for the Sunday brunch crowd, the room was nearly empty, as were the breakfast dishes for four set on the large round table.

In compliance with Lucas's request, Michael, Rob, and Rob's lady friend, Melanie, had arrived at the hotel an hour previously. As if by prearrangement—and it probably was— Melanie had left the table as soon as she'd finished eating, ostensibly to unpack, leaving the three men to talk in private. Although Lucas had arched one brow on seeing his youngest brother's companion, he had remained silent, accepting Rob's decision to have the young woman accompany him to the supposed welcome-home party.

"I talked to him on the phone late Friday afternoon," Lucas finally replied. "Will said we can look for him in three weeks." He paused to take another, deeper swallow from the coffee cup.

"He's driving east from Montana, said he'd give me a call from wherever he stops for the night on Saturday evening."

"Mike tells me you're turning your townhouse over to him until he finds a place of his own," Rob said, picking up the silver coffee pot to refill his own cup. "Does that mean you're going to be spending most of your time working here in Philadelphia from now on?"

Lucas drained his cup, then held it out to Rob for a refill, his third. Deciding it was time to apprise his brothers of his plans, at least his personal ones, he answered, "Yes, and I hired Will to take my place in the Reading office."

"You don't think we can handle it?" Though Michael's tone was mild, there were threads of hurt and anger woven through it.

"Can you?" Lucas asked, a new, gentle note in his voice. "You're both expert in your particular fields, but is either one of you ready yet to assume the position of C.E.O.?"

Michael sighed, then admitted, "No."

Rob let a negative shake of his head answer for him.

"But we could learn."

"I know, and you've both done a fine job since I've been out of the office," Lucas praised their efforts. "But there is still a lot for you to learn, and that's why I'm bringing Will Denton into the firm."

"How do you know he can handle it?" Michael asked in his normal, practical manner.

Lucas gave him a chiding smile. "I did my homework." He shrugged. "When I offered Will a job, I didn't know whether I'd slot him into the Reading office or here, at The Cutting Edge."

"But the results of your homework decided the issue?" Rob asked, frowning.

"Yes, partly. Turns out Will is a true steel man, knows the business every way from Sunday. He can guide you as well as I could over the rough spots until you're ready to assume control. But that isn't the only, or the main, reason I'm installing him in my former office. I could have gone on as before, dividing my time between Reading and Philly. But not anymore."

"Why not?"

Lucas smiled, then tossed his bomb.

"I'm getting married."

"You're kidding!" Michael exclaimed, grinning.

"Way to go!" Rob cheered.

"Who's the woman?"

"You'll be meeting her later this afternoon. We'll be announcing our engagement at the party."

"But who is she?" Michael persisted.

"Frisco Styer." Lucas raised his cup to his mouth, to conceal the twist of regret on his lips.

"Harold's daughter?"

"Yes."

While Rob smiled and shook his hand, Michael looked pensive and concerned.

Knowing Mike had been fully aware of his intention to take over The Cutting Edge, Lucas made a mental note to be very careful while his brother was in town. More to the point, he decided he had better ask Frisco to be careful.

Frisco. It hurt to think of her, of the shock and insult he had inadvertently inflicted upon her.

Stupid ass, he admonished himself, for about the hundredth time. She had given herself to him so very passionately, so beautifully, he had begun to hope—to believe—she might yet give him her love.

Lucas swallowed a sigh with his coffee. Just one week of seeing Frisco force a smile for her parents while tolerating his lightest caress, a week of wanting her, needing her, yet knowing she held him in contempt, had effectively deflated his male ego.

He loved her so very much. The last thing he wanted to do was hurt her in any way, and her contempt for him sliced into his mind like a weapon, lacerating his emotions.

His wife.

The pain dug deeper into Lucas, into his very being.

He'd set her free, even now, if he could. But it was too late. In all probability, Frisco would reject such an offer. They had taken the irrevocable step; they had told her mother they were in love. And Gertrude had been so thrilled and delighted by their news, so eager to plan a wedding.

Lucas was certain that Frisco would rather tolerate him than disappoint her mother.

Christ, he thought, condemning himself. What an unholy mess he had made of everything.

The only hope he now had left was that somehow, in some way, he could, with time and patience and unqualified love, untie the noose he had fashioned for himself. Because if he couldn't bring Frisco around, hear her laughter, taste her passion, see himself in the depths of her eyes, he would be lonely for the rest of his life.

For a man like Lucas, a man used to going his own way, accustomed to being on his own, the prospect of spending his life alone should not have seemed so bleak. But now it scared the hell out of him.

He loved Frisco so very much.

"Congratulations."

Feeling like a fraud, Frisco flashed her most brilliant smile and offered her cheek for yet another kiss, along with her murmured thanks.

Her father, one arm encircling her mother's waist, had announced the engagement moments ago. Frisco had been deluged with good wishes and kisses, not all on the cheek, ever since.

Melanie's hand clasped in his, Rob sauntered up to her and Lucas after the initial crush abated. "I think you've started something here, big brother," he said, in what Frisco had already learned was his usual flippant way.

"Yeah? And what would that be?" Lucas asked, casually but possessively draping an arm over Frisco's shoulders.

"I just proposed to Melanie," Rob answered, unabashedly raising her hand to press her fingers to his lips.

The gesture was so courtly, so tender, Frisco was hit by a sudden sting in the eyes, a tightness in the throat . . . and an unfamiliar twinge of envy.

"Well." Lucas raised his eyebrows and extended his right hand. "Let me return the congratulations."

"And let me return your kiss, Melanie," Frisco said, slipping away from Lucas to embrace the girl.

"Your ring is so beautiful," Melanie said on a sigh, after the• exchange.

"I hope you're not expecting one on the same order." Rob gave a rueful laugh. "A rock that size would damn near impoverish me."

"Maybe your brother will give you a raise," Melanie suggested, smiling timidly at Lucas.

"Then again, maybe he won't," Lucas retorted, softening his words with a reciprocal smile.

Rob heaved a sigh. "Well, honey, it didn't work, but it was worth a . . ." He broke off as a young woman brushed by him to confront his brother.

"So, you're the MacCanna."

"And you're Jo," Lucas said, dryly. "And you're late, as well."

"I knew that," Jo said airily, thrusting her hand out to him. "You're a lucky man, MacCanna," she said, giving his hand a no-nonsense shake. "But I'm warning you here and now, you'd better take care of Frisco."

"Jo!" Frisco exclaimed.

"Jo, really!" Karla scolded, coming up beside the tall woman. "Will you ever learn to behave?"

"Probably not." The observation came from Karla's husband, Danny.

"I hope not," Lucas drawled, grinning at the militant woman. "You're a kick, Jo."

"A dangerous kick, Lucas." She grinned back at him, baring perfect white teeth.

"What kept you?" Karla demanded of Jo.

"I was on duty."

"Oh, sorry." Karla smiled. "I'm afraid you missed the announcement . . . not to mention the champagne."

Jo leveled an arch look on Lucas. "You skimped on the champagne?"

He laughed aloud and shook his head.

Frisco answered for him. "No, Jo, we didn't skimp on the champagne. There's plenty."

"There'd better be," she muttered. "I'm off duty, and thirsty as hell."

"Oh, Jo." Karla rolled her eyes.

"At your service, ma'am," Michael said, strolling into the group, a tray of filled glasses in hand.

"Ah, the bartender"—Jo made an obvious inspection of this tall, dark-suited, somber-faced figure, then lifted her eyebrows—"or is it the butler?"

"It's the brother," Michael responded, his voice low and as somber as his expression.

"Another MacCanna?" Jo glanced from Michael to Lucas. "How interesting."

There was an undercurrent, something in Jo's cool voice that made Frisco uneasy. Praying her friend would not cause a scene, she looked to Lucas to respond.

"There are three of us," he said, the gleam in his eyes in conflict with his bland tone.

"And you have to be the third," Jo drawled, her gaze homing in on Rob.

"Guilty," he confessed, shifting his eyes to Melanie. "And this is—"

"I'll take care of that," Lucas interrupted, gesturing to Michael to distribute the champagne.

While Michael handed around the wine, Lucas made formal introductions, and Frisco studied her future brothers-in-law. She had categorized them at first meeting, and as the day progressed, their opposite and individual manners appeared to prove the accuracy of her first impressions.

From the beginning, she had suspected Rob's breezy, light-hearted attitude concealed a quick, sharp, intelligent mind. By comparison, Michael was quiet, thoughtful, reserved. He had actually said very little, but a close look at his eyes revealed the same bright intelligence present in his brother.

The insight didn't surprise Frisco; were they not siblings of the vaunted legend?

Of the three, Michael was the last one she would have expected Jo to eye so warily. Yet that was precisely what Jo was doing.

Strange.

"So," Jo's voice drew Frisco from her reverie. "Have you set a date for the wedding?"

Frisco opened her mouth to say no. The words didn't make it past the tip of her tongue.

"The first Saturday in June," Lucas said decisively.

The first Saturday in June! Frisco clamped her lips together, denying the exclamation voice.

"Why, that's only a little over a month away!" Karla didn't so much as hesitate in voicing the exclamation. "Exactly four weeks from yesterday, as a matter of fact." She turned astonished eyes on Frisco. "And you didn't say a word about it at dinner Wednesday evening."

"Yes, I know, but you see . . ." Frisco began, raking her mind for a reasonable excuse for not revealing a date she hadn't yet known herself.

"That's because we didn't decide until just yesterday," Lucas calmly explained, gazing lovingly at his soon-to-be bride. "Did we, my love?"

My love! Frisco was pierced by a stab of pain, followed by a sudden, violent urge to slap the love-struck look off his deceitful face. Choosing prudence over violence, she gave him a saccharine smile instead. "Yes, my darling, we did."

His eyes flashed a warning, which she decided she had better heed. Saving face by tossing her head in disdain of the angry glitter in his eyes, she deliberately turned away from him to address her friends.

"I would be truly honored if you, Karla, would consent to being my matron of honor, and you, Jo, to being my maid of honor."

"Oh, Frisco," Karla cried. "I was hoping you'd ask us both."

"I'd like to see you try to get married without having us attend you," Jo weighed in.

"I wouldn't dream of it." Frisco smiled at them, then sent a quick glance at Lucas. He slanted a droll look at her. "I wouldn't consider myself really married if you two weren't there," she continued blithely, speaking to them while digging at him.

His eyes narrowed.

She angled her chin.

Fortunately, before the situation deteriorated into either a verbal or physical confrontation, her mother rushed up to whisk Frisco away to speak to more late arrivals.

It was a lovely party. Frisco knew it, and everybody who attended said it was. But finally it was over. She heaved a deep, if silent, sigh of utter relief on closing the door after the last departing guest.

"Wasn't it a wonderful party?" Gertrude slid her arm around her husband's waist as the four of them returned to the living room.

A muffled groan escaped Frisco.

"Careful," Lucas murmured.

"Yes, my dear, it certainly was," Harold replied with gentle indulgence. Leaving her side, he went to the bar the caterer had set up in front of fireplace. "And now I'm going to pour all of us a fresh glass of champagne, so we can drink a private toast to my daughter and prospective son-in-law," he announced, proceeding to do precisely that.

"What a wonderful idea!" Gertrude exclaimed.

"And then I'm heading for home," Frisco said before her mother could initiate a party postmortem, which she knew Gertrude would do, given the opportunity.

"Oh, must you?" Gertrude asked, obviously disappointed. "I thought we could begin planning the wedding."

"I'm beat, Mother." That was the truth; after playing the excited fiancée for what had seemed forever, Frisco was worn out. "We'll have to do it later."

"Suppose we come for dinner one evening this week to discuss it?" Lucas suggested, smiling as he accepted a glass of wine from Harold.

"Tomorrow evening?" Gertrude said eagerly.

"Yes, Mother," Frisco agreed, stifling yet another sigh. "We'll come here straight from the office."

Chapter Twenty-nine

"Well, I personally prefer having the wedding here in our garden, rather than in the church," Harold said, closing the door behind his daughter and future son-in-law. "And the early June weather should be perfect, not too hot, not too cool."

"I suppose." Gertrude offered him an uncertain smile. "But I've always dreamed of a big, beautiful church wedding for Frisco," she added plaintively.

"I know, my dear," Harold said, soothingly, gently ushering her into the living room. "But there simply isn't time to plan a large wedding, and really, we must credit Lucas for coming up with the idea of our garden."

"Hmmm, yes, Lucas is being very considerate of our feelings on the matter." Gertrude turned to gaze at Harold, a frown tugging her finely arched eyebrows together. "I'm concerned about Frisco, though, I think she looks tired and pale. And she barely touched her dinner this evening. Come to that, I don't recall seeing her eat a thing at the party yesterday. Did you notice?"

"Now, now, my dear, you're not to worry." Harold forced a chuckle, tamping down his own sense of unease about his daughter's well-being. "Frisco is newly engaged, and planning to wed within a few weeks. If she's a trifle pale and has no appetite, it's only because she is excited, I'm sure."

Harold prayed to God he was right, because if he wasn't, and this arrangement turned out to be a disaster, he would be more to blame than Lucas.

"You see?" Lucas said, shifting in his seat to smile at Frisco after he had brought the car to a stop in the parking lot of her condo complex. "A little compromise on everybody's part and everybody is satisfied."

Actually having to work to keep from grimacing at him, Frisco gave him a deadpan look.

"Is everybody satisfied?"

"Aren't they?"

"It seems to me that every time you suggest a compromise, you end up winning," she observed caustically. "While I end up doing the compromising."

"Are you telling me you wanted the lavish church wedding your mother had in mind?"

Frisco shook her head. "No, but—"

"What?" he demanded when her voice trailed away to nothingness. "I distinctly recall you informing me that you did not want to be married in some official's office or even a judge's chambers."

"Yes, but . . ." Frisco's voice faded; what Lucas had said was true, she had told him exactly that. Still, she couldn't help feeling that she and her mother were the only ones making compromises.

"But what?" Impatience laced his voice. "As it is, this wedding will be a sham, a show put on for your mother. In case you've forgotten, we're already married."

"I haven't forgotten." Frisco's voice was icy. "It's legal, binding, and *consummated* . . . right?"

Lucas sighed. "Frisco—"

"Which reminds me. It's getting late, and we both have to work tomorrow." She pushed open her door. "You certainly don't want to let things slide . . . not now that you've married the owner's daughter to get them."

"Dammit, Frisco!" Lucas swung the driver's side door open and thrust one leg out.

"Don't bother," she said. "I can find my own way to my apartment."

"Frisco, we have got to talk." Lucas angrily stepped out of the car.

"Not tonight." Waving him away, she started for the tenants' elevator. "Good night, Lucas."

"Damn it to hell."

Frisco heard his muttered curse as the elevator doors swished together.

So, Mr. Compromise is not happy with my attitude, she thought. Tough. She was the one paying the price in sleepless nights and raging hormones, thanks to his manipulations.

She wouldn't allow herself to even think about how she would handle the situation after the second wedding, when her parents would naturally expect her to set up housekeeping with Lucas.

And she adamantly refused to acknowledge, let alone consider, the cause of the anticipatory shivers skipping along her spine.

Frustrated sexually, emotionally, and psychologically, Lucas stared at the closed elevator doors for several seconds before slamming back into the car.

He didn't relish returning to the hotel. Despite its amenities, its excellent service, it was still just a hotel, impersonal, lacking real warmth.

For the first time in his adult life, he desired a home of his own. The townhouse he had occupied for the previous ten years or so had never been one. It was shelter, a place to sleep and, on rare occasions, eat a light meal or snack.

For his needs at the time, it had sufficed. But things were different now. He had had a taste—an appetizer only—of the marital state, and now he hungered for the full marriage meal.

And, dammit, Frisco was his wife. She belonged with him—in his life, his home, his bed.

Lucas consoled himself with the reminder that in less than five weeks they would go through the motions once again; they would be, in effect, doubly married.

And then . . .

His body tightened in the obvious place, and in response, his jaw set in determination.

Though she didn't know it yet, sometime next week, he and Frisco Bay were going house shopping.

Despite Frisco's less than clear thinking, the succeeding days passed productively, as well as swiftly. There was much to accomplish, both in the office and in preparing for the wedding.

One thing that had to be decided was the question of residence. The day after they had dinner with her parents, Lucas set her mind spinning with an abrupt announcement.

"We're going to take off one afternoon this week to begin looking for a place to live."

"I have a place to live," she said, not too brightly, frowning at him.

"I don't," he chided. "And I'm getting tired of living out of a suitcase."

"But what's wrong with my place?" Frisco had not only assumed he would move in with her after the wedding, she had pictured him in her place, next to her, in her bed.

"It's too small."

"Not for me," she said, taking offense despite the fact that she had felt cramped for space at times.

"My point exactly." Lucas smiled. "We'd likely be bumping into each other all the time."

Frisco experienced a flutter in her stomach at the exciting suggestion. Telling herself to grow up, she decided to do what she actually longed to do, but without giving herself away in the process. Heaving a noticeable sigh, she suggested an alternative.

"There is so much yet to be done, couldn't we at least wait until after the wedding to go house hunting?"

"You wouldn't mind sharing that small amount of space with me?"

Not wanting to appear too eager, Frisco carefully worded her answer. "Lucas, couples have been known to start married life together in one room. I think we can survive for a while in a three-room and bath-and-a-half condo. Don't you?"

"Of course."

Frisco's spirits plummeted. His voice sounded so casual, so unconcerned, she was tempted to smack him. Because there wasn't a thing casual or unconcerned about the way she felt about him.

That incident was just one of those cluttering up Frisco's mind throughout the weeks before the wedding.

Since she had been denied the joy of planning a large church wedding and an even larger reception, Gertrude set happily about arranging the perfect intimate affair, to take place in her own garden.

As a form of appeasement for thwarting her mother's dearly held dreams of a lavish wedding, Frisco simply agreed to everything Gertrude wanted.

While she would have been content to wear a regular dress or even a suit—the one she was originally married in would have been fine—her mother was appalled at the very idea.

"I will see you married properly dressed in a white bridal gown, Frisco Bay Styer," Gertrude said, adamantly. "Even if it is off the rack."

Frisco, Karla, and Jo went shopping for traditional wedding garb.

It was during their first jaunt to the bridal shop that Frisco became concerned about Jo. And after their second jaunt, this time for shoes, she called Karla to ask if she had noticed something odd about Jo's behavior.

"You mean odder than usual?" Karla asked, obviously rhetorically, since she added, "I couldn't help but notice. She's rather subdued, isn't she?"

That was it precisely; Jo was exceptionally subdued, which in and of itself was odd.

"Do you think it could have something to do with her work?" Frisco wondered aloud.

"Well, maybe . . ." Karla sounded skeptical, and proceeded to say why. "But you know Jo. As a rule, when something's bugging her, she just explodes, spewing invective over anyone within hearing range."

True, Frisco allowed. Uncomfortable for anyone who happened to be in the vicinity of Jo's verbal eruptions, but true, nonetheless.

"You know," Karla mused aloud. "Jo has been acting kinda weird ever since you announced your engagement. You don't suppose she feels betrayed or something?"

"Betrayed? In what way?"

"Oh, you know, some such drivel or other about giving in to the enemy," she explained. "You know how she gets on my case about lowering myself by giving up my career to be a homemaker . . . as if that's something to be ashamed of."

Frisco couldn't buy the theory, and said as much. "Oh, I don't think so, Karla. And really, I don't believe Jo seriously believes you lowered yourself by choosing to keep house. In fact, I'll go so far as to claim she secretly admires your staunch belief in the rightness of what you're doing." She laughed softly, then added, "But she does enjoy needling you about it."

"I always thought so, too, but . . ." Karla sighed. "If it isn't that, what is troubling her?" Before Frisco could respond, she suddenly said, "Oh! You don't suppose she still believes Lucas somehow coerced you into marriage, do you?"

Truly concerned, Frisco echoed Karla's sigh. "I don't know. She seemed to get along all right with Lucas—and his brothers, especially Michael."

"Well, Michael is very easy to get along with," Karla said. "He's so quiet and nice."

"I know." Frisco smiled. "When I noticed them talking together off in a corner, I was kind of hoping some of Michael's low-key demeanor would rub off on Jo. I should have known better."

"Jo is Jo," Karla murmured.

"But not lately, and it worries me."

Frisco's concern for Jo intensified as the days leading up to the wedding diminished. Instead of improving, Jo's attitude appeared on a downward spiral; she went from sharp and brittle to reticent and morose.

And Jo couldn't have picked a worse time to sink into what appeared to be a frightening state of depression if she had planned it, and Frisco was convinced she hadn't. Jo was outspoken at times, but she had never to Frisco's knowledge indulged in spitefulness.

Still, her odd behavior came at an inconvenient time for Frisco, simply because she and Lucas were, somewhat amazingly, getting along quite well in their free hours as well as at work.

In fact, Lucas was displaying gentler, more accommodating qualities.

Could it be possible he was courting her?

The question teased Frisco, teased and tormented her. She simply didn't have time to explore the possibilities, encouraging as they were. She had too much to do to give her undivided attention to their relationship.

Indeed, the entire situation was enough to make the angels weep, Frisco decided. And she thanked heaven, and Lucas, for the short amount of time allowed to arrange the wedding. If she had had to endure such craziness during the usual preparation time of a year, or even longer, she was certain she'd have ended up in a small room with padded walls.

Then again, she mused, unamused, she still might.

Chapter Thirty

"You'll be all right while I'm gone?"

Frisco leveled a get-serious look at Lucas. "I think I can muddle through in the office without you for a few days," she said dryly.

"I wasn't referring to the office." He returned her look with interest. "And I think you know it. After nearly a month of working with you, I'm convinced you could run the entire operation by yourself."

He had meant the remark as a compliment, she felt sure. At least, she hoped so. Otherwise, she could think of only one other reason for his making it.

And that didn't bear thinking about—except that Frisco now could think of nothing else.

Could Lucas possibly be considering a permanent return to his Reading firm, leaving her on her own, both in the company and . . .

She shivered.

He noticed.

"Are you cold?" He frowned. "I didn't think the air was too cool in here."

The "here" he referred to was Bookbinder's restaurant. Lucas had asked her to choose a place to celebrate; they would be married one month on Monday.

It was now Saturday, exactly one week from the big day, their second wedding day.

"No." Frisco shook her head. "I'm not cold. I . . . er, just felt a momentary chill."

"Someone walk over your grave?" he asked, obviously teasing her with the old saying.

"I suppose." She smiled; it wasn't easy. "What time are you leaving in the morning?" She had deliberately changed the subject.

"Early." Lucas took a swallow of his afterdinner coffee. "Will should get into Reading fairly early, too. When he called late this afternoon he said he was going to stop for the night in Pittsburgh. He said he planned to get a jump on the rush-hour traffic in the morning by leaving around five or so." He shrugged. "Accounting for breakfast and rest stops, I figure he'll arrive around noon or soon after."

"I'm still surprised he decided to drive rather than fly. It's a long haul from Montana to Pennsylvania."

"Yeah, but he told me he wanted to bring his stuff with him." He smiled. "That is the stuff he wanted. Everything else went into storage or was sold."

"That also surprises me," Frisco said, frowning in disbelief. "I mean that he'd sell his home, and practically everything in it."

"It shouldn't, you know."

"Why not?" Her frown deepened.

"Will told us in Hawaii he'd been considering relocating there—before I offered him a job, that is. If you'll recall, he said that since his wife died there wasn't anything to keep him in Montana."

Frisco had completely forgotten the conversation, which wasn't surprising; she had had other things on her mind at the time, like getting married to a man she barely knew . . . for business purposes.

And since returning home, she had had many other pressing things to contend with; the welcome-home party, the wedding arrangements, and most pressing of all, the conflicting fear/hope that she might have conceived Lucas's child during those wild, passionate, unprotected hours they had spent together in the hotel room after their first wedding.

The possibility of pregnancy had disappeared with the appearance of her period exactly on time a few days after the party. Frisco had heaved a sigh of relief, but also had known a pang of regret.

"He said he's bringing his wife's lace bridal veil and train with him," Lucas was saying, ending her moment of introspection. "He's already shipped her wedding gown to his son in Honolulu."

"Will's a nice man," she observed, giving him a worried look. "I hope Michael and Rob have no trouble accepting him in the office."

"I don't believe they will," Lucas said, smiling in a way that told her if they did they'd have even more trouble with him. "From what I've gleaned about Will's expertise, he should be able to cover my desk with Mike and Rob hardly noticing the transition."

His confidence relieved Frisco's mind on two counts: her concern about his brothers' acceptance of Will and her more immediate and personal concern about Lucas's intentions. Evidently, he had no plans to return to his Reading office within the near future.

Suddenly, Frisco's coffee had a richer, more full-bodied aroma and taste.

"And you'll be back on Wednesday, right?" Her voice held a lighter, more carefree note.

"Hmmm," he murmured, in the process of taking another swallow from his cup. "Probably late in the afternoon," he continued, cradling the cup in his hands. "Would you mind if I came directly to your place? I'm going to be bringing some of my stuff with me," he went on to explain before she could answer.

"Of course not. I'll give you my extra door key now instead of on Saturday." She raised her eyebrows. "Some of your stuff?"

"Don't panic, Frisco Bay," he said, smiling. "There's not all that much."

She smiled back, and this time it was easy; Lucas had called her Frisco Bay for the first time since they had returned from Hawaii.

The days which had seemed to fly by during the previous weeks, slowed to a dragging pace for Frisco while Lucas was away. She was occupied and at the same time distracted, busy yet with too much time on her hands.

She missed him. It was as simple and uncomplicated as that. And, along about mid day Tuesday, she discovered an age-old truth: love did strange things to people.

For Frisco, it was strange to realize that all at once she hated living alone.

But Wednesday finally came, and for the first time in her working life, she found herself watching the clock, urging the hands to move faster.

Lucas was waiting for her when she arrived home. And he wasn't the only thing waiting for her. A mouth-watering aroma permeated the apartment.

He had cooked dinner for her.

"I could become accustomed to coming home to this very quickly," she said appreciatively, seating herself at the carefully laid table.

"It's nothing fancy," he warned, placing a still bubbling pan of lasagna on the table.

"It smells wonderful." She inhaled the spicy scents of cheese and tomato sauce. "I had no idea you could cook."

"My repertoire is limited." Lucas grinned and handed a bowl of tossed salad to her. "The bread's from the French and Italian bakery in Reading," he confessed, indicating a long, crusty loaf with a movement of his head.

"Did you warm it?"

He gave her a look.

She laughed.

It was a very congenial, enjoyable meal.

They were still at the table, sipping the last of the dark red wine, when the phone rang.

"It's probably my mother," Frisco said, rolling her eyes and pushing her chair back. "Two to one she just thought of something new to add to the program."

"I'll pass," Lucas drawled.

Frisco was wrong; it wasn't Gertrude. It was Jo, and she sounded close to hysteria.

"I'm sorry, but I can't participate in your wedding," Jo declared.

"What?" Frisco was unable to believe she had heard correctly.

As if he had been zapped from the table in the tiny dining alcove into the kitchen, Lucas was standing beside her near the wall-mounted phone.

"Trouble?" he asked softly.

Frisco lifted her shoulders and slanted a helpless look at him, while trying to absorb what Jo was saying.

"I said I can't be in your wedding," her friend repeated, her voice rising. "I just can't."

"But . . . Jo, I don't understand. Why can't you be in the wedding?" Frisco repeated for Lucas's benefit. "Are you sick or something?"

"I sure am," Jo answered, her voice growing shrill. "I'm physically ill, hurling my guts out, and I'm something else; I'm mad as hell."

Frisco shot Lucas a look that silently cried, This isn't Jo's style at all.

Then she spoke calmly, soothingly, "I need a better answer than that, Jo. Please, can't you tell me why you're sick—and why you're mad?"

"I'm sick because I'm pregnant!" Jo shouted. "And I'm mad because that son-of-a-bitch brother of your groom forced himself on me and made me pregnant!"

Frisco was jolted. Brother? Which brother? Jo didn't give her time to ask.

"And I can't be in your wedding because I can't bear to look at Michael's face!"

"Michael?"

Frisco and Lucas spoke in unison; she in disbelief, he in flat denial.

"Michael," Jo repeated the name like a curse. "I could kill him . . . or myself."

"Jo!" Panic clutched at Frisco. "Don't talk like that. You don't mean it, and you're frightening me."

"Welcome to the club of used and frightened females," Jo retorted. "Hell, you're a charter member." She laughed and Frisco shivered. "You know all about being used, don't you, dear friend?"

"Jo, I'm coming over," Frisco said, fighting to keep her voice free of the fear gripping her. "You had better be there. And don't you dare do anything foolish. I'll be at your place in a few minutes."

Without waiting for a response, afraid of what it might be, Frisco hung up the phone and turned to Lucas.

"I've got to go." She moved to circle around him, but he caught her arm, holding her still. "Lucas! I have to go to her!"

"I know. I know." His voice was cool and collected, exactly what she needed to hear. "I'll take you in a moment. But first, I want to call Mike."

"What good will that do?" Frisco demanded, resisting his hold. "Michael's in Reading, for God's sake!"

"No, he isn't." His grasp on her arm held firm. "He drove down with me this afternoon. He's at the hotel, and I think he needs to be told."

"Then let me go in my car." She again tugged against his grip, unsuccessfully. "You can follow in yours after you've talked to him."

Lucas gave a sharp shake of his head, then, one-handed, cradled the receiver and punched in a number with his thumb.

Though it seemed to Frisco to take much longer, only seconds were required for the hotel switchboard operator to connect Lucas to his brother's room.

"You've got trouble, Mike, big trouble," he said bluntly. "Frisco has just had a call from her friend Jo, who has accused you of raping her and, in the process, making her pregnant."

"I don't want an explanation now," he snapped, obviously in-

terrupting whatever his brother had started to say. "Frisco is
frantic with worry, because Jo talked wildly of killing you or
herself. Don't interrupt," he said harshly. "We're leaving now
to go to her place, and you had better haul your ass over
there, too."

Lucas hung up without saying another word.

"Okay, we're out of here." Still grasping her arm, he strode
for the door.

Fortunately, none of Jo's fellow officers were around as he
broke the speed limit racing across town. Frisco was out of
the car an instant after he pulled to a stop in front of the row
of brownstones which had been converted into apartments.
Lucas was right behind her as she mounted the steps of the
house in which Jo had lived since joining the force.

The scent of garlic tickling her nose, Frisco ran up the narrow
staircase to the second floor and along the hallway to the rear
apartment.

"It's Frisco, open the door," she called, stabbing her finger
into the bell.

To her relief, the door swung open at once; to her dismay, Jo
looked awful. Her eyes were red and puffy, her face was chalky
white, and her lips were set in a tight, hard, defiant line.

"Ah," she said, curling her lip in a sneer. "I see you've
brought the MacCanna with you."

"Jo, honey, you look terrible." Frisco stepped inside and
immediately gathered her friend into her arms.

"I feel terrible," Jo muttered, backing out of the embrace,
but not before giving Frisco a quick hug. "You can't imagine
what it's like to throw up every fucking time you put something into your stomach."

"Oh, I'm sorry," Frisco commiserated, moving into the
small, immaculately clean living room.

"Not as sorry as I am," Jo retorted. "And not nearly as sorry
as that bastard Michael is going to be." Narrowing her eyes,
she shifted a stony look at Lucas, who had remained standing
just inside the open door. "Since you're here, you may as well
come all the way in."

As if forgetting the open door, Lucas crossed to stand beside Frisco.

Jo followed his every step with her hard stare.

"I don't understand any of this," Frisco said, feeling her way. "You and Michael seemed to get along fine at the party."

"Oh, of course, so long as there was an audience, he was charming." She sneered. "It was later, when we were alone, that he revealed himself—literally and figuratively."

"But . . ." Frisco shook her head. "Rape, Jo?"

"No."

The emphatic denial came not from Jo, but from the man standing in the doorway. Frisco fleetingly wondered how far above the speed limit Michael had driven to arrive there so quickly.

"Yes!" Jo cried in contradiction, swinging around to confront him.

"Oh, you look terrible," Michael said in a concerned murmur.

"No shit," Jo snapped. "So the opinion's unanimous. Now shut the goddam door."

"Your language, sweetheart," Michael cautioned softly, closing the door with a gentle backward kick.

Sweetheart? Frisco frowned, thoroughly confused by the endearment and by Michael's loving tone. She glanced at Lucas. He lifted his shoulders and gave her a look that said, Don't ask me, I'm only his brother.

"Sweetheart, my ass," Jo snarled. "You raped me and knocked me up. And I'll use any language I choose."

"Jo," Michael said in a quiet, steady voice, "I did not rape you and you know it. You were a willing, one might say eager, participant."

"You raped my mind!" she accused loudly.

What? Frisco's own mind reeled. "Jo, what in the world are you saying?"

"You should know better than anyone."

"Me? I?" Frisco frowned, but before she could demand that Jo clarify her remark, her friend directed scathing looks at Lucas and Michael.

"Are blackmail, coercion, and mind games family pastimes of the MacCannas?"

Frisco felt Lucas tense beside her, as a glimmering of Jo's intent sparked in her mind. She had thought, hoped, Jo had revised her opinion after meeting him, but apparently Jo still harbored the belief that Lucas had forced Frisco into an unwanted marriage.

He had, of course, but . . .

"Jo, I still don't understand," she said, drawing her belligerent friend's attention away from Lucas—and the subject of his motives. "In what manner did Michael . . . er, mess up your mind?"

"In the time-honored, male supremacy way," Jo declared, swinging back to glare at Frisco. "You know, the usual routine. Seduce the bimbo's mind by telling her what she wants to hear; in this instance that he"—she indicated Michael with an insulting jerk of her head—"was in complete sympathy and agreement with my beliefs, my position on the cause of feminism and equal rights."

"That was the truth," Michael inserted.

"Sure," Jo said disparagingly, not bothering to spare a glance at him. "And then," she went on to Frisco, "after I was lulled into a feeling of security with him, he seduced my body, over and over again, throughout the night of the party and straight through Monday and Monday night."

The scenario Jo described was so similar to the one played out in the hotel room in Hawaii, Frisco experienced an eerie chill along her spine.

Frisco slid an uneasy glance at Lucas. He met her gaze without flinching, then moved his head in negation of the questioning accusation in her eyes.

And, rightly or wrongly, brightly or stupidly, Frisco believed his silent message of reassurance.

"What you've described doesn't sound like rape to me, Jo," she pointed out.

"It wasn't," Michael said. "And she knows it."

Jo again whipped around to confront the brothers. "Maybe not physical rape, but it was coercion of a type." Her hard stare settled on Lucas. "Along the lines of the type you used to get control of Frisco's family's business by getting her to marry you."

Lucas didn't deny her charge; he didn't get the chance to so much as open his mouth.

Without consideration or hesitation, Frisco stepped in front of him, chin lifted, the light of battle in her eyes, prepared to protect and defend.

"You're off base, Jo," she said, quietly but firmly. "I agreed to marry Lucas because I wanted to." In that instant, she realized her claim was the absolute truth; secretly, in her heart of hearts, she had wanted to marry him, to stay with him.

"Maybe you did want to," Jo conceded, raising a skeptical brow. "But why?"

There was an instant of stillness; or was she imagining it? Did she imagine as well that she could actually feel Lucas holding his breath? No matter. The time was past for playing games, of any sort. Looking her dear friend straight in the eyes, Frisco answered with adamant certainty.

"Because I love him."

Lucas's hand closed around hers, and Frisco smiled at the sense of rightness settling inside her. But it wasn't the proper setting for exploring the sensation. That would come, she thought, drawing strength from his touch—strength to deal with Jo's problem.

But then Michael took the initiative.

"And I love you, Jo."

Five tiny words, and before her eyes Frisco witnessed the first crack in her friend's tough facade.

"You lie!" Jo cried, betraying uncertainty with a quick flick of her tongue over her lips. "You walked out of here that Tuesday morning and never looked back, never came back, never even called!"

"I was waiting for you to decide whether or not you wanted to take a chance on me," Michael explained, moving around Frisco to stand directly in front of Jo. "I was hoping you'd call me."

Frisco felt a gentle tug on her hand. Glancing over her shoulder, she nodded in mute agreement with the suggestion Lucas whispered: "Let's get out of here."

Backing toward the door, Frisco watched and listened in fascination to the byplay between her friend and her brother-in-law.

"You . . . you—"

"Do you have any idea how intimidating you can be?" Michael asked. "You scare the hell out of me, lady, do you know that?"

"I do?" Jo's blue eyes still glittered, but Frisco suspected the gleam was more from incipient tears now than anger.

"You do." Michael paused, then blurted out, "Do you want to have an abortion?"

"No!" Jo cried, one hand moving protectively over her belly. "Never."

Hovering in the doorway, Frisco sighed with relief; Michael echoed her sigh.

"Good." He held out a hand to her. "I love you, Jo, and I already love our baby." He smiled. "At the risk of sounding trite, old fashioned, and traditionally male, will you marry me?"

"Oh, Michael." Jo held out a moment longer. Then, ignoring his hand, she stepped up to him, encircling his waist with her arms. "I guess I'd better say yes, before I do something really radical . . . like cry."

Stepping back, Frisco pulled the door shut, leaving the couple in privacy.

Chapter Thirty-one

"Did you mean it?" Lucas said, standing taut and still just inside her apartment.

Frisco had been expecting the question ever since they'd exited the scene at Jo's place.

"Not just about loving me," he went on before she could respond. "But about wanting to marry me?"

"Yes," she answered with simple honesty.

"The first time, in Hawaii?" he persisted.

"Yes, Lucas. May I sit down now? It's been an emotionally draining evening."

A slow, sexy-as-the-devil smile teasing his lips and lighting his eyes, Lucas moved, closing in on her. "Like Henry Ford, I've got a better idea." Coming to a halt in front of her, he bent and swept her up, into his arms. "Why sit down when you can lie down?"

Frisco curled her arms around his neck, rested her head on his shoulder, and murmured, "I like your idea a lot better than Ford's."

Moments later, their clothing scattered all over the bedroom floor, Lucas settled Frisco carefully on the bed, then covered her with his warm body.

"At the risk of sounding exactly like my brother," he murmured, brushing her parted lips with a teasing kiss. "I love you, Frisco Bay."

"I'm glad," Frisco whispered, gasping in delight when his tongue flicked her lower lip. "Because I love you back, Lucas MacCanna."

"It's been so long, over a month since we've been together like this," he said, settling between her thighs. "I've been going crazy with wanting to be with you, inside you, loving you."

"We have all night," she said, arching her hips in invitation for his possession.

"We'll need it," he said, savoring his slow entry into her silken sheath. "And all the nights ahead."

Except to dash into the kitchen at odd hours to feed a different, but as demanding, kind of hunger, they didn't leave the bed all that night, or all day Thursday and through Thursday night.

They reluctantly parted company early Friday morning, but only because each had last-minute things to do before renewing the vows they'd taken the month before, and because she had agreed to her mother's suggestion that Frisco spend Friday night at her parents' home, sleeping in her old bedroom.

Friday virtually flew by for Frisco. It was nearly dinner time before she arrived at her parents' house, loaded down with a nightgown, an outfit to change into after the reception, and of course, the wedding gown.

Eschewing virginal white for the reenactment, Frisco had chosen a severely cut, long-sleeved, high-necked silk and lace sheath in a creamy shade of ivory. Upon viewing the dress for the first time, both of her parents exclaimed their delight.

"Oh, darling, it's absolutely beautiful," Gertrude sighed. "And, even though it is more modern in design, it will work perfectly with the lace veil and train that that nice Mr. Denton sent along with Lucas."

"Sophisticated, yet traditional," Harold proclaimed, examining the gown judiciously. "Your mother is quite right; it will work perfectly."

Lucas called her on the phone twice between after dinner coffee and bedtime. Both of his calls were made to deliver the same message.

"I love you, Frisco Bay."

And, both times, she gave the same response.

"I love you back, Lucas MacCanna."

Though aware on some level of consciousness of the odd, slightly furtive looks her father slanted her way during the course of the evening, Frisco was too content to speculate on whatever might be rattling around inside her father's head. She retired early, floating within an aura of anticipation.

The first light tapping against the door came moments after she had entered her room. Immediately following the tap, the door was opened a crack.

"May I come in, dear?" Gertrude asked, rhetorically, since she proceeded to do precisely that.

"Sure," Frisco answered, smiling impishly. "Is it time for the time honored mother-daughter pre-wedding talk?"

"Well, something like that," Gertrude admitted, smiling in return.

"Are you going to instruct me on the correct behavior of a wife?" Frisco asked, still smiling.

"No." Gertrude's smile vanished. "Each woman, each new wife, must decide her own behavior, in concert with her lifestyle and her husband's character. And that is what I wanted to talk to you about . . . your soon-to-be husband's character."

Uh oh, Frisco thought, her sense of euphoria rapidly dissipating. Had her mother somehow, in some way, figured out that love had precious little to do with the original agreement she had entered into with Lucas?

"His character?" she repeated, her voice ringing weak to her own ears.

"Yes." Gertrude fluttered one hand in a gesture of helplessness. "I personally like Lucas very much. He has impressed me as an honest, forthright man." She paused to sigh; her daughter echoed it in silent relief, as her mother continued.

"But I am not marrying him, you are, and by now you should have a clearer picture of his character."

"I think I do," Frisco concurred. "And I also believe he is' forthright and honest."

"But do you love him?" her mother asked urgently. "Are you in love with him."

Ah hah! There it was, the root of her mother's concern. Having gone to her own groom with adoration in her heart for him, Gertrude desired the same for her daughter. The realization brought a thickness to Frisco's throat and a soft smile to her lips. She crossed the room to embrace her mother.

"Yes, Mother, I am in love with him," she said with firm conviction. "Deeply and completely."

Gertrude gave her a quick hug, then stepped back, blinking against the tears sparkling in her eyes. "I'm glad, because marriage by its very nature is difficult to maintain. Loving helps retain the balance, even when one of the partners is less than one had hoped." Smiling, she opened the door and stepped into the hallway, murmuring a soft, "Good night, darling."

She knew! Frisco stared at the closed door in stunned amazement, feeling certain that her mother knew, had known all along, or at least from early on, that her husband was hardly the stuff of heroes. And still she loved him, supported him, stood by him.

The far from heroic man tapped on Frisco's door less than a half hour later.

"Frisco, are you awake?" Harold called in a lowered voice.

"Yes, Dad," she answered, wondering what form of advice he might wish to impart to her. "Come on in."

"I've been thinking," he said the minute he crossed the threshold. "About this wedding."

"What about it?" Frisco eyed him suspiciously as she tied the belt of her robe securely around her waist. "I hope you don't want to make some eleventh-hour changes," she said, only half jokingly.

"No, no." He shook his head; it mirrored the motion of his hands, revealing the extent of his inner conflict and nervousness. "Er . . . no, it's not that."

On the spot, Frisco decided that if he broke down and confessed to once again being in financial trouble, she would verbally, possibly even physically, tear a strip from his hide.

When he just continued to stand there, literally trembling all over, she braced herself for hearing the worst, if he ever got to it.

"What is it, Dad?" she finally asked, after a lengthy, nerve agitating silence.

"Frisco, baby . . ." He broke off on sight of her frown at the endearment. "I'm sorry"—he shrugged—"habit, I guess." He drew a breath, then began again. "I . . . er . . . I wanted you to know that you don't have to go through with this wedding, if you don't want to. I'll manage . . . somehow, to repay Lucas for covering my debts."

Frisco sighed. "I'm already married to Lucas, Dad, and you know it. I overheard the end of your conversation with him that morning in Hawaii." Knowing that Lucas loved her, she could now smile without rancor at the memory. "I heard him tell you then that the marriage was, and still is legal, binding . . . and consummated."

"Nothing is irrevocably binding."

"What do you mean?" She had an inkling, of course, but she had to hear it from his lips.

"Annulment. Divorce." His smile was meant to look encouraging, she knew. To her, it appeared reminiscent of the father of her childhood, thus endearing. "It can be accomplished quietly. Your mother, your friends, no one need ever know."

"And if you lose the business?" she asked, fighting the sting of tears in her eyes. "What then?" she went on in an emotion-choked voice, knowing it wouldn't happen, yet needing to hear his answer.

"We'll survive," he answered, bravely, she thought, but without bravado. "As long as I have your mother by my side, we'll survive." He smiled again; his saving-grace smile of pure love for his wife. "Your wonderful mother is stronger than you might believe."

Oh, no, Frisco thought, a tear slowly rolling down her cheek.

An hour ago, she wouldn't have believed, but not now. Now she knew better, and felt better . . . about a lot of things.

"I want to go through with this wedding as planned," she said, easing his conscience and his fears.

"But, why, if it's not necessary?"

"But it is necessary," she said, laughing through her tears. "Necessary for me, not for you, or even Mother. Because, you see, I love Lucas, Dad, as much, maybe even more, than Mother loves you."

It was a perfect day for a wedding. The sun was warming, but not hot. The breeze was gentle, not too brisk. The setting was beautiful.

"You've outdone yourself, my dear," Harold complimented his wife, bending to bestow a gentle kiss on her excitement-flushed cheek.

"Thank you, darling," Gertrude said, her smile brilliant as she gazed up at him. "Everything is lovely, isn't it?"

"Indeed," he agreed, glancing around at the changes she had wrought in the house and garden—with a good deal of expert assistance, of course.

They were standing just inside the open French doors leading from the dining room to the garden. Having chosen the dining room rather than outdoors for the serving of the food after the wedding, Gertrude had directed the caterer to utilize the available space in any manner he deemed most attractive.

And he had done a superior job. The long formal table was draped in snowy linen, in its center a four-tiered wedding cake, decorated with delicate icing vines and wildflowers. Picking up the motif, live vines and wildflowers were festooned around the table's sides.

The large hutch had been removed from the far end of the room, and in its place a bar had been set up, its front also strung with vines and wildflowers; two white-jacketed bartenders stood ready to serve.

But the most impressive change of all was the one made by the florist in the garden. It was now a veritable bower of flowers, all manner of cultivated blooms: roses, gardenias, carnations, pure white lilies, and many other varieties.

In the open center of the bower, chairs had been set up in rows, a four-foot-wide aisle having been left to lead from the dining room to the altar erected at the end of the garden. A latticed trellis arched before the altar; under it the bride and groom would stand to exchange their vows.

Both the altar and the trellis were festooned with vines and wildflowers. Their fragrances blending with the profusion of scents of the other blooms perfumed the soft late spring air.

Satisfied with his visual inspection, Harold glanced at the slim gold watch on his wrist.

It was almost time. In a few moments, Rob MacCanna would come to escort Gertrude to her seat. That would be his cue to go to the foyer, where his daughter, his baby, would descend the staircase to him.

Had he done right by her in agreeing to this arrangement? Her first marriage, undertaken in secret, could easily be annulled. But this wedding, attended by family and friends, was different, more real.

A wave of last-minute panic washed over Harold, leaving him trembling, staring blankly into a fear-induced abyss.

"There's Lucas—and Michael," Gertrude said, her voice piercing the terror blocking Harold off. "And here comes Rob."

His eyes homed in like a laser on Lucas. The sight of MacCanna standing before the arched trellis, tall, confident, responsible, was a reassurance in and of itself.

Lucas would take care of his baby; Harold couldn't have explained how he knew it for a certainty, but know it he did.

Gertrude was on her way to her seat, gone, and so was Harold's panic. Heaving a silent sigh of relief, he made his way to the foyer. At the base of the staircase, he stopped and glanced up. Frisco was poised on the second-floor landing, ready to descend. The picture she presented drew a soft heartfelt exclamation from him.

"Oh, baby, you look so very beautiful!"

* * *

Quiet as it was, Frisco heard her father's compliment. A gentle smile curved her lips, for the man she had adored throughout her youth and had despaired of since entering adulthood. Acceptance settled in her mind, and she no longer wished he were like Will Denton or any other man; he was her father, and she loved him.

It occurred to her that perhaps being in love, deeply in love, the way her mother had always been with Harold, changed one's perceptions—or scrambled one's normal reasoning powers.

Her smile growing bright, lighthearted, Frisco started down the stairs to him. All was well; her sense of humor remained intact.

"I'm confused," Karla murmured from two steps behind Frisco, where she was positioned to hold aloft the trailing, delicate lace veil Will Denton had delivered to the house that morning.

"About what?" Frisco asked, laughing softly; Lord, it was unbelievable how good she felt!

"You, for one," Karla said. "I can't understand how you can be so calm; I was a nervous wreck the day I got married. Come to think of it, so was Danny!"

Reaching the foyer, Frisco paused and turned to smile at her friend, improvising with, "I'm older, more mature than you were at the time."

Karla looked skeptical.

Behind her, holding aloft the end of the lacy train, Jo laughed indulgently.

"And you've got me really confused," Karla said, glancing over her shoulder at Jo. "You're like a different person so . . . so pleasant, even your language!"

Frisco and Jo exchanged meaningful glances, and then they both laughed.

"Come along, lovely ladies," Harold put in urgently. "We don't want to be late for the wedding."

Frisco and Jo again exchanged glances, both grateful for Harold's timely interference; Jo had insisted that not a word be uttered about her intent to marry Michael until after Frisco's wedding.

Lucas was waiting for her in the midst of the bower, looking handsome and formidable, and to Frisco like everything wonderful.

Her hand resting on her father's arm, she slowly traversed the aisle to him. Her father placed her hand in Lucas's, and she and the groom stepped beneath the arched trellis. The somber-faced minister began speaking.

This time, Frisco heard every word.

They were twice married.

Her eyes were bright with unshed tears when she and Lucas turned as man and wife to greet their guests.

Gertrude's face was glowing with love, and wet from tears of joy. Even Harold's eyes held a suspicious watery film.

Frisco smiled in understanding when she glanced at Will. Unabashed tears rolled down his scored face. Frisco knew Will was not really seeing her, but the woman who had last worn the lace veil and train so many years ago.

The reception commenced immediately following the ceremony, and seemed to Frisco to go on forever. But, at last, her mother murmured that she and Lucas could change clothes and then slip away, if they liked.

They liked.

"Where are you going on your honeymoon?" Rob called out as they were getting into the car.

"None of your business," Lucas retorted, drawing a burst of laughter from the crowd.

"Honeymoon?" Frisco asked as he drove away from the celebrants. "Honeymoon? You didn't say anything to me about a honeymoon."

"It must have slipped my mind."

"Right." She pulled a stern expression. "Out with it, Mac-Canna. What did you have in mind?"

He tossed a suggestive grin at her.

"Besides that."

"Would you like to go back to Hawaii?"

"Yes, someday—but not today," she admitted. "I can't face that long flight again so soon."

"Glad to hear it, because I can't either."

Frisco laughed. "You haven't made any plans at all, have you?"

"No." He flashed another grin. "But I'm open to suggestions—keeping in mind, of course, that we agreed to take only one week off from work."

"Well . . ." Frisco said, drawing out the moment. "We could go to several nearby vacation spots—the mountains, the seashore, or . . ."—she sent a grin back to him—"we could just hole up in the apartment, while allowing everyone to believe we went to one of those places."

Lucas produced a sexy-sounding growl from deep in his throat. It was all the response she needed.

"More?"

Frisco stretched and shook her head. "I've had enough, more than enough. I feel like a self-indulgent pig."

Lucas chuckled, and set the plate of sandwiches aside. "You can diet next week."

"You're all heart." Frisco swallowed the last drops of her champagne.

"Er . . . not all heart," he said, laughing at the look she threw at him.

"Braggart." Frisco moved, pretending she was getting up from her pillow-propped position against the headboard of the very rumpled bed.

Still laughing, Lucas held her in place by curling one arm around her waist. "You, more than anyone, should know I'm not a braggart. Not about that."

"So, okay," she conceded, laughing with him. "You're ah . . . shall I say, well endowed?"

"I think the expression is 'hung,' " he instructed, fighting to keep a straight face.

"And I think we should change the topic of conversation," she retorted, repressively.

"All right," he readily agreed. "I have a question I've been itching to ask you since the day we met."

"A question?" Frisco frowned. It was now Friday, and they had been talking, pouring out their innermost thoughts to one another, off and on, ever since they'd returned to the apartment after the wedding the previous Saturday. Unable to fathom what remained to be explained, she invited, "Ask away."

"Why did your mother ever name you Frisco Bay?"

Having expected something deep, dark, and serious, Frisco was sent into peals of laughter by his question, along with his baffled expression. After she had regained a measure of composure, Frisco recounted to him the misty-eyed, romantic origins of her name.

Lucas frowned.

"What?" she prompted.

He shook his head. "I was just wondering."

"About what?"

"About you possibly having conceived sometime during this last week."

Uh-oh, Frisco thought, feeling her stomach lurch. They again hadn't used any form of protection, and while they had discussed and agreed upon having children . . .

What if Lucas didn't particularly want to start a family so soon?

In that instant, Frisco realized she did want to be pregnant, just like her mother, made pregnant during the rapture of her honeymoon by the man she loved more than life itself.

So, of course, she had to ask, had to know.

"And if I have conceived?"

"If the child's a girl," he said, a frown of consternation tugging his brows together. "Are you going to insist on naming her Philadelphia?"

"Weeeell . . ." Frisco said, a relieved, teasing smile curving her lips as she curled her arms around his neck and snuggled closer to his hard warmth.

"Weeeell, what?" Lucas asked, eyeing her warily.

"Maybe we can compromise."